THE HOUSE IN HAVANA

ANNETTE LEIGH

Also by Annette Leigh

The Bayswater Series

The Raging Fire (novella)

The Whispering Palms

The Curlew's Scream

The Three Wishes Series (novellas)

A Christmas Wish

A New Year's Wish

A Valentine's Wish

Prologue

The house witnessed it all. No one else was watching.

No one.

Not from the windows.

Not from the balcony.

Not even from the stone wall.

No one saw the figure in black slip around the edge of the house, cloaked in shadows, using the moonless night for cover.

No one heard the scream—just one—cutting through the silence like a barn owl's screech.

Only the victim felt the pain of the first blow, tasted the metallic tang of their blood, spilling life over the jagged rocks.

He waited until he was sure. Sure that all life had drained from the body. Sure that its secrets would be safe.

He turned. Left the body wedged between the rocks, waiting for the sea to claim its prize.

And leaving the house with yet another secret.

Chapter One

2016

Miami in summer; blue cloudless skies and a relentless sun—an-all's-well-with-the-world kind of day—except for me, it wasn't. I stood at the edge of the grave, droplets of perspiration beading between my shoulder blades and running down my spine. I'd pinned my long dark hair on top of my head to escape the heat, but shorter strands had broken free and fallen in damp curls around my face. I pushed them behind my ears as I tried to focus on the priest's final words about my *abuelita* —my grandma, Alicia. As a young child, I'd struggled to say *abuelita*, so I called her *Ita*.

Wiping away a tear that had escaped under the sunglasses hiding my grief, I glanced around those gathered to say good-bye. We were a small crowd, a handful of Ita's friends who'd left Cuba with my grandparents during the chaos of 1959, a couple of extras they'd collected along the way, and me, her granddaughter, Cate.

Scooping up a handful of the freshly turned earth, I let it slip through my fingers and rain onto the lid of the coffin. Its patter, almost drowned out by the distant drone of a lawn mower, was a reminder that death waits for no one. I turned away from the sunshine to wait in the shade of the fig tree for the rest of the congregation to finish their goodbyes.

Graciela, my grandmother's closest and oldest friend, joined me. "Catalina—Cate," she quickly corrected herself, folding me into her arms and pressing me close.

"Graciela," I whispered, my eyes filling with tears. My loss was so raw, so painful, that any small show of kindness broke the fragile façade of my composure.

Graciela released me, and I flicked the tears away with the back of my hand.

"Are you coming back for something to eat before you leave for Fort Lauderdale?" she asked.

Graciela took my silence as agreement. "Good. I'll see you at our place, then. Would you like me to come with you?"

"You go. I want to say goodbye to Father Paul first."

Graciela squeezed my arm again and joined the others.

I walked over to Father Paul, his black robes swamping his thin, wiry frame. Clutching his Bible like a shield in front of him, he gave me a smile. A smile meant to provide comfort. A smile that rested somewhere between "I'm sorry for your loss" and "time heals." I stopped him before he could put his smile into words.

"Father, thank you. Are you joining us at Graciela's?"

He shook his head. "Unfortunately, no. I have another service in twenty minutes. But I would like to speak to you. You know, your grandmother was more than a member of the congregation to me." His voice slowed like he was strolling through the streets of old memories. His face told me not all of them were good. "She was a dear friend."

"I'll be back in Miami in a few weeks."

I turned to leave, and he grasped my hand, his thin, bony fingers wrapping around my wrist as if willing me to remain. "We will talk soon?" There was an urgency to his words that unsettled me.

"Of course," I reassured him. His hand loosened, sliding away like a boat slipping its moorings.

I crunched my way down the gravel path past the single-story pink building that housed the administration and then to the parking lot. My car sat by itself, surrounded by now-empty spaces, baking in the relentless sun. I opened the door and waited a couple of minutes to allow the hot air to escape before jumping in, and cranking up the air-conditioning, and driving the twenty minutes through the afternoon traffic to Graciela's place.

Graciela and her husband, Mario, lived in the house they'd bought when they first moved to Miami. Like my grandmother, Graciela refused to move away from those who had welcomed them into their hearts when they'd arrived from Havana.

I could hear voices as I knocked on the screen door and was about to call out when Graciela appeared.

"Catalina," she said, ushering me into the black-and-white-tiled room she always referred to as the "Florida" room. Today, the doors and windows were folded open to catch the trade winds. The floors created an invitation to the past, as did the clumps of palm trees dotted around the walls and between the white cane furniture.

"Sit down, here on the sofa," one of their friends urged, moving over to make room for me.

"What can I get you?" Graciela picked up a plate of sandwiches and rushed over.

I knew the empty feeling in the pit of my stomach, which had been there since I'd woken up, wasn't going to be fixed by food. "I'd love *un cafecito*."

"Mario! *Un cafecito* for Catalina," Graciela directed operations, then turned to me. "You must have more than coffee. Here, try one of these." Graciela thrust a plate of small cakes toward me, and I reluctantly took one, putting it on one of the small plates and sliding it onto the coffee table in front of me. Even though I'd had nothing to eat since early morning, my appetite had disappeared.

"And what about that nice young man of yours?" the woman seated next to me said. "Graciela said you're engaged now?"

"Liam? He really wanted to come to the funeral, but he had some big business meeting he couldn't reschedule." My words were apologetic, but the tone in my voice held the resentment of someone abandoned. Liam should have been here. "You know what it's like?"

Everyone nodded sympathetically as if they understood. I wished I could.

"He and Ita got on so well together," I added, attempting to make amends for his absence but failing miserably.

One of the men sitting opposite me raised his eyebrows at his neighbor in a covert operation I might've missed if I hadn't looked over at that very minute.

"Which reminds me, I've got something for you," Graciela said, her voice low—sharing-a-secret low. She beckoned me, and I followed her down the hall to her bedroom, where she opened the closet door and pulled out a package, which she handed to me.

"What's this?" I asked.

"It's from your grandmother. She wanted me to give it to you if something happened to her."

"Why didn't she give it to me herself?"

"That I do not know."

I sat down on the edge of the bed, the package in my lap, my hands hovering over the string that bound it.

My name had been scrawled on the front. There was no doubt that it was Ita's handwriting.

The string came away easily when I pulled one of the ends, and I peeled back the brown paper. The package contained a sepia-colored photo and three envelopes—a thick, official-looking envelope with a US Government stamp and two letters, one addressed to my grandmother and the other addressed to me. I held up the photo to show Graciela, who was now sitting on the bed beside me.

The photograph was of a family gathered on the steps of what looked like a two-story house. Three young women stood together on one step in front of their parents. I studied the photo closely, trying to pick up the nuances of their facial expressions. Two of the women were smiling at the camera, but the third stood slightly apart—unsmiling, disinterested, detached—her gaze fixed on someone or something beyond the frame.

There was a definite family likeness between them. I turned the photo over and recognized my grandmother's writing: "*Mi familia,*" I read aloud. A lump formed in my throat. I'd never seen any photos of her family before. Ita had always said she'd left them behind in Havana when they emigrated.

I looked up at Graciela, who smiled. She pointed to the woman in the middle of the photo. "The three sisters. That's Marielle standing next to your grandmother and that's Rosa beside her." Her voice softened when she mentioned Rosa, and a chill passed through me. I looked at the photograph, searching their features for any resemblance to mine. The similarities were uncanny. We were all tall and slender, and although Rosa's hair was cut short, there was no doubt that we were related.

"Rosa doesn't look as if she liked having her photo taken."

"Rosa loved having her photo taken." Graciela's voice took on a disapproving tone. "She was going through a difficult time."

Laying the photo carefully to one side, I checked the wad of papers from the "official" envelope. As I unfolded them, a silver chain and disc fell onto the floor. Graciela picked it up and handed it to me. On one side, there was an engraving of a woman rising out of the ocean.

"Who is this?" I asked.

"Our Lady of Regla." Graciela lowered her voice, as if saying it aloud would unleash events she could not control.

"Yemayá. To some, she's the Black Madonna of Regla, and to others, she is one of the orishas of Santería. She is the protector of women and keeper of secrets."

"I don't remember Ita wearing it," I said.

"Neither do I." Graciela shrugged. "But she obviously wanted you to have it."

I placed it to one side and picked up the two remaining envelopes. I put the first aside and opened the letter from my grandmother, reading through a mist of tears.

Mi querida Catalina,

I know you will have received this after my passing. Please don't be sad. I want you to know you brought such joy to our lives, and I want only happiness for you. I have left everything I own to you, including the claim to property that your grandfather and I owned in Cuba before we left. One day, it may be worth something. Until then, keep it safe from others who would do anything to get it.

Con mucho amor,

tu abuela.

I put it to one side and picked up the official envelope that had been included in the package. Inside was a document from the Foreign Claims Settlement Commission. I read through it and discovered that my grandparents had made a claim for a villa in Havana and a farm in Matanzas that had been confiscated after they left for the States in 1960.

"A house in Havana?" I handed the papers to Graciela. "And a farm—*Finca Grande.*"

"I knew that your grandparents had made an official claim when they left Havana and moved to the States." She took the paper from me and studied it. "From memory, the farm was a wedding gift from your great-grandmother's family, and they bought the villa from them just before they left for the States."

Excitement bubbled in the cauldron of my stomach, brewing the creation of a plan. Question after question raced through my mind. Was a claim the same as a deed? I picked up the photo again and looked at the house that had been the backdrop to my grandmother's early life. I couldn't help wondering why she hadn't told me, and more importantly, why the lawyer I'd spoken to earlier hadn't mentioned anything about the claim. I folded the piece of paper and returned it to the envelope.

"Do you think we should be getting back to the others? They must be waiting for us," I said.

"Yes, you can have a closer look at everything later," Graciela said.

I rewrapped the letters and the photograph in the brown paper and put the chain around my neck before rejoining the others, who were in the middle of reminiscing about the old days.

"Your coffee will be cold by now. Let me get you another one," Graciela said.

"Are you still teaching?" one of the men, Luis, asked, including me in the conversation.

"Yes, I love it."

"I don't know how you do it these days. When I was young —" Mario was about to launch into one of his popular stories about discipline dealt out by the Jesuit priests when he was interrupted by Graciela.

"You know your grandmother's sister was a teacher?" she said.

"Which one? Rosa?"

"No. The youngest sister, Marielle."

"I didn't know that. But then there are a lot of things I don't know about Ita's family. She never spoke about her sisters, or her life in Cuba, for that matter."

"It's a shame she never went back to see them," Luis added.

"Do you think that any of Ita's relatives would still be alive?" I asked.

"I'm not sure. I haven't heard that Marielle has passed away, so she might still be alive," Mario said.

Graciela flicked him a warning look and changed the subject. "Would you like to stay the night?"

"Thank you, but I have to go back. Liam's expecting me."

"Then you must make sure to keep in touch and visit us often."

"Of course I will."

The conversation eventually shifted away from me to Ita, and I spent the next couple of hours listening to stories about my grandparents' lives that I'd never heard before—stories about their farm in Matanzas, stories about grand balls, stories of privilege and wealth. Stories that piqued my curiosity.

"You know, Ita would never talk about her life in Cuba, and I never really understood why," I said. "Whenever I asked, she would always say that her life was in the States now."

I caught a glance between Mario and Luis, but no one

provided an explanation. And if they did know, they weren't sharing.

The shadows had lengthened and disappeared while we'd been celebrating Ita's life, and by the time I was ready to leave, the afternoon had melted into twilight, that place between day and night, that time of reflection between action and rest. After saying goodbye to everyone, I went to ring Liam and saw that I'd missed three calls from him. I dialed his number.

"I've been trying to call you!" Liam yelled over the loud music playing in the background.

"Sorry. My phone was on silent for the funeral, and I forgot to turn it back on."

"Everything okay?" he asked.

"Sorry, what did you say? I can barely hear you."

"Wait a second." I heard some muttered conversation as if he had his hand over the speaker. "Just wondering how everything is going?"

I took a moment to gather my thoughts, but it was apparently a moment too long. Liam had already moved on.

"Still coming home tonight?"

"Yes, tomorrow I'll have to sort some things out with the lawyer."

"Of course you will. Honey, look, I've gotta go." His voice was distracted, as if telling me he had a better offer. "I'll talk to you when you get back." He ended the call, and I was left staring at a blank screen.

Resentment trickled into the vacuum left by his call and by his absence at Ita's funeral.

I pictured Liam in the bar, surrounded by his work

colleagues, who nowadays seemed to see more of him than I did.

Disappointment that Liam would choose work over supporting me cut deeply, but not having the time to talk to me on the phone cut deeper. I resisted the urge to call him straight back. It could wait until I arrived home, but then… we needed to talk.

Chapter Two
____

I opened the door of Liam's apartment and dropped my suitcase inside. Twice as large as mine, with twice the view and twice the price. But mine was just a couple of minutes away from the school where I worked in West Palm Beach, another hour's drive north.

With Ita's inheritance, Liam and I might finally have enough money to put down a deposit on an apartment immediately. Then we wouldn't have to wait any longer to get married, and I could look for a permanent position in Fort Lauderdale.

I could understand Liam wanting to make sure that we were financially secure before getting married, but time was slipping by—five years, in fact. Long enough to be driving between Fort Lauderdale and West Palm Beach, long enough to be living between two places.

Jet the cat meowed a hole in the silence, rubbing against

my leg, arching his back, and pushing against me. I wasn't the boss of him—I didn't belong.

A lamp in the corner sent a soft glow across the room. The furniture, like the apartment, was all glass and angles. The curtains were open, and the city sparkle shone through the plate-glass windows. It was state-of-the-art modern, but I couldn't wait for us to buy a place together, one that was ours.

"I'm home," I called out. My voice bounced off the walls of the apartment. "Liam?"

No answer. No Liam. Just a note sitting by itself in the middle of the glass dining room table.

Hi Cate,

Gone out to grab a bite to eat. If I'm not home when you get in, join us at The Reef Club.

Liam

Disappointment grabbed my heart and crushed it. I'd had one of the worst weeks of my life, and my fiancé was out with his work colleagues. Again. The fact that he'd left details about where he was should've made me feel better … but it didn't.

I didn't want to spend time with Liam's friends. Exhaustion was pulling me toward a hot bath, but grief was pushing me toward spending time with Liam.

I put my bag in the bedroom and took out the parcel that Ita had left me. As I looked through the contents, I realized I hadn't read the second letter, which I now opened.

.   .   .

June 6, 1959

Querida *Marielle,*

I hope you are all well. Life here is much changed; it is so lonely on the farm, and I never see Mama and Papa. I am desperate for company. I feel so alone. I miss you so much.

Please write back to me with all your news. I can't wait till I see you all again.

Con cariño, tu hermana,

Rosa

My grandmother had never spoken of her family in Cuba, but she'd kept this letter from Rosa. Kept it for over fifty years. Kept it for me.

I felt the pendant around my neck. Yemayá. Protector of women … and secrets.

I filled the bath with hot water and submerged myself, washing away the grief of the last few weeks. My mind started to wander and ended up in the streets of Havana. The door to the world of "what if" slid open. What if I went to Havana? Found the house there. Found my relatives.

The planets seemed in alignment; the summer holidays would start in a couple of weeks, and I wouldn't have to be back to start the new school year until September—it was a perfect time to go to Havana. I could find out more about the house there and track down any remaining family at the same time. Surely Liam could take some time off work as well. The hot bath had done its trick.

I was a strong believer in striking while the iron was hot,

sometimes even when it was only lukewarm. Ita always said, *"El que espera desespera*; he who waits, despairs." It was a mantra that resonated with me and one I easily adopted. Liam thought I used it to excuse what he considered my impulsive actions.

I stood up, wrapped a towel around me, and grabbed my black dress out of my bag. I'd always prided myself on being able to get dressed in ten minutes, and tonight was no different.

I ordered an Uber while I was waiting for the elevator and couldn't believe my luck when it pulled up at the curb at the same time I did. *Yes, the planets were in alignment.*

Nearly thirty minutes later, I arrived at the entrance of *The Reef Club*. Tonight, it looked more chicken coop than swanky bar. I pushed through the noise, the crammed bodies, and the cocktail glasses in search of Liam. Smoke clogged my throat— Fort Lauderdale might have some of the strictest smoking laws in the country, but they didn't apply here; it was a stand-alone bar that didn't technically serve food. I pushed my way around the edge of the dance floor but still couldn't see Liam or his colleagues.

Applause and whistling filled the space left behind when the band stopped playing. A squeal erupted from the tables nearby, and I stopped in my tracks. A woman continued to dance on one of the wooden coffee tables, even though the music had stopped. She was petite and slim, with spiky short hair framing her elfin face. Her red chiffon dress floated around her as she moved in time with the music still playing inside her head. Carly.

"Carly, get down." A man had risen and held out his arms toward her.

Those sitting nearby joined his entreaties but were drowned out by the band starting their next song. Carly ignored everyone.

A second man stood up. He wasn't facing me, but I recognized him immediately—his short dark hair sculpted by his favorite barber, Leon, and broad shoulders a result of regular gym visits. The crowd around Carly was cheering her on.

"Get down, Carly," he demanded. Carly stopped dancing, took one look at Liam, and jumped into his arms, grabbing him tightly around the neck, her weight pushing him backward toward me.

Carly's lips latched onto his like a vacuum hose on full power. My blood started a slow simmer. I began counting. Stopped when I reached ten. The slow simmer had shot to boiling. The rest of Liam's friends, who appeared to be enjoying the show, saw me and stopped laughing.

Ben, Liam's closest friend at the law firm where he worked, recognized me and gave me a smile, an I-can't-wait-to-see-what's-going-to-happen-next smile. I didn't disappoint. I grabbed Liam's arm and pulled him toward me. He was still holding Carly, but when he turned and saw me, he managed to get her to stand on her own feet.

"Hello, Liam." My voice had a faux-fun feel, a-fancy-seeing-you-here kind of feel, a-what-the-hell-are-you-doing feel.

"Cate." His blurred eyes widened in their sockets, like a woolly lemur in the crosshairs looking for a flight path. Expressions ranging from surprise to guilt and everything in between flickered across his face. Carly just looked confused. Liam pushed her away into the arms of one of the other men. "Let's go outside," he said, grabbing my elbow and ushering me through the crowd to the door. "Why didn't you call? I could have met you at the airport." Liam asked.

"What was going on in there?" I demanded.

"What do you mean? Nothing was going on."

"It didn't look like nothing to me. In fact, it looked very much like something."

"You're overreacting. And stop giving me that look. I'm not one of your students."

"Overreacting?" I could hear my voice getting louder. I ignored the comment about "the look."

"Shhh." Liam pulled me out of the way of the crowds on the sidewalk into the recessed doorway of a shopfront.

"Don't *shhh* me."

"Cate, I promise you there is absolutely nothing going on between Carly and me. You saw her. I was just trying to stop her from making a fool of herself." He slipped his arm around my waist. "Come on. Let's go home," he said.

I pulled away from him, but he tightened his hold. We stood looking at each other. I searched his gray eyes for answers, but the shutters were up, the curtains closed, and the truth? Nowhere to be seen.

We had to walk a couple of blocks before we could find a taxi, and by the end of the ride home, I'd managed to calm down considerably. The scene with Liam and Carly played over and over in a loop in my head. Had I overreacted?

Liam made coffee and we stared at each other awkwardly on either side of the glass dining room table, as if we were on our first date and not sure what to say. I pushed aside the note he'd written earlier. A pregnant pause hung between us while we drank our coffee.

"I'd like to go to Havana," I said.

Liam looked surprised at the change of conversation, and I could see the tension leave his shoulders as he realized I'd called a truce and he'd escaped a bullet.

"Havana. Why Havana?"

I paused, trying to translate my emotions and thoughts into words that Liam might understand. "There's a chance that Ita's sister is still alive, and I'd like to find her. Now that Ita's gone, I have no one."

"Rubbish! You've got me."

"I know … but … today I listened to the stories Graciela and her friends were sharing, and I realized how little I knew about Ita and her life. I want to go and see where she grew up, see if any of my relatives still live there."

He leaned back in his chair. "You've always wanted to go to Paris and Venice. Are you telling me you'd rather go to Cuba?"

Liam was right. I'd never mentioned wanting to go to Cuba before. "I'd love to go to Paris and Venice, but I feel the need to go to Havana as soon as possible. So much of my grandmother's life is a mystery, and if I don't go soon, I'll miss the chance to find anyone who knew her."

Liam stood up, poured himself another coffee, and leaned against the bench. "You know your grandparents were quite wealthy when they were in Cuba. They owned a lot of property before they came to the States," he said.

I froze, my cup stalling mid-air like an elevator caught between floors. "How do you know that?"

"Your grandmother told me once when we were visiting."

"I don't remember that."

"Don't you? She also told us that she had a claim to the property they left behind."

"I don't remember that either. But I did find out about the claim when I was in Miami. That's another reason I want to go to Havana."

Liam's eyebrows started to rise, but he caught them and pulled them back into line.

He came around the table and stood behind me, his hands massaging my neck. "You know, this claim of your grandmother's is going to be worth something someday. And that someday may be sooner than we think. If relations between the States and the Cuban government improve one day, there could be a resolution to the embargo. And if that happens, there would be a real chance that you—we—could end up being quite well off. We could finally get a place of our own together."

I placed the cup softly on the table. "Liam, I don't believe you. I've just buried my grandmother, and all you can talk about is money."

Liam sat down and leaned forward, entwining his fingers in mine. "It would definitely help us achieve our goals. Maybe we should go to Havana. The sooner, the better."

"What do you mean?"

"You know, to find out what's happened with the house

and the farm. I know this guy who represents Americans with unresolved claims, and there's definitely money to be made," Liam mused. "I'm sure he would give us a good deal."

"How does that work?"

"He buys up the claims and then sells them to third parties who are interested in one day developing property in Cuba—it's kind of like an investment in the future when the claims are settled. I could talk to him."

My chest tightened. Things were moving far too quickly. Did I really want this? "There's no rush, is there?" I tried to steer the conversation back to my original idea. "But I'd still like to go to Havana. Do you think you could get some time off work to come with me?"

"Maybe…" His eyes swerved away from mine, dodging the question, and he loosened his grip on my hands.

"Yes, I do know how it is. You're always working, and we hardly get to see each other anymore." Indignation had lit a fire in my belly, and every word Liam said was stoking it. "In fact, you spend more time with your buddies from work than you do with me." I heard the whine in my voice and hated myself for it.

Liam shrugged. "It's my job, and let's face it, we need all the money we can get."

"Then you won't mind if I go over for a couple of weeks," I said, throwing down the challenge.

"You'd go without me?"

I didn't skip a beat. "If you're too busy."

I watched the second hand crawl around the clock's face while I waited for his answer.

Liam straightened in his chair. "You go, then. I guess if things ease up at work, I'll join you there."

I pushed back the chair from the table and walked over to the kitchen sink, aware that Liam was following my every move.

"Okay, I'll book tomorrow." *El que espera, desespera.* There was no hesitation in my voice. And no response from Liam.

Chapter Three

The taxi's lights swept over the faded yellow façade of the
Hotel Copacabana as it pulled into the driveway. Built in the
sixties, it was well-known, but not as well-known as the one
made famous in the song by Barry Manilow. There were more
luxurious hotels in Havana, but this one was reasonably priced
and located in Miramar, not far from Ita's family home.

The illuminated image of a toucan rested on the side of
the Copa's stucco wall, standing guard, its one eye staring into
the night.

Watching.

Before I even had time to get out of the taxi, the driver
had swung my bag out of the boot and handed it to the doorman, who gave me the briefest of smiles—one that vanished
like it had somewhere better to be—before motioning me to
follow. I dragged my luggage up the ramp, pushing through
the wall of salsa music, trying to escape each time the auto-
matic doors opened.

A curtain of black-and-white pendant light shades hung at various lengths, separating the lobby from the bar area. The lights cast a soft glow over patrons who lounged in wicker chairs, watching dancers pressed hard against each other on the dance floor.

The doorman waited patiently beside my bags while I checked in, then took off through the plate-glass doors. I followed him outside, past the floodlit pool, up two flights of stairs and down a dark corridor, where he stopped in front of a wooden door. He twisted the key in the lock and finally managed to open it, scraping it across the tiled floor.

"You're very lucky, *Señora*. You have a very nice room." He stood proudly at attention inside the door and waited for me to enter. Then he strode to the wall of faded curtains, before pulling them apart and wrestling open the sliding door.

"There, *Señora*, I told you. A very nice room with a view of the pool and … the ocean. And here …" He crossed quickly to the bathroom. "A very big bathroom."

The "very nice room" had many virtues, which he continued to list, and when he'd finally exhausted all of them, we stood together in awkward silence until I realized he was waiting for a tip. I hadn't had a chance to change any money, so I shamefully handed him a couple of US dollars.

"Thank you, *Señora*." The smile that flashed across his face was genuine and not so eager to get going this time. Money was money—and it appeared that US dollars would do.

Alone at last, I called Liam, and when he didn't answer, I stepped out onto the balcony.

The warm, sultry evening wrapped itself around me. I thought of Liam and wished he could've been here with me.

I'd been hoping to recapture some of the magic we'd felt when we'd first met. His recent promotion had taken over his life, and now it seemed to be an endless round of business meetings, working late, and being on call twenty-four hours a day.

There was no doubt that my decision to come to Havana against Liam's wishes had taken him by surprise. I'd even surprised myself a little.

The pool below was floodlit and reflected the white sculptures rising from its depths—two figures entwined holding a baby at one end and a number of dolphins destined to remain suspended in time over the bridge spanning the pool at the other end. The warm ocean breeze from the Straits of Florida caught the sound of laughter and music and carried them up to my balcony. I breathed deeply, letting the salty ocean air invigorate and energize me. "I am finally here," I whispered into the dark Havana night.

Daylight had transformed the scene from my balcony. The sculptures that had looked ethereal last night rose pure and white out of the diamond-sparkle surface of the pool. The sun was already beating down on the blue-striped towels stretched across rows of empty sun lounges in preparation for a long day in the sun. Waves pounded the walls of the ocean pool attached to the rock wall of the resort, the breaking white water swirling through the broken stone balustrade.

My stomach rumbled—it had been a long time since the wrap I'd had on the flight last night. I quickly showered and dressed, pulling on a denim skirt and cotton t-shirt. I swept my long dark hair—striking a contrast with the fair skin I'd inherited from my mother's Spanish side of the family—up into a ponytail.

After a quick glance in the mirror, I checked the time and then dialed Liam's number—no answer. The call went straight to voicemail. He was probably on his way to work. I'd give him a call later.

After a breakfast of toast and black coffee, I grabbed Marielle's address, my hat, and a water bottle, and approached the reception desk.

"Excuse me, *Señora?*" I asked. The receptionist was busy tapping on the computer, her long red nails flying across the keys. She bundled a pile of papers together and slipped a rubber band around them. Then, and only then, did she glance up.

"*Sí?*"

I pushed the paper with Marielle's address across the desk. "*¿Sabe si esta dirección está cerca de aquí?*" I mustered all the Spanish I could remember from school.

The receptionist's eyebrows drew together, bookending the two lines forming above the bridge of her nose. *Maybe I hadn't done such a good job with the Spanish.* She held out her hand for the map and drew a circle around the hotel. "You are here." She traced a line along the road parallel to the coast. "The place you're looking for is somewhere near here," she said, drawing a cross. "Sometimes the house numbers, they can be complicated. It is best you take a taxi." She pointed toward the glass doors. "The doorman will be able to help."

"*Gracias, Señora.*" I looked at the map and gauged the distance between the hotel and the villa. I was tempted to walk but changed my mind as soon as I hit the wall of humidity—humidity so thick, so heavy, so sticky I felt I was wading through jelly.

"*Señora*, can I help?" The doorman from last night had been replaced.

"*Sí, necesito un taxi por favor.*"

The only car to be seen was an old red Lada parked in the center. A man was polishing the hood with a piece of cloth.

I turned to go back inside to ask the receptionist to call a taxi when the doorman gave a piercing whistle. The man tucked the polishing cloth into his back pocket, jumped into the red car, and screeched over to the hotel's entrance.

Thinking my Spanish wasn't as good as I thought, I repeated myself in English.

"I would like a taxi, *por favor*."

"This is a taxi, *Señora*," the doorman said.

"It doesn't look like a taxi."

He shrugged. "No, not a registered taxi," he conceded. "But it is a taxi all the same."

The driver jumped out of his car, perspiration drenching his cream suit. His dark eyes were almost hidden by a curtain of straight black hair falling over his forehead, and a neatly manicured mustache framed a smile of perfect white teeth.

He walked toward me, swept his hair out of his eyes, and secured it on top of his head with his hat. As he came closer, I could see he was older than I first thought; I put him around fifty, although it was hard to gauge his exact age. He stood in front of me, his left hand on his heart, then bowed.

"Pedro *a su servicio!*" he declared.

The doorman waved me toward the open door, urging me

to get inside the vehicle. I walked toward the box-shaped car. A handwritten sign stuck to the windscreen assured me it was a taxi.

I slid into the back seat, and after three attempts to close the door, Pedro seemed satisfied and slipped into the driver's seat. I looked around the inside of the taxi. It had definitely seen better days. Days when you probably couldn't see the bitumen through the small hole in the floor. I bent over to have a closer look. Yes, as I suspected, it wasn't the only one. I positioned my feet carefully on what I thought were more solid sections of the floor.

"Where I take you, *Señora?*" he asked.

I handed him the address and prepared for the drive as best as I could by gripping the front seat. Pedro released the clutch and the "taxi" screamed out of the parking lot, pushing me hard against the back seat.

As we neared the address, Pedro slowed down. Each house, except the one outside where we stopped, had been newly renovated, freshly painted in pastel colors, and protected by neat, wrought-iron fences and gates.

"The Villa Marquez-Fuentes." Pedro beamed a smile so bright it could light up New York in a blackout.

The Villa Marquez-Fuentes, like Pedro's taxi, had also seen better days; its history and wounds lay exposed for all to see.

While the other Art Deco houses were surrounded by gardens and shrubs that had been clipped and cropped, the villa was shaded by a neighborhood of giant banyan fig trees and almost hidden by a tangled garden of bamboo, hibiscus, and passionflower fighting for space and domination.

Pedro didn't waste any time and jumped out of the car to open the door for me. "I wait for you here."

"It's probably better not to wait, Pedro. I'm not sure how long I'll be." Excitement, anticipation, and trepidation were doing battle in my stomach, leaving the butterflies exhausted. I didn't want to share this moment with anyone else.

Pedro drove off, albeit reluctantly. I took my grandmother's photograph out of my backpack and held it up to compare it with the house that stood in front of me. Nearly sixty years had made a difference, but through the tangle of plants and bushes, I could still see that it was the same house; the twin curved bay windows on either side were shaded by palm trees.

Vines gripped the side of the wall, searching out fresh, unexplored stone to cover, and thick curtains covered both windows. The wooden fence, unlike its neighbor's, needed a fresh coat of paint, and the gate, hanging by its hinges, gaped open.

I turned, looking over my shoulder, trying to imagine who or what had caught Rosa's gaze as it was taken.

Clenching and unclenching my fists to stop the tingling in my fingers, I pushed my way through the gate and walked up the marble steps to the door. I wiped my hands, sticky with perspiration, on my skirt. My fingers explored the cool twists and turns of the metal door knocker of the villa before I finally knocked loudly.

A parrot nesting in the branches of the nearby tree screeched and flew away. No answer and no sounds of anyone inside.

I fought my way through the overgrown path to the side of the house. Another set of stone steps led to a veranda that stretched along the entire side to a closed door. I tried knocking, but there was still no response. Disappointment surged through me. I was about to head back to the hotel, but stopped. I'd come too far to give up now.

I continued down the veranda and tried the second door, almost hidden among a clutch of pot plants. Still no response. I looked out on the garden filled with palm trees and tropical plants and waited for someone to answer the door.

The sound of the sea lured me toward the back of the house. A cool breeze flew off the water, whipping my hair around my face. I pushed the long strands that had escaped back into the elastic band and walked to the stone wall at the end of the property. I stood still for a couple of minutes, hypnotized by the waves crashing and clawing their way over the rocks—the white horses of the high tide jumping the wall, their bid for freedom short-lived as the water slipped back through the rocks into the sea.

I broke the spell of the crashing waves and forced myself to continue to the other side of the house. There was no veranda here, only a stucco wall with windows set high off the ground. The corner of one of the curtains had come loose from its rod and had left a small section of the window exposed.

I tried to ignore the small voice urging me to take a quick look inside to see if anyone still lived here. I glanced behind me and saw that the entire property was protected from prying eyes by a wall of greenery. Even though there were houses on either side, I couldn't see or hear anyone else.

"*El que espera …*" I murmured.

No amount of jumping or clinging to the wall helped me

to see inside. I needed something on which to stand, so I returned to the other side of the villa and dragged one of the garden chairs back to the window. Placing the chair under it, I tested my weight, and even though its legs sank into the soft grass, I thought I could balance on it long enough to at least see inside.

The chair wobbled back and forth as I shifted my weight to control my balance. With one foot on either edge of the chair, I gripped the top sash of the window to pull myself higher to see through the gap. Just another inch or two. A bit higher.

"Can I help you?" a voice powered through the humidity, demanding attention. I turned and snatched a glance at a man glaring at me—flashing dark eyes, black waves of hair brushing the collar of his shirt, broad shoulders, and a hands-on-hips-what-the-hell-are-you-doing stance.

I yelped in fright as my sudden movement tipped the chair backwards and I fell heavily, my ankle collapsing under my weight. A cry of pain escaped. I moved my foot slightly and wriggled my toes. Luckily, nothing appeared to be broken. The pain transformed itself into anger.

"You scared me!" I exclaimed, ignoring his question and building a barricade of indignation around me for protection. I dragged myself to my feet, using the upturned chair, and leaned against it to save putting too much weight on my injured ankle. We stared at each other, and I pulled my eyes from his before I became lost in their dark depths. My heart was racing, and I wasn't sure if it was only due to being caught in an embarrassing situation.

"What do you think you're doing?" The man towered over me, making me feel at a distinct disadvantage. I squared my shoulders, straightened my back, and winced as I put extra weight on my foot.

My face caught fire as heat rushed up from my neck. "I was checking to see if anyone was home."

"And this is how you check if someone is at home? You do not knock on the door? Wait to be invited inside?" His dark eyes narrowed. "Why are you sneaking around like a thief?"

My face flamed hotter. "I was not sneaking. I knocked, but there was no answer."

He shrugged. "Of course. You didn't think that if no one answers, then that is because there is probably no one at home?" Cracks were beginning to form in my wall of indignation, and I was beginning to feel exposed. He paused. "I have just this minute arrived to find you breaking into my home."

There was no way I could refute the claim. Caught red-handed and red-faced, and wishing the ground would do the decent thing and swallow me, my only course of action was to apologize.

"I'm sorry. I wasn't sure if anyone lived here anymore. I think my grandparents used to live here once … in this house."

"Here? I do not know." He paused. "But Marielle Marquez might know. She's not here now. You will have to come back." His voice took a break from indignant and suddenly turned helpful.

"Marielle Marquez-Fuentes? She still lives here?" Hope pushed my voice higher. Faster.

"*Sí.*" He was looking at me strangely now.

I held my breath, trying to calm the excitement rising at the thought that I was finally going to meet Marielle. "My name is Catalina Johnson." I introduced myself and held out my hand. "Marielle *Marquez-Fuentes* is my great-aunt. My grandmother, Alicia—" I began.

"I'll make sure she gets your message." His words cut me off, his dark eyes narrowing as they traveled down the length of my body like a panther sizing up its prey.

I was dismissed like a naughty schoolgirl, and I didn't like it. He swung the chair over his shoulder and turned to walk away.

"Will Marielle be home this afternoon? I can come back later."

He turned and gave a do-as-you-want shrug. "Three o'clock. But next time, knock on the door."

I straightened my dress, tucked my embarrassment into my bag, and limped out of the front gate, which squeaked in sympathy behind me. I stopped beside the blue Chevrolet now parked out front and turned to take one last look at the house.

The curtains twitched in the front bay window.

A fleeting movement.

A woman?

Marielle?

Chapter Four

___

I started in the direction of the hotel but had only hobbled a block when Pedro and his "taxi" slid to a stop beside me.

"*Señora*, jump in and I take you back to the Copacabana."

With my ankle throbbing and my pride and ego bruised, I was grateful to slide into the back seat.

"Would you like me to show you Havana? I am a very good driver, and I do a great price."

"I don't know, Pedro. I've hurt my ankle …"

He looked at me in the rear-view mirror, caught my eye and probably the guilty blush I could feel flushing my face.

"No matter, *Señora*. You see Havana from the back seat of my taxi? No? No walking. You just sit and relax and enjoy. Pedro will do all the work."

We negotiated a price, and I spent the next couple of hours in a whirlwind tour driving past Fifth Avenue, the gardens, the Colón Cemetery, and the Malecón, before finally ending up in Old Havana. Pedro slowed to a stop-start pace, squeezing his taxi through the narrow cobblestone streets filled with tourists and budding entrepreneurs selling a slice of Havana Past.

"My uncle has a very nice café near here. You want, we can stop for something to eat?"

I checked my watch. It was one-thirty—plenty of time to grab something before heading back to the Villa Marquez-Fuentes.

After a ham-and-cheese sandwich, Pedro drove me back to the villa and gave me a scrap of paper with his name and phone number on it. "My business card. I can come whenever you need me, Señora."

"Thank you, Pedro, and please call me Cate." I put the paper in my bag and waited for three o'clock.

I watched the minutes tick by from under the shade of an African Tulip tree diagonally opposite the villa and calculated the time it would take me to get to the front door.

Five minutes to go.

Two minutes.

I took a deep breath and crossed the road. I hesitated when I reached the gate, but only for a second, then strode up the steps and knocked on the door. Forcing myself to breathe slowly, I waited. Eventually, the door inched open to reveal an elderly woman. I could immediately see the resemblance to the young woman in my photo.

She stood straight and proud, her head tilted to one side, her white hair pulled back severely from her face, and her dark eyes searching my face, questioning. "Can I help you?"

"My … my name … is Catalina Johnson." My words became tangled with my emotions and were trapped in my throat. I forced them out. "I think my *abuela* … Alicia … used to live here."

A look of confusion, then a slow dawn of recognition spread across her face. "You are Alicia's granddaughter?"

"Yes."

"Catalina." Marielle opened her arms, and it seemed so natural for me to walk into her embrace—an embrace filled with the love I could no longer show my grandmother.

Marielle stepped back and held me at arm's length. "Let me look at you." She studied my face closely and hugged me again, then held her hands to her heart. "What am I thinking? Come in. Come in. We will talk inside."

Just as Marielle turned to go inside, the man I'd met earlier in the day appeared from the shadows behind her. Scowling, he pushed past us, acknowledging neither myself nor my earlier transgressions. I watched him head down the steps and slam the gate behind him before jumping into the blue convertible. He revved the engine, then roared off, leaving a trail of fumes and smoke behind him.

"That's Antonio," Marielle said by way of an introduction, "my godson. He came to live with me when he was twelve … that was twenty years ago. He's obviously in a hurry."

I wouldn't have been so charitable in describing his behavior.

"Let's go inside." Marielle turned, and I followed her into the villa.

The hallway was wide with dark timber floors and paneled walls. A rainbow of colors flooded through the stained-glass windows above the door, spreading across the floor on either side of the doorway.

"This is the sitting room." Marielle led the way through the first door on the right. I followed her into a room with furniture upholstered in faded jewel-colored fabrics. One wall was completely covered with a bookcase, and photos crowded the shelves of a smaller bookcase on another wall. The bay window reached almost to the ceiling.

A huge mahogany desk and chair filled one entire corner, but still left enough space for a sideboard and four comfortable armchairs to be positioned around a coffee table. "I'll make coffee and then, Catalina, you can tell me everything." Marielle pointed to one of the chairs near the coffee table. I sat down, struggling to find a comfortable place between the aging springs while Marielle disappeared into another room.

Within fifteen minutes, Marielle returned with a tray carrying delicate china cups of coffee. I took a sip, thought of Ita, and could feel tears starting to pool in my eyes. "You know my grandmother … passed away recently?" I stumbled over the words and tried to keep the tremor from my voice.

Marielle nodded. "Father Paul contacted me."

"Father Paul?" My voice reared up like a startled foal. I was surprised that he would even know how to contact my grandmother's family in Cuba.

"Yes, he and your grandmother went to university together, and so we both knew him well."

I was even more surprised. He hadn't mentioned this at the funeral. Was this why he wanted to talk to me? Between sips of the strong, dark coffee, the door to the past opened, and we shared memories of my grandmother—her sister.

"You know, I visited her once in America?" Marielle said.

"You didn't want to stay like Ita?" I asked.

Marielle hesitated before answering. "No, not really. I thought I might, but then I realized paradise was here, in my own backyard … and anyway, by then it was too late," she added in a low whisper.

I thought about my grandmother. "It must have been hard for her to leave her family and friends and live in a strange country." I wasn't sure I could ever find that kind of courage.

"It was hard. Very hard. But then … it was hard for all of us." Marielle changed the subject. "Where are you staying while you are here in Havana?"

"At the Hotel Copacabana."

"Nonsense! You are family, and you will stay here with me."

I started to shake my head.

"I insist. We have plenty of room. Come, let me show you the rest of the villa." She stood up and led the way down the hallway.

Marielle gave me a tour of each room. Next to the sitting room was a formal lounge room, and opposite was a dining room. The kitchen opened onto a veranda and a short flight of steps that led down to the garden I'd discovered previously.

Further down the hall, there was a large office and closed rooms, which Marielle referred to as reception rooms. At the end of the hall, a staircase curved its way to the first floor.

We climbed the staircase to an internal gallery that ran around the entire floor, exposing the hallway below. Closed doors stretched down both sides. "The bedrooms are all on this floor." She nodded at the closed door at the end. "That's Antonio's room. And this one belongs to Haydée. You'll meet her soon. She is the daughter of a close friend in Viñales and is staying here while she goes to university. I thought that maybe she and Antonio …" Her voice held the whisper of a wish. Then she shook her head and continued down the gallery.

I found myself strangely interested in whether Antonio and Haydée were in a relationship or whether it was just wishful thinking on Marielle's part. Antonio was certainly attractive, if only he could do something about his anger.

"This will be your room," Marielle said, opening the door before drawing open the curtains to let in the daylight.

I looked around. Although the furnishings were dated, the room was light and airy, very different from the ones I'd already seen. The antique furniture was beautifully carved and stylish, although not as ornate as the other rooms.

"It's beautiful." I went to the window and looked outside into a canopy of trees and the ocean beyond.

"This used to be your grandmother's room. Of course, it needs new curtains, but you know, times here are difficult and it's not so easy to buy things now," Marielle said.

I didn't care about the curtains. In fact, I loved the idea of staying in Ita's old room.

"Are you sure I won't be imposing?" I turned to face Marielle.

"Of course not, Catalina," she said, giving me another hug. "I'm looking forward to you staying here. Our family together again."

"Will Antonio mind?"

"Antonio will not care," she reassured me.

I remembered our last encounter, and I wasn't so sure.

We walked around the gallery to the other side.

"Are these bedrooms as well?" I asked.

"Yes, but we don't use them. We keep a couple of rooms made up ready for guests, not that we have many these days. Having you here will be like having Alicia with us again."

"Where does Aunt Rosa live?" I asked.

She stopped mid-stride and placed her hand on the railing beside her. "Rosa?" Marielle turned to face me, one hand on the railing and the other playing with the strand of pearls at her throat like worry beads. "Rosa doesn't live here." She turned and walked down the gallery to the staircase.

"Does she live in Havana?" My question hung in the air like a bubble, wistful and full of hope.

"We don't know," Marielle said, stopping and turning toward me again. "We haven't heard from Rosa since nineteen fifty-nine." Her sharp words burst the bubble, hope seeping from the cut.

"Now, let's have another coffee," Marielle said, her tone telling me that she had finished discussing Rosa.

"I'd love one, *gracias*." I was happy to drop the topic … but just for now.

We returned to the living room, but there was no more talk of Rosa—only of Liam and my plans while in Havana.

"It's a shame that your young man wasn't able to come with you. I'd love to meet him."

"He's going to try to get away, but his work is pretty busy at the moment. If he can't make it this time, we'll definitely come back so you can meet him."

"You know the old saying—if a man loves you, he will move heaven and earth to be with you, even if he is working."

I smiled, remembering that Ita would say the same thing.

Maybe there was some truth in it. Either way, I was still waiting.

I rummaged around in my bag and took out the photo I had brought with me. "I found this in my grandmother's things."

Marielle stared at the photo, and a melancholy Mona Lisa smile spread across her face.

"I remember this photo. It was taken on the front steps of the villa. We were about to visit your great-grandparents in Matanzas. Our last Christmas together. That's me." Marielle pointed to the young woman to the left of the family grouping. "I was the youngest," she mused. "Yes, those were the days. We were so happy and … so naive. We had no idea what the future was going to bring."

I could feel Marielle slipping away from me into the past.

The front door slammed and reverberated through the villa, bringing us back to the present with a jolt. I glanced up to see Antonio stomp past the door and disappear down the hall. A frown flashed across Marielle's face, then disappeared behind a mask of practiced politeness.

"I think I'll go back to the hotel and arrange to check out early."

"I'll expect you sometime tomorrow." Marielle squeezed my arm. "I can't tell you how good it is to see you."

She walked me to the door. I glanced around, but there was no sign of Antonio. I wondered what lay behind that tough, angry exterior and hoped he wasn't going to make it difficult for me to stay at the villa. Marielle and I gave each other another hug, and I left her to deal with Antonio.

The sun was still high in the sky, but the breeze had stalled.

No sign of a taxi. And no sign of Pedro. I arrived at the Copacabana exhausted but happy. I'd found Marielle, my grandmother's sister, and the Villa Marquez-Fuentes—my grandmother's home.

I paused at the gate. Marielle knew about my grandmother's death. But did she know about the claim my grandmother had made on the villa? The claim I had inherited.

Chapter Five

I arrived at the Villa Marquez-Fuentes early the next morning with my luggage and hopes of getting to know my great-aunt. I knocked on the door and caught a familiar perfume, sweet and gentle on the breeze. Frangipanis, my grandmother's favorite flower. A voice behind me scattered the memories that were beginning to take shape.

"*Sí?* Can I help you?" A young woman was standing behind me at the bottom of the steps, one hand resting on the marble pillar, the other holding a carry bag.

"*Buenos días*, my name is Catalina Johnson. Marielle Marquez is expecting me."

I caught the hint of an eyebrow lift, and then her brown eyes went blank. "*Bienvenida*, I'm Haydée," the woman said. Tall, well-proportioned but with curves that were squeezed into tight jeans and a jersey top, Haydée climbed the stairs and pushed past me to open the door. "This way," she tossed over her shoulder.

I hesitated on the threshold, but the lure of the past was too strong. I grabbed my bags and followed Haydée down the hallway to the kitchen, where she put her carry bag onto one of the two benches that lined the walls. She picked up a piece of paper from the middle of the table and read it.

"Marielle's out, but she'll be home later."

"I could come back." I looked at my pile of luggage and hoped that Haydée had noticed it as well.

"No need. You're here now. This way."

I shrugged my backpack onto my shoulders and pulled my suitcase down the hallway behind her.

I could hear voices coming from the room on our left—male voices, angry. I glanced through the open doors of the reception room. Antonio and two other men were seated at a table poring over a large piece of paper, while a fourth man stabbed it with his finger.

I paused at the open door.

"It's these buildings here. Right on the plaza," one of the men said.

Antonio slammed his fist onto the table, pushed back his chair, and towered over the other men. "Impossible! We must —" Antonio looked up, his eyes locked onto mine like a homing missile, and my heart stumbled, skipped a beat, and tried to avoid the strike. The other men turned and followed his gaze. Antonio started to stride toward the door.

"This way," Haydée called to me from halfway up the flight of stairs.

I started after her, the door slamming behind me and masking the rumble of raised voices continuing to battle each other. I climbed the winding marble staircase, lugging my bags one step at a time and wondering what I had just witnessed. Haydée waited at the top of the staircase, leaning against the balustrade, watching my awkward progress but not offering any help.

My excitement at moving in with Marielle was decreasing by the minute, by the step. Despite what Marielle believed, it appeared neither Antonio nor Haydée was at all enthusiastic to have me as a house guest.

"This way," Haydée barked.

I followed her to the room Marielle had shown me yesterday. After I'd dragged my suitcase through the door, I turned to thank her, but she'd already disappeared. I sat on the bed and looked around the room. Ita's room. A lump stuck in my throat, heavy with grief, but I refused to let it overwhelm me. I dragged my suitcase onto the bed.

With my clothes unpacked and my private documents secured in the locked cupboard, I slipped the key into the pocket of my shorts, grabbed my backpack, and went downstairs. No voices, angry or otherwise, and no sign of Haydée or Antonio.

It was so hot I was melting faster than ice in a mojito, so I escaped to the shade of the garden to wait for Marielle. The minute hand dragged its way around the numbers until I could stand waiting no longer. I mentally flicked through the list of places I wanted to visit. With only two weeks, I didn't want to waste a minute.

I decided on the Colón Cemetery. Not just for its historical significance—I needed to find where my family was buried and pay my respects. Perhaps I might find Rosa's name there. I checked the map in the guidebook and realized that it was too far to walk, especially now that it was mid-morning and the heat was worsening.

I quickly dismissed the thought of walking to the Copacabana on the off chance that a taxi might be waiting for me, so I rummaged through my backpack and found Pedro's card. A part of me, the part that remembered the sawn-off seatbelts and the hole in the floor, hesitated, but the impulsive part of me had me reaching for my phone and dialing Pedro's number. Pedro pulled up in front of the villa within a couple of minutes.

"*Señora* Cate, Pedro at your service." He levered open the door and wiped the seat with a clean piece of cloth before helping me into the back seat. After he was sure I was safely inside, he slammed the door shut, then gave it a second shove with his hip to make sure it was closed.

"Where to, *Señora?*" he asked. He was looking at me in the rear-view mirror, and I could tell from the crinkles at the sides of his eyes that he was smiling.

"Colón Cemetery, please, Pedro."

We were soon hurtling through the crowded streets toward the cemetery. In the absence of any seatbelts, I adopted the brace position against the back of the seat in front of me each time Pedro accelerated, turned a corner, or changed lanes. Miramar slipped past me; tree-lined avenues and restored villas against a background of blue skies and blaring horns.

"Crazy drivers." Pedro accelerated and switched lanes, adding his car's horn to the woodwind section of the action unfolding around us.

Pedro didn't slow down until the yellow wall separating the living and the dead came into view. The head and wings of an angel peeked over the top of the Colón Cemetery wall, perhaps keeping an eye on the living in her spare time. He found a space between the oncoming traffic, slammed his foot on the accelerator, and swung the taxi around before skidding to a stop in a storm of gravel outside the cemetery's entrance.

There was a rush of men toward the car, but Pedro was faster than all of them and had opened the door and helped me climb out before they reached us.

"They want to be your guide." He nodded at the group closing in around us. He rubbed his thumb against his fingers, indicating that this service would come at a price.

"Thank you, Pedro. How much do I owe you?" When he named an amount, I paid him and added a tip.

"*Señora* Cate, thank you," he said, pocketing the money before revving the taxi and leaving me to do battle with the crowd of potential guides.

I chose the closest, who introduced himself as Marco, and we negotiated a price that made me realize that I was severely underpaying Pedro.

"You wait here. *Un minuto.*" Marco held up one finger. "I'll be back." He disappeared inside the office at the side of the main entrance, while I stood there, looking down the avenue Cristóbal Colón toward the Central Chapel.

The sun pounded the cobblestones between the graves and reflected off the marble tombs, which marked the final resting places of many of the great families of Havana. After a quick introduction, Marco began his well-rehearsed tour.

Our first stop was at the fireman's memorial dedicated to the bravery of the men who had died in a fire in 1890. It was large—large enough to ensure that they wouldn't be forgotten. We then moved on to the central chapel.

"We cannot go inside right now because there's a funeral in progress. Not everyone can use the chapel—it's reserved for those whose families have served the state," Marco explained before moving on.

While I lingered at each of the tombs, fascinated by the artistry of the stone masons, Marco waited in scraps of shade wherever he could find them. Now, he was huddling in a circle of shade cast by one of the small trees struggling to thrive in the gardens of alabaster angels and lost souls.

Marco wiped the sweat from his face with a piece of cloth and then replaced it in the belt loop of his jeans and waited for me to catch up. He kept up a fast pace, stopping only briefly at key points of interest to explain the funerary art and the history of the great families of Havana, most of whom had left the island in the years following the Triumph of the Revolution.

"You seem to be very familiar with the cemetery and its history," I said.

"I spend a lot of time here. It's a very big responsibility."

"Is there any way I can find my family's crypt?"

Marco started to shake his head. "Maybe … There are many graves here. What is their name?"

"My grandmother's surname was Marquez-Fuentes. Her family was originally from Spain."

Marco's eyebrows contracted while he thought about my question. "Marquez-Fuentes." He stretched out his response. "*Sí*, I know the name." His face lit up with a smile. "I think I may know the resting place of the Marquez-Fuentes. If my memory is correct, and most times it is, they were a *familia muy importante, no?* Very … how you say? Well-off … influential. Yes, come this way, and I can show you some other graves on the way."

I followed Marco past a number of tour groups, each one accompanied by their own version of Marco. Everyone, that was, except a man with a white hat, standing by himself and staring in our direction. Surely, he couldn't be looking at us. I quickly glanced behind to see what he could be watching, but when I looked back, the man turned, disappearing behind one of the mausoleums.

I gulped some water from my bottle and wiped the perspiration from my forehead with the back of my hand.

"It is getting too hot for you, no?" Marco asked.

"It is hot, but I'm fine."

"That is good because now we see something special."

We walked through avenues of angels and crosses until we arrived at a grave surrounded by people. I turned to check if the man in the white hat was following. He was standing near one of the graves we had passed. An uneasiness started in my stomach—only Pedro knew where I was. I grabbed my phone and quickly snapped a shot of him before he could disappear.

Marco stopped in front of a grave covered in flowers. Women in brightly colored dresses had made themselves comfortable sitting on the surrounding graves.

"It looks like we have interrupted a funeral?" I whispered to Marco. "Should we leave?"

"No. Is no funeral. This is the grave of *La Milagrosa,* and these," he gestured at the people milling around, "are people looking for a miracle."

"A miracle?"

"Yes. Watch, and you will see."

I looked to where he was pointing and saw a man walking backwards from the grave, bowing. When he returned to the group of women, one of them rose and took his place at the foot of the grave and used the brass ring to knock three times.

I opened my mouth to ask Marco a question, but he raised his fingers to his lips to silence me and nodded toward the grave. I watched the woman place a bunch of flowers on top of the bunches already there, then whisper some words that couldn't be heard. I watched her walk backwards to where she started. This was repeated by the next person … and the next.

Marco led me away from the gathering.

"What is happening?" I asked when we were a safe distance away.

"It's a long story … and a sad one," Marco began in a low voice. "Amelia was the wife of a wealthy man, but she died while giving birth. Sadly, the child also died. And the husband? He was distraught. Amelia and her child were both buried together, the baby at Amelia's feet. Every day, the husband would come and knock on the grave to let Amelia know that he was there and would spend hours talking to her. When it was time to leave, he would walk backwards because he refused to turn his back on his wife and child."

Marco wiped the perspiration from his forehead. "And then, after a year, they opened the grave to bury another family member." He lowered his voice. "And do you know what they found?" I shook my head. "They found the baby was no longer at Amelia's feet but was now in her arms. So, it is said that if you have a strong desire for a miracle, then you must come to Amelia's grave and make your wish." I looked over at the growing pile of flowers on the grave. "You make your wish now?" Marco asked.

My wish? Life with Liam? Finding Rosa? Getting to know Marielle? "Maybe another time," I said.

"*Sí*. No problem. But a word of warning. You must be very careful what you wish for because that is what you will receive." He walked away without waiting for an answer.

Before leaving, I took one last look at Amelia's grave and saw the man with the white hat standing near the group of women watching us.

"Marco?" He looked around at me. "See that man over there?"

"Where?" Marco turned and looked in the direction I was pointing.

"Over there. The man with the white hat. Near Amelia's grave. I noticed him when we first came in, and I think he's been following us while we've been here."

"He's probably just following the groups around to listen to their guides. It happens all the time. Some people just don't want to pay the money for their own guide." I looked over to where the man had been standing, but he was no longer there. "Besides, why would he be following you?"

"Good question." I couldn't think of a single reason. "I'm probably just being hyper-vigilant, thinking I was back in Fort Lauderdale."

"Now, then, onto the crypt of the Marquez-Fuentes."

We retraced our steps to the more grandiose crypts and headed down the second avenue, making a couple of turns. Looking at the thousands of graves in each direction, I was grateful that I had a guide because I was pretty sure I wouldn't be able to find my way without one.

After many turns, we stopped in front of a massive stone structure with glass doors. Two angels stood on either side, their wings wrapped around their bodies.

"This, *Señora*," he stood with one arm encompassing the crypt before us, "is the resting place of the Familia Marquez-Fuentes." His voice reverberated through the silence like a ringmaster announcing a performance. I felt overwhelmed by the scene before me, while Marco squeezed himself into yet another small square of shade to wait for me.

I recognized my great-grandparents' names in the long list that connected me to the past. Here, in front of me, were many lifetimes about which I knew absolutely nothing. A blanket of sadness and loss for the family I had never known wrapped itself around me like the angels' wings.

I read on. Even though I didn't expect to see Rosa's name, I still scanned the list on the front of the memorial.

It wasn't there.

Marco moved closer, wiped his forehead again, and looked at his watch.

I walked around the crypt to see if there was a second section on which names might be found and I became aware Marco was following behind me.

"*Señora?* You are looking for something in particular?" he asked.

"I expected my great-aunt Rosa's name to be here, but I was wrong." I grabbed my phone out of my backpack and snapped a couple of photos from different angles.

When I'd finished, we headed back toward the main

entrance, past Amelia's grave, past the firemen's memorial, and finally to the tomb in the shape of a pyramid. I memorized the route— signposted by angels and crosses—so that I could return to my family's crypt, maybe even return to make a wish by Amelia's grave.

Just as a taxi was dropping off a group of tourists, Marco darted out of the entrance, grabbed the driver, and quickly negotiated a fare for me to Miramar.

I slid into the back seat, the taxi idling and waiting for a gap in the line of traffic. While we were waiting, I glanced out the side window. The man with the white hat was speaking to Marco under a palm tree at the entrance.

A shiver tingled up my spine, then fell to the pit of my stomach.

The taxi driver glanced at me in the rearview mirror. "Is there something wrong, lady?"

I met his eyes in the mirror. "No, nothing." I smiled, trying to convince both of us that everything was fine, but my stomach remained empty and hollow.

Something wasn't right.

Chapter Six

I tried to shake off the uneasy feelings that had traveled back with me from the cemetery. When the taxi pulled up in front of the villa and I paid the driver, I headed toward the front door. Butterflies darted and danced beside me and through the tangle of green that bordered the path. The key Haydée had given me slipped easily into the lock, and I pushed the wooden door open and stepped into the welcome cool.

I had hoped Marielle would've returned from visiting her friend, but emptiness greeted me when I entered the hall.

I'd just made a cup of coffee when the door to the garden opened. A woman I had never met stood inside the doorway. She had a smile that caused her brown eyes to crinkle at their corners, but otherwise her olive skin on her round face was almost wrinkle-free.

"Oh, *perdón.* I gave you a fright. I'm Isabelle, Marielle's friend, and you … you must be Catalina." She didn't wait for confirmation, launching herself toward me, wrapping her arms around me and kissing me on both cheeks. "*Bienvenida a Cuba.* Come. Come, bring your coffee out and join us in the garden. We've just been to the markets." She picked up a plate of *galletas*—cookies dusted with sugar—from the table, and I followed her outside.

"Look who I found," Isabelle announced as we joined Marielle.

"Don't be ridiculous. You didn't find her at all." Marielle brushed away her announcement like a mosquito in the Havana heat.

"I hope I'm not intruding," I said.

"No. No. Sit down. You are not intruding," Marielle assured me.

"It looks like you've been out," Isabelle commented.

I tucked strands of hair that had escaped into my elastic. "Yes, I decided to visit the Colón Cemetery."

"You came all this way to see The City of the Dead?" Isabelle asked, her tone making it clear she thought it an unusual choice.

"Yes, I did. I really wanted to visit the family crypt. I know Ita would have wanted me to do that."

A slight frown traced its way over Marielle's forehead, and I wasn't sure if it was caused by the mention of Ita or the family crypt.

"And did you find it?" Isabelle asked.

"Yes, eventually. Marco, the guide, helped me."

"I'm amazed you found it at all," Marielle said.

"I hope you have plans to see more of Havana than the cemetery while you are here," Isabelle said.

"Oh yes. I intend to see as much as I can. I don't want to waste a minute. And I want to see the countryside as well."

"You know your grandparents owned a farm in the country, in Matanzas?" Isabelle said.

I could've told them then that I already knew about the farm—that I knew about my grandmother's claim on the villa and the farm.

But I didn't.

And I didn't know why.

"I'd love to visit it. See where they used to live. Is Matanzas far from Havana?"

"Not so far, but I don't know whether it would be worth the trip. There's not much of the farm there anymore," Isabelle said. "Is there, Marielle?"

"I don't know … I haven't been there for years. Just the house and a couple of outbuildings, I think," Marielle replied, shaking her head. "Like everywhere in Cuba. No one wants to work on the farms anymore. That's young people nowadays. No commitment to helping our country. They're only interested in life in the big city," she added softly.

Isabelle reached over, covered Marielle's hand, and shook it slightly. "Marielle, young people today are just the same as they used to be in our day. Have you forgotten? You and Rosa never enjoyed visiting the farm. You much preferred the fun and excitement that was to be had in Havana." Isabelle smiled. "Remember those stories Rosa would tell about the Hotel Nacional and the Riviera? So exciting." She turned to me. "You can't imagine what it was like," she said. "Rosa would tell us all about the movie stars, the dresses and jewels … Frank Sinatra."

"It sounds like it was an exciting time," I said to Isabelle.

"Marielle can tell you some stories too. Can't you, Marielle? I never went to the nightclubs … or had fancy clothes, for that matter."

"I'd love to hear what it was like growing up in Havana."

"Me? I didn't grow up in Havana. I grew up on the farm in Matanzas," Isabelle said.

"My grandmother's farm?" I asked.

"Yes. Isabelle *worked* for your grandparents." Marielle emphasized the word "worked" and added a full stop, which signaled the end of the conversation.

Isabelle threw back her head and laughed—a laugh that was as full and as round as she was—then reached over to take Marielle's hand once more.

"My dear friend, you don't have to protect or stand up for me. Yes," Isabelle said, looking at me. "I did work for your grandparents at their farm. My family didn't have much, but we did have each other. And while I may not have had fancy dresses or gone to nightclubs, I still used to enjoy hearing about Rosa's exploits."

I looked at the two women together. Marielle and Isabelle —the yin and yang of friends. Isabelle, robust with dark hair, Marielle silver-haired, fine-boned and fragile. I wondered about the twists and turns their lives had taken over the years.

"I'd love to know more about those times … and about Rosa."

Marielle stood and started clearing the table.

"Sit down, Marielle." I was surprised by the authority in Isabelle's voice. "Marielle doesn't like talking about the past or about Rosa, do you?" Isabelle turned to Marielle. "But I think it's about time she did." The two women exchanged a glance that was impossible for me to read.

"Another time, perhaps," Marielle said, her voice suddenly weary.

"Marielle, time is running out. We aren't getting any younger," Isabelle said, picking up the tray. "Why don't you show Catalina Rosa's room?" She tossed the idea like a hand grenade into the silence, then she left us and headed toward the kitchen with the tray rattling with empty cups and saucers.

"Rosa's room? I'd love to see it." I jumped into the silence, desperate to find out more about my family … and Rosa's disappearance.

But I wasn't just searching for my family roots, for Rosa. I also needed to know what had caused my grandmother to cut all ties with her family.

"No one has been in Rosa's room for nearly sixty years." Marielle was dodging my request like Pedro dodges cars.

"That's a long time."

"My parents were so distraught by her disappearance, they locked up that part of the house … and it's remained closed. We've never needed the room because the house is so big."

Isabelle reappeared in the doorway, her bag over her arm. "I'm off now. I'll leave you two to get to know each other." She blew us both a kiss, but the look she gave Marielle was for her alone—a look that was both encouraging yet unyielding.

"I'd really love to see Rosa's room," I said, "but I understand if it's too upsetting to go up there after so many years."

Marielle hesitated. She looked toward a door at the end of the veranda, then sighed. "Perhaps it is time, like Isabelle says, to face the past. The room holds memories. Both good and bad. Wait here." Marielle went inside the house and returned with a key. "Come with me."

I followed Marielle down the veranda and waited while she struggled with the lock. "Can't you get to Rosa's room from inside the villa?"

Marielle looked at me. "No. Originally, this used to be guest accommodation for Papá's business colleagues when they visited Havana, but Rosa claimed it for herself when she turned eighteen. She was always Papá's favourite."

Finally, she pushed it open and switched on the light. These stairs, unlike the main staircase, which was circular and made of polished wood, were much steeper, allowing only one person at a time to climb them. With no railing to hold on to, I copied Marielle's movements, using the wall as a guide. We reached the first-floor landing and stopped in front of the closed door. I wasn't sure if she was catching her breath or gathering her strength to step into the past.

Her keys jangled in the silence, and I held my breath as she fumbled with the lock. After a brief struggle, she pushed open the door to Rosa's room.

Marielle walked into the room, then stopped, stood silently, and looked around. Years of darkness and damp greeted both of us. After crossing to the heavy rose-colored velvet curtains, she pulled them apart to let the sunlight enter. Flecks of dust disturbed by the moving curtains floated on the sunlight flooding the room, eventually settling on the floor and the antique wooden furniture.

It had been nearly sixty years since Rosa disappeared, and this room looked as if nothing had been touched during that time.

The dressing table was filled with bottles; many appeared to be filled with perfume that had become amber-thick with age. In the center of the dressing table was a photo.

I picked it up and studied it. Rosa stared into the camera lens, confident and proud, head slightly tilted and lips smiling. Her dark hair was pulled back from her face, and I caught a glimpse of the flower pinned to the nape of her neck. Her fitted strapless dress fell in folds that skimmed the ground, and around her neck, she wore a heavy jeweled necklace of red and white stones.

"She was beautiful." I studied the photo. "So was the dress. And that necklace looks stunning." I handed the frame to Marielle.

"It is," she said. "Wait, I can show you." She lowered her voice and walked over to the tall chest of drawers and cupboards near the door. She pulled out the second drawer filled with scarves and handkerchiefs and carried it over to the bed before returning to the bureau. She slipped her hand into the space where the drawer had been, then turned toward me, holding a black velvet box in her hands.

Marielle beckoned me over to the dressing table, then sat me down on the stool in front of the mirror. She opened the box to reveal the same necklace Rosa was wearing in the photo. When she held the necklace up to the window, the light danced and sparkled through the stones.

"Try it on." She placed the necklace around my neck, fastening the clasp. It sparked a chill on the back of my neck, despite its brilliance and the light that shone from the stones.

"Catalina, it looks beautiful on you."

I glanced at the photo of Rosa and then at my reflection in the mirror, touching the stones gently. "They are beautiful."

"They should be. They are rubies and diamonds. Our father gave them to Rosa at our last Christmas together as a family. Each of us received a piece of the jewelry that had been handed down through the generations. My father always said it was part of a pirate treasure, but then again, he was always good at making up stories."

My grandmother had never mentioned receiving any jewelry from her father, and I certainly had never seen anything like this before. "And you've never thought of selling them?"

A frown creased Marielle's brow, and she straightened her back. "Never! No matter how difficult things are—Antonio." Marielle looked toward the door, and I glanced in the mirror and saw the reflection of Antonio behind me. He was leaning against the doorframe, his arms folded and lips curled up at the corners like he'd caught us in between bases without anywhere to run.

"Catalina wanted to see Rosa's room," Marielle explained, and I wondered why she felt she needed to.

"And her belongings as well?" Antonio came toward me and towered over me. "You must be very special. No one is ever invited up here."

I couldn't tell whether he was mocking me or serious, but either way, I wasn't prepared to give him an advantage over me. I faced him, unflinching. He reached out and lifted the front of the necklace, his fingers grazing my skin and making my heart race. I hoped he couldn't feel it as well. I glanced over his shoulder and saw Haydée enter the room.

"What's going on here?" Her voice was cold and measured, steeling itself for battle.

Antonio smoothed the necklace against my skin, his feather touch brushing my shoulders and pushing my pulse rate even higher. He turned slowly, and I caught a flicker of annoyance cross his face.

"I'm showing Catalina Rosa's room," Marielle said.

"You shouldn't be here," Haydée said, glaring at me. I wasn't sure whether she meant Rosa's room or Havana.

A flash of guilt hit me, slowing my racing pulse. It was innocent enough, but I understood the way it must look, especially if she and Antonio were in some kind of relationship. My mind conjured up images of Liam and Carly at the nightclub. The last thing I wanted was to cause Haydée unnecessary concern.

"Come on," Antonio said to Haydée. "We'll leave them to it." He turned Haydée around by the shoulders and moved her toward the door. Haydée glanced back as she left, and there was no mistaking the scowl she flashed at me. I looked to see if Marielle had caught it as well, but she was busy returning the necklace to its box.

"Is it safe there?" I asked, nodding toward the bureau. "Shouldn't you put it somewhere more secure?" I was thinking a bank vault.

"It's been here for fifty years, and no one's taken it yet."

"I suppose." Havana was obviously a very different place from Fort Lauderdale. "I don't think Haydée is happy about me staying here." I changed the subject.

"Don't worry. She's just not used to sharing with others."

I wondered if Marielle was talking about the villa or

Antonio or both. I'd certainly detected a hint of jealousy in her actions.

While Marielle was walking around the room, picking up items and then replacing them, I sat down on the four-poster bed, which was covered with a gold-and-pink brocade bedspread, and looked around. A small painting hung on the wall to my left.

The image was of a woman enveloped in a blue gown and cloak that flowed over the wooden, engraved pillar, hiding everything except her black face and hands. In them, she held a baby, also clothed in blue. The woman's face, a picture of serenity and contentment, was the same one I was wearing around my neck.

Marielle picked up one of the perfume bottles, took off the lid, and smelled it. "This used to be her favorite," she said.

"Is this Yemayá?" I asked, pointing to the painting.

Marielle continued to check the different bottles. "These certainly haven't stood the test of time," she said, wrinkling her nose.

"Marielle?" I persisted.

She glanced at the painting to which I was pointing.

"That? That is Yemayá."

"She's the protector of women and their secrets, isn't she?"

"Nothing but mumbo jumbo," Marielle replied.

My hand flew to the pendant around my neck. "You don't believe in her?"

Marielle bowed her head and shook it slowly. "Rosa was always putting her faith in the wrong place. Like that …" She was about to say something more, but she closed her mouth firmly, her lips pressing against each other and refusing to give her words their freedom.

I grabbed the opportunity to ask more about Rosa. "I don't understand how Rosa could disappear, and no one know where she is."

Marielle straightened, looked around the room, and walked slowly to the dressing table to pick up the photo of Rosa.

"When did you last see her?" I asked.

"Wednesday, January seventh, nineteen fifty-nine." Marielle's voice sounded remote, detached, rehearsed. "Rosa was going out with her friends like she did most nights of the week, but this time it was different. It had been a week since the Triumph of the Revolution, and many of our friends had already left for the States."

Marielle clasped Rosa's photo to her chest. "That night she and her friends were going to the Hotel Riviera for dinner and then on to the casino. During the evening…word came through that Fidel and his troops would be in Havana the next day.

Chaos erupted in the streets. Everyone who could leave Cuba did." She replaced the photo on the dressing table. "That night was the last time I saw her."

"You think she left Cuba?"

"I wish I knew."

"That was the last time you saw Rosa? January eighth, nineteen fifty-nine?" My voice took on a cross-examining tone.

"Yes. The last time anyone saw her."

A chill started a slow crawl up my spine. The letter I'd found with the pendant and the claim was clearly dated in

June of that year—five months after Rosa had disappeared. "But …"

Marielle walked over to the windows and closed the curtains, shutting out the dark, heavy clouds and cutting off my questions.

"I think it's time we go." She ushered me out of the room, leaving the memory of Rosa—and my unanswered questions —behind the locked door and away from prying eyes.

Chapter Seven

Armed with a freshly brewed coffee, a quiver full of questions, and snatches of dreams from a restless night still haunting me, I searched for Marielle and found her in the garden.

She had allowed me glimpses into her early life, allowed me to see Rosa's room, but the mystery surrounding my great-aunt was growing. Unanswered questions were one thing—lies were another.

"Good morning, Catalina. You look lost in thought," Marielle said, turning and hooking her arm over the chair as I approached.

"I can't stop thinking about what has happened to Rosa."

"Catalina, look at me. I have lived my life. It hasn't been easy, but I know one thing—the past is past. It is only the present that matters," she said.

I wasn't sure that was true, but I knew it would do no good to disagree. "I guess … Marielle, I'd really like to visit Ita's farm in Matanzas."

"Whatever for? You heard Isabelle. The only thing remaining is the villa. After your grandparents left Cuba, their farm was confiscated."

"Was the villa here in Havana confiscated as well?"

"It came close. Your great-grandfather sold the villa to your grandfather just before the Triumph of the Revolution because he wanted to build a house closer to Vedado and the university. But after your parents left, we were allowed to remain here because Papa abandoned the idea of building another house."

"Didn't you mind losing the farm?"

"It really wasn't mine to lose, and Isabelle was right. Only Alicia, your grandmother, loved the farm. Besides, there were so many who were less fortunate than we were."

The villa that once belonged to my grandparents now belonged to Marielle. Would the claim Ita had given me risk the relationship I was building with Marielle?

"I'd still love to visit the farm to see where my grandparents lived." I let the thought settle between us. "Would you come with me?"

"I don't enjoy traveling so much any longer, and as I said, I don't think it helps anyone to go back to the past." Marielle paused. "No, Catalina, I'm not interested in returning, but if you would like to go, I'm sure Antonio will take you."

I wasn't sure Antonio would be as willing as she thought he would be. "Is it far from here?" I asked.

Marielle thought for a minute. "Maybe one and a half hours by car. Maybe a little longer."

"Is there a bus or train?" I asked.

A second shrug.

"Or maybe I could hire a car."

"I'm sure Antonio wouldn't mind," Marielle assured me.

"Antonio wouldn't mind what?" Antonio appeared behind us.

I twisted in my seat so I could see him more clearly. My heart skipped a beat as my gaze skimmed over his blue jeans and collared t-shirt, which hugged his body.

"Catalina would like to visit the farm where her grandparents lived. I thought you might be able to take her if you have time."

Antonio looked from Marielle to me, opened his mouth to say something, then closed it firmly.

His silence said it all. I didn't need or want him to waste his precious time taking me to Matanzas. "I'm sure I can find my own way. Pedro will take me."

"I've got to go out for a while," Antonio said to Marielle, then gave me the briefest nod and a smile that could have been mistaken for a grimace.

"Antonio doesn't like me staying here," I confided in Marielle after he'd gone.

"It's not you, Catalina. Antonio, like many Cubans, doesn't think very highly of those who left to live in America. He views them as traitors. He's also very concerned about what the future holds for us."

"I see." I thought of the claim sitting in the locked cupboard in my room and felt guilty that I had come to Havana with a view to investigating my supposed inheritance.

"And ..." Marielle continued. "It doesn't help that his wife left him to live in America. They're divorced now, but he has never got over her leaving. I will talk to him, because regardless of his feelings, you are my family."

Marielle might see me as family, but that wasn't going to change Antonio's opinion of me.

The afternoon sun was flagging, and so was I. Twilight crept through the garden, chasing away the heat and creating pools of shadows. I was sitting in one of the squatter's chairs on the veranda, feeling frustrated and disappointed. I'd spent most of the day investigating ways of getting to Matanzas. Pedro already had a booking, the day tours to Matanzas weren't operating, there were no hire cars, and public transport didn't appear to be very reliable.

The hairs on the back of my neck prickled. Someone was here. Watching me. I looked around. Antonio was leaning against the stone column at the top of the stairs to the kitchen, silent and unmoving.

We looked at each other, summing one another up, watching and waiting to see what the next move would be.

"How did you go organizing your trip to Matanzas?" he finally asked.

"I'm working on it." I was determined not to play the helpless female.

"I'm not working tomorrow. I can take you there if you like."

Surprise pushed up my eyebrows. I was sure I could find my own way to Matanzas, although I appeared to be quickly running out of options. An image of Ita reminding me not to cut off my nose to spite my face appeared, and a tug of war took place between my ego and logic. Logic eventually crossed the line a winner.

Besides spending time together, the trip might help Antonio and I to get to know each other better. We could put our first meeting behind us. I thought of Haydée and what she would say when she found out that Antonio had offered to drive me to Matanzas. She didn't have anything to be concerned about. There was no denying I was attracted to Antonio, but I was engaged to Liam.

Antonio coughed, and I looked up to catch him checking his watch. I needed to make a decision, and he appeared to be running out of patience.

"Thank you, that's very kind of you," I accepted, and threw in a generous smile I hoped exuded gratitude. "Of course, I'll pay for petrol and any other expenses." I didn't intend to put myself in a situation where I owed Antonio anything.

"Are you okay to leave early?" he asked.

"How early is early?"

"Eight o'clock? The earlier we start, the earlier we can get back."

"That would be great. Have you ever been to the farm?"

"No, but I'm sure I'll find it." He turned away. "See you at eight tomorrow," he called over his shoulder.

I rang Liam after dinner to let him know how things were going and was surprised he was already home from work. I described my visit to the cemetery and finding my family's crypt. "But something strange happened. This guy was following us around the cemetery," I said.

"You sure?"

"Marco said that people often do that so they don't have to pay for a guide. But then I saw him talking to Marco as I left the cemetery."

"You've got to be more careful," he said. "Anything can happen in Havana."

"Don't worry about me. I'm perfectly safe." I decided to change the subject. "Tomorrow I'm going to see my grandparents' farm in Matanzas … and you don't need to worry about my safety. Antonio is taking me."

"And who is Antonio?" The sharp edge of his voice sliced through the air.

"Marielle's godson—he lives at the villa."

"I don't like the thought of you driving around the countryside with strangers."

"Antonio is not a stranger," I tried to reassure him. "Anyway, I'll ring and let you know how it goes."

True to his word, Antonio was ready to leave by the time I arrived downstairs close to eight o'clock. I'd overslept and didn't want the day to get off to a bad start by asking if I had time to make a coffee. I ignored my stomach rumbling its dissatisfaction as we headed to Matanzas.

It was a slow escape through the traffic in Havana, but I didn't mind. I was enjoying the drive down the Malecón— waves throwing themselves onto the pavement, glimpses of life in Havana captured from the window of the moving car.

The windows were down because the air-conditioning

didn't work, but at least the seatbelts and the engine did. The smell of petrol fumes and blaring horns swirled around us as we drove past.

After leaving the noise of the city, we drove into the green of the countryside accompanied by the crackle of static from the radio. The warm wind streamed through the window, my hair flying and whipping my face. I grabbed my hair and tied it back so I could at least see the road ahead. Antonio hadn't said a word since we'd left the villa, and I was beginning to think he'd regretted his offer to drive to Matanzas. I leaned over and twisted the dial on the radio, looking for some music to fill the silence between us. The crackling grew louder.

"Sorry. It died a couple of weeks back." Antonio didn't seem to be sorry at all.

We saw very few cars along the way, but every so often, large groups of people were gathered on the side of the road.

"Is that a bus stop?" I asked, making conversation. Antonio turned his head to look where I was pointing.

"No. They're waiting for people to give them a lift. In Cuba, it's a luxury to have a car, so we always help out those who don't have one. You'll see lots of people waiting along the highway for a lift. Even in Havana."

I couldn't imagine that kind of thing happening in the States. If you stopped for a stranger there, you'd probably end up minus your wallet … and your car. "I'd never think of doing that in Fort Lauderdale," I said.

"Of course not. But here … here it is very safe." Antonio looked at me and raised his eyebrows. "It's much safer in Cuba than in your country."

So, that was how it was going to be? My country, his country. Battle lines were drawn. So much for starting afresh.

We continued along the coast—through small pueblos, their whitewashed houses fenced with cactus hedges, with glimpses of the ocean through the trees. My stomach's internal clock had been rumbling since we'd left this morning and now was turning rebellious, demanding food. I started to get excited when I saw a collection of buildings.

"Do you think …?" Too late. We'd passed it. My stomach groaned in protest, and I hoped Antonio couldn't hear it. He continued driving. He had said he would take me to Matanzas and lunch wasn't part of the deal—it was an extra and it didn't look like it was going to be an option anytime soon.

"We have to turn off the highway before we get to Matanzas." Antonio slowed, checking for side roads. He drove for another three miles. "I'm sure from Marielle's directions, the turn is somewhere near here." After another mile, he slowed and swung the car onto a dirt track that was almost concealed by shrubs and trees.

We bumped our way over the rutted surface for another half mile until I saw what would have been, in its day, a two-story country villa. Antonio drove up the wide cracked circular drive, bordered by giant banyan fig trees, and stopped in front of the marble steps leading to the front door. I leaned forward, gripped the dashboard, and peered through the dusty windscreen.

Ghosts from the past whispered around me, their invisible fingers brushing the back of my neck and sending shivers through my body.

Antonio looked at me. "You okay?"

"Sure. Is this it? *Finca Grande?*"

"It is."

"It's … it's magnificent."

"It would've been even more impressive when it was built."

"Do you think anyone lives here now? I'd love to see inside."

"Wait, and I'll see if I can find a chair somewhere."

Letting my glance do the talking and refusing to comment, I jumped out of the car and walked toward the house, wondering what it must have been like to live here … what it must have been like to have to leave it.

I strained my ears for evidence of anyone living in the house, but the only sounds I could hear were the birds singing in the huge banyan fig trees above us. I hesitated at the top of the stairs and glanced back to see if Antonio was following.

He was leaning against the side of the car, arms folded, watching me. I straightened my shoulders and knocked on the door. No one answered, so I tried again. Harder and longer. Still no answer. I turned the knob. That would have been too much to hope for. I pushed the door, willing it to open, but it held fast, so I started back down the steps.

Antonio had remained in the same position, but by the time I'd reached the bottom of the stairs, he was inside his car with the engine revving. I walked past him toward the side of the house.

"Where are you going?" Antonio called out.

"I'm going to see if there is anyone out back," I called over my shoulder. A string of Spanish words chased me around the house, and by the time Antonio had caught up with me, I was already climbing the back stairs.

The house had been built on a small rise, and while there was a set of five steps leading up to the wide veranda at the front and side, there were three times as many leading up to the back door.

"What is it with you and other people's homes? You just can't go intruding on people's privacy." He grabbed my arm to stop me going any further. Our eyes met in a silent standoff.

I shook his hand away. "I'm not intruding. I'm just knocking on the door."

I climbed the rest of the stairs and didn't look back until I'd reached the top. Antonio waited at the bottom, kicking the dirt at the base of the steps. I knocked loudly, but there was still no answer. The door and the windows were firmly fastened. I wiped the dirt from the glass and peered into the house.

No visible signs of anyone currently living there—I was tempted to prise open one of the louvers to see inside, but one look at Antonio's face stopped me.

I gazed out at the rest of the property. The land around the house was relatively flat, stretching toward the river, which meandered in great loops and disappeared in the rolling hills to the east of the house. The plantations were gone now—all that remained were traces of the old fence lines that once divided the fields.

Antonio climbed the stairs and stood on the step below me. I could feel him close to me and couldn't stop the tingling that was racing through my body. I thought of Liam and chastised myself for what seemed like an involuntary act of betrayal.

"I guess it would have been a hard kind of life," I mused, trying to get my feelings back under control.

"Hard?" Antonio laughed—a laugh that mocked, told me I was mistaken. "Your grandfather would've had his share of men and farmhands who worked for next to nothing."

I looked at him sharply. "My grandparents wouldn't have taken advantage of others."

Antonio looked at me like an indulgent father.

"Let's have a look around?" I had no intention of spoiling the day by arguing about the past. I started down the steps. Antonio stood as if he was fixed to the spot. "Come on, let's stretch our legs before the trip back," I insisted.

Antonio lagged behind as we walked down an overgrown path beside the house, through a rose garden that had gone wild and through what had probably been the vegetable patch for the farm. At the end of the garden, the path divided and led in two opposite directions. One led to the fields that I could see from the top of the back steps, and the other to a hill in the opposite direction.

"Let's see what the farm looks like from the top of the hill." I threw down the challenge and started up the path, which zigzagged its way to the summit. Antonio, probably realizing that it was pointless to argue, ignored the path and took off in a vertical direction.

I'd underestimated the incline, and it wasn't long before the blood was pumping through my body and pounding in my ears. I slowed to a walk, taking time to appreciate the view of the homestead and fields below me.

The climb to the top was longer and harder than I'd expected, and all I could think about was the bottle of water I'd left in the car. When I reached the top of the hill, I headed for a clump of trees and the shade they offered. Antonio was already waiting for me there.

"Here, have this." He handed me his bottle of water.

"Thank you." I smiled gratefully and gulped down a couple of mouthfuls.

"You keep it. I've got another one in the car." He continued to the edge of the cliff, where he stopped, hands resting on his hips, surveying the countryside. He struck an imposing figure, but I pulled my gaze away and headed further into the stand of trees.

A solitary headstone surrounded by a wrought-iron fence rested peacefully amongst the calming whisper of the wind through the trees. Beside the headstone was a marble angel lit by the dappled sunlight flickering through the leaves. I leaned over to read what was written on the stone.

Luisa Marquez-Fuentes

There was no birth date. Only the year in which she died: 1959. The same year as the Triumph of the Revolution. I reached over and touched the angel standing guard in an effort to connect to the past, to acknowledge a life once lived. I pulled my hands away from the ice-cold stone. The cawing of a crow landing in the gallery of leaves above me shattered the silence.

In all the conversations I'd had with Marielle, she'd never mentioned Luisa. A distant cousin or relative by marriage? It was strange that Luisa wasn't buried with the rest of the family, in the Colón Cemetery, and I made a mental note to ask Marielle … or Isabelle.

"Catalina," Antonio called, "it's time to leave."

I pulled my thoughts away from Luisa and the possible reasons she was destined to remain here alone with only the crows' calls and the wind's sighs for company. Sadness crept up behind me and draped its cloak of loss around my shoulders.

Antonio came and stood beside me. "It's time to …"

I turned to face him.

"What's wrong?" His tone, gentle and soft, reached out to me.

I shook my head. "Nothing." My voice cracked as the word escaped. I didn't understand the different emotions swirling inside me, so how could I begin to explain them to Antonio? He stepped closer, and to my surprise, wrapped his arms around me. I sank into his embrace, feeling his heartbeat. Strong. Steady. Soothing.

A wave of guilt surged through me as I fought against a riptide of emotions. I untangled myself, but Antonio remained close, so close I could feel his breath on my cheek.

"Ignore me. I'm just being silly," I said.

Antonio didn't say a word. His silence settled between us, stopping time, giving me space to think and speak.

"It's just … overwhelming when you spend your life not knowing about your family, and then when you do…" I stopped mid-sentence, taking a deep breath. "We should go."

"It is not easy feeling alone. The only family I have is Marielle, even though we are not related by blood."

Antonio revealed a softer side I'd not yet seen. It was as if he understood exactly how I was feeling. I did feel alone, and even though I had found Marielle, I knew it was only temporary because I was due to go back to the States in a couple of weeks.

Antonio and I were from different worlds, but somehow, we'd found a connection through Marielle.

We stood beside each other, looking down at the house where my grandparents had begun their married life together, and a strange feeling of peace and belonging crept over me.

"It's getting late," Antonio said.

I didn't want the day to end. I wanted to stay here—surrounded by peace and tranquility.

We walked down the hill in silence, Antonio beside me instead of retracing his steps down the steep incline. When we reached the car, he opened the door and waited for me to get inside before closing it. Something had changed between us. The animosity and tension that had seemed to exist before had disappeared. Antonio started the engine and headed back down the track to the main road that led out of Matanzas.

"You are hungry?" he asked.

As if on cue, my stomach rumbled. I nodded.

Just before we reached Matanzas, Antonio pulled over near a roadside stall, and we went to the counter to order.

"The options here are pretty limited," he explained. "How does a ham-and-cheese sandwich sound?" he asked.

"Coffee?"

"*Sí*, coffee also."

"Perfect. Here, let me get this." I searched my bag for my wallet.

"No." He placed the order.

"Thank you, but I said that I would cover expenses," I reminded him.

"You can get it the next time."

My pulse danced a salsa at the thought of a possible "next time."

Antonio ordered for both of us, and then we sat opposite each other on the wooden benches nearby. The sun beat down onto the cement, the faded umbrellas providing little shade. Further down the road, I could see houses crowding either side of the street and a man sweeping the pavement. We watched him work while we waited for our sandwiches and coffee.

"You are satisfied with your trip to Matanzas?" Antonio asked.

"If you're asking me if I've enjoyed my day, then the answer is a definite yes. I'm pleased I've seen the farm, but the visit has just raised even more questions for me."

"What questions?"

"Have you ever heard of Luisa Marquez-Fuentes, for one?" I asked.

"No, never. But Marielle will know."

"I'm not so sure. Marielle doesn't like talking about the past. Maybe I should ask Isabelle?"

"You could try. She knows all the family secrets because she's been with the family since she and Marielle were children. They've been through a lot together, those two."

I took a deep breath. "Do you think Marielle knows what happened to Rosa?" I asked.

"Like you said, Marielle doesn't like to speak about what has passed. And I've never heard her speak about Rosa."

Our lunch arrived, and we continued our conversation between mouthfuls of ham-and-cheese sandwiches and coffee.

"Don't you think it's just the slightest bit strange that a

woman like Rosa goes missing and no one can find her, or even seems interested in finding her? Of course, she might be in America like everyone assumes, but no one really knows, and no one really seems to care."

Antonio flicked a glance at me.

"No one except me," I whispered. I glanced over at him and caught him frowning.

"What's wrong?" I asked.

"I think that sometimes dragging up the past is not a good thing."

"That's what Marielle says."

"Then perhaps you should honor her wishes."

I thought about what Antonio had said but couldn't make any promises.

The rest of the drive home went quickly, too quickly. I was lost in a million thoughts, which were racing each other. Eventually, I just lay back against the seat and enjoyed the scenery flashing by. I must've dozed off because the sounds of peak-hour traffic and the blaring of horns woke me. I looked over at Antonio, feeling guilty that he'd had to drive while I slept. "Sorry, I didn't mean to go to sleep."

"*No hay problema.* We came back the same way, so you didn't miss anything." We rounded the corner, and Antonio pulled up in front of the villa behind a late-model black car.

"Visitors?" I asked casually.

"Not that I recognize," he replied.

He was out of the car and had my door open while I was still gathering my things. He took my bag and held out his hand to help me get out. I was just about to thank him for taking me when I heard the gate behind him slam shut.

I looked over his shoulder just in time to see Liam striding toward the car. Excitement flared—until I saw the look he threw at Antonio. I took a guilty step away from him, even though I'd done nothing wrong.

The three of us stood together, trapped in time.

Liam moved beside me—an opening move that gave him an advantage, a possession-is-nine-tenths-of-the-law advantage.

"Liam, this is Antonio …" I began, but Liam stepped forward, hand outstretched.

"Liam Rochester, Cate's fiancé."

Chapter Eight

Liam stood in front of me, looking like he'd come straight from the office—his crisp white business shirt crushed from traveling and the hot wind tugging at his loosened tie. He wiped the perspiration forming in beads of sweat on his forehead with the back of his hand.

"It must be over a hundred degrees." Liam reached out, pulled me toward him, and kissed me. I glanced quickly around and felt strangely relieved that Antonio was already heading inside the villa.

"How long can you stay?" I asked.

"Only a couple of days."

"I thought you'd be able to stay a bit longer." Disappointment slowed my voice.

"I was lucky to get even a couple of days off. Work is crazy at the moment."

"How did you know where to find me?"

Liam turned his head to one side as if the answer was

obvious. "You told me you were staying at your grandmother's family home," he said as if that explained everything.

"Really?" I'd only told him it was in Miramar—and Miramar was a pretty big place.

Liam smothered my next question with another kiss.

"Why don't you get your bags out of the car?" I suggested.

Liam held up his hand. "No need. I've got a room at the Copacabana."

"But why aren't you staying here? I'm sure Marielle would love you to."

"I don't want to cause any trouble." He ran his finger around the edge of his collar, tugging it away from his neck. "Besides, I've already checked in."

I could understand why he didn't want to stay at the villa, and I couldn't deny a sense of relief knowing that Antonio and Liam wouldn't be staying under the same roof. But confusion persisted, tiptoeing around our conversation.

"I guess I could always stay with you at the hotel." Even as I made the suggestion, I wished I could grab the words and take them back, but instead, I held my breath as they hung in the air between us, waiting for Liam to decide what to do with them. I wanted to spend time with Liam, but I also wanted to spend as much time as possible with Marielle.

"I'll have to spend a bit of time working, so it would be better if I had my own space. Anyway, the hotel isn't far. You can come and go as you please."

"O-k-ay …" No invitation to move into the Copacabana with him.

"Tell you what. I really need a shower. How about I go back to the hotel, freshen up, and pick you up in an hour?

We'll go and have something to eat, and you can tell me all about your trip to Matanzas."

I nodded.

"An hour, then." He pulled me toward him again, kissed me lightly on the lips, then slipped behind the wheel of his hire car. I turned to go into the villa, then stopped. I had a strange feeling that I was being watched. I scanned the windows on the ground and first floors, but couldn't see anyone.

I showered and threw on the plain black dress, pulled my hair into a chignon, and added a swipe of lip gloss.

A knock on my door. "Your friend's here," Haydée called from outside my bedroom.

When I arrived in the sitting room, Liam was ensconced in one of the armchairs talking to Marielle. He stood up as I entered the room and looked at his watch. "You ready, Cate?" he said, moving to stand beside me. "We'd better get going."

"Why the rush?" I asked. "I haven't even had a chance to tell Marielle about my trip to Matanzas yet."

"I've booked a table at a restaurant, and we don't want to be late."

"But …"

"Go on, you two. Go. You can tell me all about your trip tomorrow," Marielle said.

Liam placed his hand in the small of my back and ushered me out of the room.

"I won't be late," I called to Marielle as we headed out.

Liam opened the car door, and I slid into the passenger seat, ran my hands across the leather, and couldn't help but compare it to the cracked faux leather of Antonio's treasured Chevy.

"You'll love this restaurant. I've heard the views are spectacular," Liam said.

We pulled up into the driveway of a two-story building shielded from the road by towering hedges and lit by wrought-iron lamps. Two men dressed in dinner suits rushed over to open our doors, and we followed a third man upstairs, where we were met by the maître d'hôtel. Like the other three men, his navy suit was impeccably tailored and pressed.

"Good evening, *Señor*, your—" the waiter began, but Liam cut him off.

"I've made a booking. Rochester."

The waiter led us out onto the terrace overlooking the ocean and showed us to our table.

"I know it's still early, but I thought you might like to see the sun setting," Liam said. We stood together, leaning against the railing of the deck, Liam's arm around my waist as we looked over the expanse of ocean and waves crashing over the rocks below.

"Amazing, isn't it?" He pulled me closer. The sun was sinking, outlining the dark clouds resting on the horizon with a sunburst of light. The sky turned rose, then yellow and orange, before deepening into crimson as the sun took its final bow for the evening.

"Of course, a sunset is always more enjoyable with a cocktail." He looked around for a waiter, who appeared out of nowhere.

"A daiquiri, *Señor*?"

"*Sí, dos*," Liam replied.

"A daiquiri?" I asked. "I thought you only drank scotch."

"Very refreshing, very Hemingway. And when in Havana …"

The waiter arrived with the daiquiris and nodded at the sunset. "*Romántico, no?*" he asked.

"*Sí,*" Liam replied.

I soaked in the scene, collecting memories on the run to file away for the future—the smell of sea, the tang of salt, and the warm, sultry wind.

Liam raised his glass. "To Havana … and to us." Before he could take a sip, his phone began to ring. He exchanged the glass for his phone and went to the far end of the deck to take the call in private.

A cloud of voices and laughter floated from the swimming pool below. A breeze ruffled its surface, creating ripples of blue and green from the underwater lights.

Liam returned accompanied by an armful of excuses and another daiquiri each. We ordered our meal, and while we waited, I filled him in on all of the things that had been happening since I'd arrived, including my visit to the farm in Matanzas and Rosa's disappearance.

"Don't you think it's strange that Marielle doesn't want to talk about her sister?" I asked. "How can she have just disappeared?" I held my glass, twisting it back and forth as I looked at the reflection of the pool lights. Liam was preoccupied with his phone.

"Liam?"

He dragged his eyes away from the screen. "Sorry, work," he explained in a voice that might've sounded guilty if his words hadn't landed like they were routine and rehearsed. "What did you say?"

"I was asking how someone could just disappear."

"It happens all the time."

"Really?" I shot him a glance to see if he was kidding. Whatever had Liam's attention, it certainly wasn't me—or Rosa's disappearance. "Marielle refuses to talk about it."

"Families are strange things," he replied in a tone that implied that my family was even stranger than most.

Our meal arrived, and we ate it at the same table but worlds away from each other. I thought of my grandmother's claim to the Matanzas farm and villa, which was lying in my room at the Villa Marquez-Fuentes. Liam continued to be occupied with his phone.

"It's funny the way things have turned out," I said after a while. "If my family hadn't left Cuba, I could be living here in the Villa Marquez-Fuentes."

"I don't think you'd really enjoy living here, but I agree it's a magnificent villa," Liam said. "And it is, after all, part of your inheritance, for which I'm sure we'll get a good price. Fantastic location on the sea front."

I placed my cutlery on my plate while I digested what he was saying. Liam was right, the money we could get by selling Ita's house in Miami and the claim on the villa and farm might just be enough to buy our own apartment in Fort Lauderdale. We'd have enough money to get married. But unease at Liam's plans niggled at the foundation of my hopes and dreams. I realized in that moment that I could never sell the claim— never betray Marielle.

The scraping of Liam's cutlery on the china filled the vacuum growing between us. The waiter who had been hovering nearby rushed in to fill it.

"Can I get you another drink?" he asked, looking at Liam. "Another daiquiri, *Señor?*" Liam waved him away.

"We don't need to discuss this tonight. Let's enjoy the evening," Liam said. "What else has been happening?"

I'd just started into my adventures at the cemetery when a man came and stood beside our table.

"Liam, fancy seeing you here." He slapped Liam on the back. "What are you doing in Havana? I've been trying to contact you." He spoke with an American accent. Texan, I thought.

I looked at Liam, waiting to be introduced, but he jumped up and grabbed the man by the arm, leading him away from our table and through the doors of the restaurant. While I couldn't hear what they were saying, I could see by their hand and arm actions that the meeting wasn't exactly as friendly as it first had appeared. Liam kept glancing in my direction, and I watched the two of them shaking hands before the stranger disappeared among the tables inside the dining area.

Liam returned to the table and ordered a bottle of champagne. "I think celebrations are in order."

"Who was that?" I asked while we waited for the champagne.

"Stuart Landrey. He's an … acquaintance." Liam paused, searched for the right word, and landed somewhere between friend and stranger.

"An acquaintance?" The tone in my voice asked for clarification.

"I met him on the plane on the way over, and we got talking. I said I'd check out some problems he was having with his computers. But frankly, I just don't have the time."

"But are computers your specialty?"

The champagne arrived, and Liam was suddenly more talkative than usual, filling me in on what was happening at work.

"Let's go back to the Copacabana and have a drink?" Liam said when we finished dinner. He stood up, took out his wallet, and peeled off a number of notes, which he threw onto the table. He was in a rush to leave, and I couldn't help but think it had something to do with the "acquaintance" I'd just met.

I didn't buy Liam's story—there was something he wasn't telling me. As we were leaving, we had to walk past the table where Landrey was sitting with three other men. He raised his glass and nodded to Liam as we walked toward the exit.

Liam's car was already parked beside the entrance by the time we got downstairs. He reversed it out of the driveway, and we cruised down the road toward the hotel.

It was after ten o'clock, and the bar of the Copacabana was almost filled to capacity. Liam pushed through the mass of moving bodies, and we both squeezed onto the two stools that had just been vacated in the bar area.

Liam ordered the drinks while the pulsing rhythm of the music wound its way around the bodies of the dancers, fused together; arms draped around shoulders and bodies crushed tightly together to prevent the outside world from intruding.

I noticed the light flashing on Liam's cell phone on the bar in front of him. He grabbed it and looked at the display, throwing me an apologetic look. "Sorry. Work again. Be back in a minute," he leaned over and yelled in my ear.

When he returned and sat down, he was frowning.

"I thought you were on holidays," I said, my voice sounding like I'd been promised champagne and had been given a soda water—without ice. I was beginning to get annoyed at the amount of time Liam was spending on his phone. "Is there a problem?"

He picked up his drink and drained it. "Of course not. Why would there be?" Before I could answer, he pushed himself off the barstool. "I'd better get you back to Marielle's before I get into trouble."

"I'm sure she's not waiting up for me. And anyway, I've got a key to the door."

"I know, but work has sent me some emails they want me to follow up." He waved his phone at me. "They only let me take time off on the condition I could still be contacted to sort out any problems. Anyway, I thought we could get an early start tomorrow and do some exploring of Old Havana."

Liam drove me back to the villa, leaned over me to push open the door and gave me a quick kiss goodnight.

"You're sure everything's okay?" I asked. Something was bothering him. I understood he needed to keep in touch with work, but he was on edge. And the meeting with Landrey sure hadn't helped.

He flashed a smile. "Of course, everything's okay. Why wouldn't it be? See you tomorrow morning." He waved as I got out of the car.

I stood on the side of the road and watched him drive away, the taillights of the car disappearing into the warm Havana night. Strains of music drifted from the villa next door, and the smell of jasmine hung heavy in the air. I sat down on the top step and quickly became lost in my thoughts.

The breeze cooled my body and soothed my mind, but there was an uneasy feeling in the pit of my stomach … and it refused to be ignored. Liam's trip to Havana wasn't turning out as I had hoped. I'd expected to be overjoyed with him making time to be with me, but all I was feeling was apprehension.

Work was still a priority, and that wasn't the only thing flashing a warning—the conversations he'd had with Ita, for which I hadn't been present, his sudden arrival in Havana, and then there was his accidental meeting with the stranger at the restaurant, whom he'd just met but who clearly hadn't expected to see him in Havana.

I folded the feelings and voices creating doubt in my mind and pushed them back into the darkness where they belonged.

With stars filling the sky and silence filling the night, I took a deep breath of cool air and silenced my doubts.

"Seems like he was in a hurry." I jumped at the sound of Antonio's voice.

He slipped out of the shadows and sat on the step beside me, his leg lightly brushing mine. My heart hit top speed, fueled by my guilty thoughts. There was no doubt that I found Antonio attractive, but I slammed the brakes on my emotions—I reminded myself that I was engaged to Liam.

I'd just spent the whole evening with Liam, but it was Antonio who was sitting beside me under the full moon, Antonio commanding the silence, Antonio making my heart race. Was it the romance of being in Havana making me feel this way, or was it something more?

"It's complicated, no?" Antonio asked. The invitation to talk was seductive and enticing.

"*Sí*, complicated," I replied, adding, "and I don't like complicated." The floodgates were trying to open and release the thoughts and feelings that had been weighing me down since Ita had died. I was about to speak, but then for some reason, I flicked the switch, and the gates locked. It would be a betrayal to talk to Antonio about Liam. "I think I'd better turn in."

I stood up, and Antonio followed.

"Catalina?" His tone was low. Sultry. Inviting.

I turned to face him. "Yes?"

Antonio wrapped his arms around me and pulled me into his embrace. My breath caught in my throat, and my heart pounded so loudly I wondered if he could hear it. I looked up into his eyes, and then felt his mouth crushing mine. My arms slid over his shoulders, my fingers combing through his hair and pulling him closer, my lips hungry for more.

The sound of the door opening pushed us apart, and Marielle stood in the lit doorway.

"I thought I heard someone out here. How was dinner?" she asked.

"Wonderful," I said, trying to cover my embarrassment. Marielle stepped back and waited for me to come inside. I glanced over to see if Antonio was following, but he had disappeared into the shadows.

I said goodnight to Marielle and climbed the staircase to my room, my stomach a roller coaster of emotions. I'd crossed a line, even if only momentarily, and I wasn't sure I'd be able to go back. My actions had unleashed a Pandora's box of passion and longing, my guilt no longer able to contain them. Eventually, I drifted into an uneasy sleep.

Something woke me—I lay disorientated, trying to work out where I was. As my eyes became accustomed to the darkness, I recognized the outline of the dressing table, the windows, the smell of jasmine on the breeze. Then the memory of Antonio on the veranda and Marielle interrupting us hijacked my thoughts. I checked the time on my phone on the bedside table and groaned. Two o'clock. I rolled over and was just drifting off to sleep again when I heard the voices.

I strained to hear them in the silence. No, I wasn't dreaming. Someone was outside, under my window. I climbed out of bed and padded across the soft rug and cool timber floor and peered through the windows, which looked down onto the tangle of garden between the villa Marquez-Fuentes and the villa next door. I stood still, holding my breath beside the open window.

I was sure that one of the voices floating through the night air belonged to Haydée, and she didn't sound happy. I strained to recognize the other voice. My stomach lurched at the thought it might be Antonio, but I quickly reminded myself that there was nothing between us.

Anger pushed Haydée's voice higher and louder. I tried to catch what she was saying, but the words were blurred by the wind in the trees and the sounds of waves crashing on the rocks. Silence, another low murmur, then four words separated themselves from the background noises, clear and distinct: "Danny's ready to sign."

The second voice responded, the volume turned to conspiratorial low, so low I still couldn't recognize either the owner or the words. I leaned out of the window to see who was talking.

Haydée stood on the edge of a pool of light that streamed through the drawing room windows, but the second person remained hidden. The next minute, Haydée merged into the shadows and disappeared into the darkness. There was no sound, no movement, and no voices—only the click of the front door closing.

I returned to bed, but my mind refused to let me go back to sleep. It didn't matter what I tried; nothing would stop my mind as it skipped from one train of thought to another—the disappearance of Rosa, the stranger in the cemetery, Liam's interaction with the man at dinner, and now a strange meeting in the garden between Haydée and an unidentified man … And who was Danny? And what was he ready to sign?

The image of Antonio kissing me flashed through my mind again. I pushed it away, determined to make sure I didn't give him the wrong message. I thought instead about Liam and our future together.

Our life in Fort Lauderdale was so different from Havana. Lots of events, lots of dinners and friends, though mostly Liam's friends. I hadn't really seen much of my own lately. They appeared to have drifted away, becoming involved in their own lives. I resolved to rectify that as soon as I got home.

When the sun rose, I put myself out of my misery and changed into a pair of shorts and T-shirt, then tiptoed downstairs and outside for a run. Making sure the door was locked behind me, I started off at a brisk pace, and the blood was soon pumping as I pounded Fifth Avenue and skirted past the clock tower. I turned around when I'd reached the end of the avenue.

It had warmed up considerably, and by the time I'd returned to the villa, perspiration was dripping from my body. I was longing for a large glass of water but welcomed the aroma of coffee that greeted me like an old friend as soon as I opened the door. It wasn't long before I had joined Marielle in the cool oasis of the garden to shelter from the already burning sun.

"How did you sleep?" she asked.

"Went to sleep immediately but was woken up in the middle of the night. Did you hear anyone outside last night?" I asked.

"No," Marielle said. "But once I'm asleep, I generally don't hear a thing."

"I thought I heard Haydée talking to someone." I enjoyed the semi-bitter taste of the coffee.

Marielle thought for a minute. "It might've been her. She went out earlier in the night, but I'm not sure what time she came home. I'll have to ask her to be quieter, now that you are sleeping upstairs."

"No," I jumped in. The last thing I wanted to do was to let Haydée know that I'd overheard her conversation. "It was no problem really; I went straight back to sleep."

"What have you got planned for today?" Marielle asked.

"Liam and I are exploring Havana."

"He seems like a lovely young man," Marielle said.

"Yes. Very." Now wasn't the time to share my doubts, which seemed to be increasing with each day.

I checked the time on my watch. "I'd better get ready, or

he'll be here and pacing the veranda outside. He doesn't like to be kept waiting." And I didn't want him running into Antonio.

I flew up the stairs, and by the time I'd quickly showered and dressed, Liam was already waiting for me in the car with the engine running. I quickly settled myself in the front seat and gave him a peck on the cheek.

Liam rested both hands on the steering wheel and looked at me. "Have you been to the old part of Havana?"

"No, but it is high on my list of things to see."

We drove through the tunnel joining Miramar to Havana Nuevo and Vedado, then down the Malecón, passing men fishing from the wall on one side and buildings being restored on the other. We drove as closely as we could to the old quarter, and Liam squeezed the car into an impossibly small parking space between a 1958 Ford and a 1957 Chevy.

Liam took my hand, and we walked along the cobblestones of the oldest section of Havana. Music flowed out of open windows and doors, and every turn we took led us to another secret space that time had forgotten. Every now and then, a car would hurtle down the narrow roads, forcing us to jump from the cobblestoned roadway and walk single file along the cement sidewalks. We crossed from one side of the street to the other, narrowly avoiding the dripping water pipes from the roofs of houses.

"Do you know where we're going?" I asked.

"I checked the map before I picked you up. You know me, always prepared." He gave a three-fingered Boy Scout salute. "I hope that's clean water dripping from those pipes!" Liam exclaimed, wiping drops of water from his face.

"It's probably rainwater."

"I hope so."

We spent the hour walking and exploring the streets of Habana Vieja, some of them more than once, because despite Liam's boy-scout preparation, we got lost. "And just when I'd finished complimenting you on your remarkable knowledge of the streets," I joked when we passed the chocolate shop for the third time.

"I'm doing my best." Liam shrugged.

"I think it's a sign that we're meant to get some supplies." I led Liam inside and bought some chocolate to share with him and a large rabbit for Marielle.

Ten minutes later, we arrived at the Plaza Vieja. Unlike the Plaza de Armas, which was filled with giant leafy trees, the Plaza Vieja was bereft of any trees or shade. The sun beat down on the expanse of stones, intense and unrelenting. Even the marble fountain surrounded by fencing in the middle of the plaza looked exhausted.

A wide blue door at one end of the square swung open, and schoolchildren dressed in maroon and white spilled out. The excited voices of children set free from their lessons bounced off the stone walls of the buildings and echoed through the plaza. I wondered what it would be like to teach here.

We walked through the swarms of children to the other end of the square. A man dressed as a waiter leaned against the lamppost in front of the restaurant, looking as if even the exertion of holding the menu was too much for him. He jumped to attention as soon as we entered his field of vision and moved toward us, greeting us like old friends.

"*Señora, Señor*, we have many lovely dishes. Come this way; I will show you a lovely table."

Liam took out his phone and turned to me. "Sorry, I've just remembered I've got to make a call. You go on up, and I'll be there in a minute," he said.

"I can wait …" I began, but Liam was already walking away and talking into his phone.

The waiter looked at me expectantly, and I followed him upstairs and onto the narrowest of balconies, from which you could see the first floor of the nearby terraced houses bordering the plaza.

A woman carrying a washing basket stepped through the white louvered doors of one of the buildings, the doors pinned back against the mint-green balcony walls. She wrestled the sheets onto the clothesline, despite the wind tugging at them and urging them to escape.

A storm was brewing; strong winds from the harbor had blown dark clouds across the tops of the buildings in the plaza. I wondered what it would be like living above the square under the prying eyes of tourists waiting for their fiancés and their lunch.

With the sheets firmly pinned on the line, she tucked the strands of long black hair into the clip at the back of her head and stood with her hands on her hips, looking down into the square. Something had gained her attention. She raised one hand and waved to someone below. A friend? Husband? Lover?

The woman blew a kiss then went back inside, pulling the doors closed against the sun. A couple of seconds later, Liam arrived and collapsed in the chair opposite me, placing two mojitos on the table.

"To the future." He held up his glass in a toast, his eyes flicking to the now-closed louvered doors across the plaza.

I followed his glance. A prickle of suspicion crawled up my spine. I shivered.

"You cold?" Liam asked.

"No." I shook my head and picked up the glass he'd placed in front of me. I couldn't shake the feeling that he knew the woman on the balcony. But how was that possible? Liam had never been to Havana before. Doubt challenged reason to a duel, and reason lost.

"Do you know the woman who lives in the building over there?" I nodded in the direction of the shuttered doors.

Liam flinched, then seemed to hesitate—a beat of silence that didn't belong. "Don't be silly, how could I know her?"

I shrugged. How could I explain the feeling?

I opened my mouth to say something, but Liam held up his hands, stopping me. "I've got good news. I've heard from the boss. He said that he could probably spare me for a few days at the end of the week if you want me to come back. Maybe we could go to one of those resorts at the beach. Just you and me." He brushed his fingers down the length of my arm. "What do you think?"

"I know things are more relaxed since the States loosened their restrictions, but I didn't think you could just come and go as you wanted."

"You still can't. Not officially. I came in under the family visit waiver—thanks to your grandmother. It's a stretch, but it gets me past immigration. So far, it's worked. So… what do you say to a few days in a five-star resort?"

Liam appeared to be doing everything he could to please me. I'd been complaining about us not spending time together, and now he was offering to take me on a romantic getaway—and here I was hesitating.

As much as I wanted to spend time with him, I also wanted to spend time with Marielle …and solve the mystery of Rosa's disappearance. I couldn't do that in a resort. "Why do you have to go back? Can't you stay here?"

"There are some things I have to do in person. I'm lucky they let me take time off in the first place."

"I'd love for you to come back, but can't we stay in Havana?"

Liam reached over, pulled my chair closer, and put his arm around my shoulders. "To be honest, Cate, I've seen just about all I need to of Havana. I want to see what the rest of the country can offer." His words turned our possible trip into a business transaction.

"But I'm just getting to know Marielle."

"You're always saying that we never have enough time to spend together." The tone in his voice challenged me to disagree.

"You're right, I guess." I leaned over and kissed him.

"That settles it then," Liam said, pushing back his chair and pulling his hand away.

"Okay, but only for a couple of days."

Chapter Nine

Liam and I sped back to the Villa Marquez-Fuentes, past the
Hotel Nacional and its twin towers, the 1850 Club, and
through the tunnel to Miramar. Liam spent the drive extolling
the virtues of the resorts at Varadero, painting a picture of
blue skies, bluer waters, and even adding in a few whispering
palms for good measure. I spent the drive trying to work out
what had happened to Rosa.

We pulled up outside the villa behind two police cars. My
heart slammed into my ribs. "This doesn't look good." Not
waiting for Liam, I jumped out of the car and ran down the
path, barging through the open front door and looking franti-
cally for Marielle. For anyone.

"Marielle?" My voice croaked, paralyzed by the fear that
something had happened to her. I stopped at the door to the
sitting room and gasped. Books had been tossed onto the floor.
Cupboards gaped open, and drawers had been pulled out,

their contents spilling everywhere. Unable to move, I gripped the doorframe.

"What's going on?" Liam asked from behind me.

"There's been a break-in." Antonio joined us at the door to the sitting room. "We need to wait outside while the police check the rest of the house." He ushered us through the kitchen door and down into the garden, where Marielle was sitting in one of the chairs, a policeman standing nearby. I rushed over and knelt beside her.

"Are you okay?" I asked, gripping her hands.

"She's had a nasty shock," the policeman answered for her, his hand resting on his sidearm, maybe to reassure us there would be no more nasty shocks on his watch.

"Someone broke into the villa this morning while Marielle was at church," Antonio said.

A policeman came out of the villa and stood at the top of the steps. "*Señor Ruiz.*" He beckoned to Antonio. "*Un momento?*"

I tightened my grip on Marielle's hands. "You're sure you're okay? Can I get you something? A cold drink?" I could feel her trembling, and I rubbed her arm gently. "Everything will be fine. I'm sure the police have got everything under control."

"It appears that some property has been taken during the break-in," the policeman nearby explained. I looked at Marielle, who was still staring into space, then turned to the policeman. "A family heirloom," he elaborated. I looked at Marielle again and saw a tear spring to the corner of her eye. She lifted her head, an act of defiance preventing its escape.

"Rosa's jewelry?" My voice was hushed, not wanting to say the words because it would make them real. Marielle nodded.

Antonio and the policeman he'd been speaking to
joined us.

"*Señora*, I have to inform you that, unfortunately, your
room has been ransacked as well. Can you go and see if there
is anything missing?" the policeman asked me.

I glanced at Marielle, who was taking a sip of water from
the glass that one of the policemen had given her. Her hand
shook as she placed it on the table. "I'd like to wait for a
minute to make sure Marielle is okay, and then I'll check."

"If you wouldn't mind checking now, please, *Señora?*" His
tone altered slightly, letting me know that it was more than a
request. "It is for the report that we have to write," he
added.

"Of course." I turned to go back into the house and saw
Liam waiting patiently on the edge of the chaos, trying to keep
out of everyone's way.

"I'm just going to check my things and see if anything is
missing from my room," I said as I passed him.

"I'll come with you."

We both climbed the stairs and walked around the gallery
to my room, where I stopped at the open door. All the drawers
had been pulled out and their contents thrown around the
room. Items of clothing that had been hanging in the
wardrobe had joined them. The locked cupboard had been
forced open, its door swinging on its hinges and its contents on
the floor.

Haydée stood in the middle of it.

She held a piece of paper in her hands and was so
engrossed in studying it that she didn't notice us enter the
room. I recognized the document at once—it was the claim for

the villa in Havana and the farm in Matanzas. Panic started to rise in my throat, forcing out my words.

"What are you doing?" I asked.

She jumped in fright. "I was just helping to clean things up." Haydée started to pick up items from the floor.

"I think Marielle might need your assistance more than me." Our eyes locked, and I thought hers glinted with hatred, her smile a snarling smirk. There was no doubt in my mind that she was up to no good.

"Thank you, Haydée," I said, snatching the paper from her hands. She said nothing as she stalked out, pushing past Liam, who had been watching from the doorway. He quickly helped me gather my belongings, then moved to look out the window.

"Looks like nothing's been taken," I said. "Can you believe that?"

"What? That someone broke in or that nothing was taken?" Liam asked absentmindedly, seeming more preoccupied with the view than with Haydée going through my personal belongings.

"Haydée going through my things, of course. You know what she was reading, don't you?" I continued.

Liam shrugged.

"The claim my grandparents made."

"Don't worry about it. She's not going to be able to do anything with it."

"What if she says something to Marielle? I swear, she doesn't like me."

"You'll just have to deal with it, but I think you're misreading her," Liam said. "C'mon, let's get back to the others."

I made sure I locked my room securely this time before heading back down to the garden.

Antonio was still talking to one of the police officers, but there was no sign of Haydée.

"I think you should come back and stay at the Copa with me tonight," Liam suggested, his arm snaking around me. "I'm heading home tomorrow."

I wondered why the sudden change of mind. Last night, he couldn't get rid of me quickly enough. I was just about to agree when I noticed Marielle hunched over in her seat, her head resting in her hands.

"I don't think I should leave Marielle now. Not when she's had such a shock."

"Antonio's here, and let's face it, he's been looking after her all these years. I'm sure he'll be able to manage," Liam replied in a tone brimming with annoyance.

"I just feel I should stay here tonight … make sure she's alright. You understand, don't you?"

"Well." Liam gave me a quick kiss. "Guess I'll see you next Friday. That is if you aren't too busy with Marielle." He was annoyed, and he didn't make any effort to hide it. I started to follow him to the car.

"It's okay." He looked pointedly over at Marielle. "I can see myself out."

A spark of anger ignited by his lack of understanding was fanned by the tone in his voice. I returned to Marielle. Antonio looked up as I joined them.

"The police have finished inside and are leaving now. They want to interview us tomorrow at the station. They're not very hopeful that they'll find the person responsible," he said.

I sat down beside them. "I can't believe there's been a break-in. It's even harder to believe Rosa's necklace has been stolen."

"One of the windows at the back of the villa has been smashed. They must have entered through there while Marielle was out," Antonio explained.

Marielle sighed and started to push herself out of the chair.

"Where are you going?" I asked.

"Where am I going?" She straightened her shoulders. "I'm going to clean up the mess."

"We can do that later, tomorrow even," I said. "It doesn't have to be done now."

Marielle wasn't giving in and pushed herself from the chair, and I had no alternative but to follow her inside, leaving Antonio to find something to cover the broken window.

"Oh dear." Marielle picked up a framed photo that had also been thrown to the ground and clutched it to her heart before placing it on one of the side tables. She bent to pick up some of the books and began placing them on the bookshelf.

I joined her, picking up books, trying to put some order in the room. "I'm so sorry, Marielle."

Marielle and I worked silently, replacing the ornaments that had been knocked over and placing the broken ones in the middle of the coffee table. The only sound was an occasional sigh and mutterings of Spanish from Marielle.

We both looked up at the sound of Haydée's voice. She burst into the room with Antonio not far behind her. Her eyes narrowed to slits of darkness as she looked at me.

"Do the police know who's taken the necklace?" Haydée asked.

"No. Marielle is very *upset*," I emphasized the word, hoping she'd get the message that now was not the time to discuss it.

"Someone must have known where it was hidden," Haydée continued. "They must have known where to look."

"But they couldn't have known about it," Marielle said. "If they did, they wouldn't have made this mess looking for it." She opened her arms wide to encompass the scene before us.

"No, Marielle," Haydée said, her voice slow and her tone patronizing—like a parent pointing out the facts to a child who couldn't understand. "I think that the person who stole your things knew exactly where to look, and they did this to throw us off their tracks."

"But how could they know? No one knew." Marielle sat down in one of the armchairs.

"Catalina knew," she spat the words at me.

I stared at Haydée, mouth open, words lining themselves up, ready to defend myself against her accusation.

"Catalina knew. You knew, I knew. We all knew," Antonio said, spreading the blame.

Haydée turned her dark glance on him. "What are you doing? Standing up for her now?" Her voice was fueled by disgust.

"I'm just pointing out the truth. There's no reason to think that this has anything to do with Catalina. Let's talk about all this later." Antonio took on the role of peacekeeper.

Haydée's anger formed an aura around her. "You're not going to get away with this!" She took a step closer to me, and it was all I could do to stand my ground. "You know,

Catalina's not what she seems to be. I can't believe that you are being taken in by her." Haydée stretched out her arm, like an actor commanding the stage and demanding their attention.

Antonio looked over and raised his hand to silence her.

Haydée took another step toward me. "Go on, tell them. Tell them why you're here."

My stomach clenched. I knew that Haydée was referring to the claim she'd found in my room.

"Don't play the innocent," Haydée spat the words at me, then turned to Antonio. "Your new friend is here for one reason and one reason only."

"Haydée …" I began.

"Go on, tell them. Admit it," Haydée said.

I tried to speak, but no words came out. Everything seemed to be crashing around me. "Now is not the time to discuss this," I managed to blurt out when Haydée took a breath.

But there was no way she was letting this go. "She's betraying you!" Her voice grew louder, urging them to take sides.

"It's not like that at all. Please. Let me explain," I begged.

"What is there to explain? Catalina's not here to meet her long-lost family. She's here to steal your home." Haydée paused for effect. "And anything else she can get her hands on, probably even Rosa's jewelry." She took a breath and turned toward Antonio.

I couldn't think of anything to say that wouldn't make things worse. I felt the silent questions of Marielle and Antonio as they looked at me.

"It's not like that." The tone in my voice begged for a chance to explain.

"Of course it is," Haydée continued, unrelenting.

"I'm sure Catalina has an explanation for this." Antonio's voice was bleeding confidence.

I closed my eyes and took a deep breath, holding onto my grandmother's charm as I began. "I came to Cuba—"

"She came to Cuba with her boyfriend because her grandparents put in a claim for this villa and the farm when they left Cuba," Haydée cut in. "I have seen it with my own eyes." She stopped as if she was expecting applause, but there was only silence. "And her boyfriend's going to sell the claims to some big business owner." Words gushed out of her mouth in a stream of hate. "And when he does, you'll end up with nothing. *Nada.* They'll come and take your home." She looked at Marielle. "Our home." She turned to Antonio.

"Marielle." I forced my voice to remain steady. "I'm in Havana because I genuinely wanted to find my grandmother's family—my family. Yes, I knew about the claim, but I had no real understanding of what it meant."

"You don't deny that you and your boyfriend were going to try to sell it?" Haydée challenged.

"You know as well as I do that this claim is useless. You're just trying to make trouble."

"Useless or not, claims are still being sold, and foreigners are still making money from them!"

"You know that's only if—"

Antonio looked at me, then turned on his heel and stalked out of the room.

Marielle, who had remained silent for most of the

exchange, put both hands on the arms of her chair, stood up slowly, and walked toward me.

"You believe me, don't you, Marielle?"

"We should talk about this another time."

"Marielle…" I began.

"Not now, Catalina. Another time." Marielle walked toward the door with Haydée following closely behind her, and as Haydée passed me, I caught the hint of a smile.

The smile of someone who knew she held all the right cards.

Chapter Ten

The next morning, I woke to sunlight, blue skies, and the dark
shadow of Haydée's accusations. There was no point in
putting off the conversations I knew I'd have to have with
Marielle and Antonio. After showering and dressing, I slipped
downstairs to the kitchen. The house was silent. I rehearsed
my speech persuading Marielle that I hadn't come to Havana
to steal her home while I was making the coffee. I sensed
someone standing in the doorway and looked up, expecting
Antonio, but the smile froze on my face when I saw Haydée.

"I thought you were Antonio," I said.

"He's gone out."

"Do you know for how long?" I asked. I'd been rehearsing
a speech for him as well.

"No, and I wouldn't tell you even if I knew," she spat.
"When did you say you were going back to the States?" Not
waiting for an answer, she took a few steps before she turned
back and threw me one of her self-satisfied snarls.

The more I replayed the conversation we'd had last night, the more I began to think that her finding the claim in my room wasn't just luck. For a start, how did she know that Liam had wanted to sell the claim and make money? Only Liam and I knew that. And why would Liam be sharing this information with Haydée or anyone else in Havana?

I took my coffee outside to the stone wall overlooking the jagged gray boulders and the swirling water below and checked my watch. Liam was already on the plane home to the States. The regular boom of the waves was tolling the death knell of my relationship with Marielle. I didn't realize how close to her I'd begun to feel in such a short time and how important it was to me to have her in my life.

I couldn't, wouldn't let Haydée ruin that. And Antonio? The cold, hard light of day was shining a spotlight on the events of last night, and I realized I'd been carried away by my emotions. I needed to get them under control before things got out of hand.

"Catalina." Antonio's deep voice drifted on the wind, igniting the memory of his kiss and his arms around me.

I straightened my back with resolve and braced myself before turning to face him. "Antonio, I …"

"I've told the police that I'll bring you down to the station to make a statement about the break-in," he said.

He caught me by surprise. Of all the things I was expecting him to say, an invitation to the police station wasn't one of them.

"Sure … but I can't add anything new."

Antonio raised his eyebrows slightly. "They still want to speak to you."

"What about you?"

"I went down first thing this morning and gave them my statement. Besides, they probably want to make sure they're being thorough, especially with a foreigner involved."

"Foreigner?" I bristled. "Don't forget my grandmother was Cuban—that makes me Cuban."

"Cuban-American," he corrected me.

My hands clenched and unclenched. "They're the same thing."

"No, Catalina. They aren't the same at all. In fact, they are very, very different." Antonio spoke slowly, stabbing each of his words into the air between us.

I resolved to prove him wrong. "Where's the station?" I asked.

"Not far. I'll drive," he said. "And don't forget your passport."

Antonio was already sitting in the driver's seat when I reached the car and settled myself onto the bench seat beside him. I glanced sideways as the engine roared. His eyes were hidden by dark glasses, and his lips were pressed together in a straight line.

The attraction I'd felt toward Antonio was still there, but the connection I'd felt after our trip to Matanzas had disappeared. And I couldn't understand the reason for the sudden change. Did he believe Haydée's accusations that I was here to take the villa away from them, or that I had something to do with the break-in?

"Just down the road" was, in fact, a couple of miles through the backstreets of Miramar. I held my hair at the nape of my neck to stop it from whipping my cheeks—a better alternative to sweltering with the windows closed.

We turned off at the sign pointing to the aquarium and took another couple of turns through the backstreets before pulling up outside what looked like a green Moorish fortress.

"Antonio." I sucked in a deep breath, searching for the courage I needed to begin the speech I'd been rehearsing for the last twelve hours. "I wanted to talk to you about … about what Haydée said."

Antonio killed the engine and then turned toward me, pushing his sunglasses on top of his head. A furrow settled between his eyes as they searched mine, as if looking for answers. "Not now, Catalina. After we talk to the police. We're late."

After crossing the road, we walked through the iron gate, up the small flight of stairs, and through the white archway. Antonio strode through the open door and nodded briefly at the officer standing guard, then continued to the front desk. He placed both hands on the railing and leaned forward.

"I'm here to see Díaz," he stated. No title, no introductions, and no explanation as to why we were here.

"He's not here. He's at—" the officer began, but Antonio interrupted.

"He said to meet him here." Antonio stood solid and unyielding in front of the desk, his voice powerful and in no mood to argue.

A couple of minutes later, an officer in a green uniform

appeared from a door to our left. He greeted Antonio with a half-embrace and a slap on the back.

"Díaz," Antonio said. "Catalina Johnson is ready to give her statement." He nodded toward the door on the left then threw me a glance. "*Un minuto*, Catalina. I need to speak to Díaz first."

"You can wait over there." Díaz nodded toward one of the bench seats running along two sides of the office. Díaz and Antonio disappeared behind the closest door. I wondered what Antonio had to say to him that was so private. Something told me they weren't organizing their next fishing trip. I thought of Haydée's allegations and shook off the notion that Antonio might be sharing them with Díaz.

Two men sat on the bench near the door, waiting their turn to be seen. I looked around the office. Pale green paint covered the plaster walls. I was moving toward the bench seat when a man walked into the station. Tall, olive skin, cream shirt, pants, and a white hat. He took off his hat and glanced over to me. Our eyes met, and I detected an almost imperceptible widening of his.

Recognition.

Brief, but there all the same. He turned on his heel, put on his hat, and joined the line of people at the front counter.

I searched in my bag, looking for my phone, and flicked through the screens until I found the photo I was looking for. It was definitely him—the man from the cemetery.

In the photo, he was standing at the edge of the crowd, beside Amelia's grave. I had my phone ready to take another photo to show Antonio when the man pulled his hat low over his eyes, turned, and disappeared out the door.

"*Señora.*" I looked up. The guard who had been positioned at the door was standing beside me. "No photos, *Señora.*" He pointed to the sign on the wall.

"But …"

"No photos. Is forbidden."

I stood up to follow the man, but Díaz opened the door. "*Señora* Johnson, we are ready for you now."

I heard the click of the latch behind me as I followed Díaz down a corridor that was also painted pale green, except for the places where the plaster had fallen from the walls. There were no voices, just the sound of our feet striking the tiled floor. The last door at the end of the corridor was open, and Díaz led me into a small interview room that held one desk and two chairs—very utilitarian.

The sour smell of damp and mold hung in the air, smothering me until I couldn't hold my breath any longer. Díaz stood behind the chair closest to the door and indicated that I should sit in the one opposite.

He sat down and picked up his pen, turning it around in his fingers, slowly, methodically. His eyes flicked up to me. "You are related to *Señora* Fuentes, no?" There was no friendliness in his voice now. No smiles.

"I am."

He checked my personal details. "And you've been staying at the villa?" I nodded. His pen scratched over the paper; the only sound in the room.

"Now …" He steepled his fingers together on top of his notebook. "Can you tell me what happened when you arrived home and discovered the break-in?"

I ran through the events of the day as I replayed them in my mind. Díaz raised his eyebrows, so I felt the need to explain further. "I went to let myself into the house, but the door was already open."

"You have a key to the house, which means you are free to come and go as you please. Is that correct?" When I said yes, he nodded and scribbled more notes, then asked me to continue.

"I went into the sitting room and saw the mess."

More writing. He placed his pen neatly beside his notebook. "Was there a reason why you went into the sitting room?" The tone of his voice changed, and the interview started to feel like an interrogation. Díaz rearranged his pen so that it was parallel to his notebook, then tilted his head slightly and waited for my response.

I looked up, losing my train of thought. "I … I guess. I didn't really intend to go into the sitting room," I stumbled. "I just looked in as I passed, and I saw the mess that was there."

"You weren't concerned for your own safety?"

I shook my head. "I wasn't alone. My fiancé was with me."

"What's the name of your friend?"

"Fiancé," I corrected him. "Liam Rochester."

"And where can I find this fiancé of yours?"

"He's had to go back to the States."

"I see." He resumed his official note-taking position. "I'll need his contact details."

I gave them to him, and he added them to his notes.

"He won't be able to tell you anything different."

Díaz put down the pen, and his eyes captured mine, fixed

and unblinking. "Why do you think your room was searched by the intruders?"

"No idea. My passport, credit cards, and documents weren't touched." My money was on Haydée. How else could she know about the claim document I'd brought with me? But I didn't mention either Haydée or the claim.

Díaz's eyebrows joined together in one line across his forehead as he tapped his pen on his notebook. He looked up and leaned forward. "And the necklace that was stolen belonging to *Señora* Marquez … you saw it previously?"

The same accusations that had been voiced by Haydée hung in the air, then fell, hitting a nerve.

"If you think I had anything to do with the stolen necklace, you're wrong."

Díaz held up both hands to stop me. "*Señora* Johnson, I do not know why you would think such a thing." More tapping. "Now, back to my question. Had you seen the missing necklace before it was stolen?"

"Yes. In fact, I even tried it on. Of course, with the permission of my great-aunt, Marielle. Antonio was there and saw it too. He also saw her take it and put it away in the same safe place where she'd been hiding it for years. Ask him, he'll tell you."

"I'm sure he will. Now, where was this hiding place?" he asked.

"In a secret compartment within the bureau."

"So, there were three people who knew where the necklace was kept. Marielle, Antonio, and … you."

"And Haydée, who also lives in the villa. She might've

known where it was kept," I said, trying to be helpful despite his intensive questioning, making me feel more of a suspect than a witness.

More scribbling, then Díaz put his pen in the pocket of his shirt. He picked up his notebook, frowned as he flipped through the pages of notes, then closed it, scraping his chair back along the tiles as he stood.

"Thank you very much for giving your statement."

I followed his lead and stood up. He went straight to the door and held it open, waiting for me to pass him.

I found Antonio in the reception area, and we walked to the car together in silence. After starting the engine, he pulled out into the line of traffic, doing a U-turn back toward the villa.

"Díaz thinks that I had something to do with the theft of the necklace," I blurted out.

"Why would he think that?" He turned his head to look at me. "I told you, Díaz is just being thorough."

I realized there was no point in continuing the conversation as I wouldn't get anywhere with Antonio.

When we pulled up at the villa, I searched my bag and found my phone. "Before we go in, I want to show you something." I flicked through the photo gallery and found the shot of the stranger I'd seen at the cemetery. "At the risk of you thinking I'm overreacting again, I want you to look at this," I said, handing him my phone.

Antonio pushed his sunglasses up onto the top of his head, revealing his penetrating dark eyes. "A man in a cemetery?"

"He was following me at the Colón Cemetery." I scanned

Antonio's face, looking for signs that he believed me, but he gave nothing away. "And I saw him again just now when I was waiting to be interviewed by Díaz. He's definitely following me."

Antonio handed back the phone. "Why would he be following you?"

That was a good question. "I don't know, but it's too much of a coincidence, don't you think?"

"I don't know what to think, but if you see him again, you must tell me." He opened the car door and went to get out.

"Antonio?"

"*Sí?*"

"I wanted to explain about last night. Can we talk for a few minutes?"

He looked at his watch. "I have a few minutes." But the tone in his voice added, *Be quick about it.*

"I promise not to take up much of your valuable time." I grabbed my bag and strode into the villa, leaving Antonio to follow me into the sitting room. I rested one hand on the back of an armchair while he stood near the doorway with his feet wide apart and hands on his hips. This was shaping up to be as difficult as I'd imagined.

"Catalina?"

I hesitated. Even though my words had been waiting for their moment in the spotlight, I suddenly experienced stage fright and struggled to get them out. "About last night … I didn't have a chance to tell my side of the story."

Antonio didn't move, didn't say anything. His eyes held mine. I took a deep breath. He wasn't going to make it easy for me.

"Some of what Haydée said is true. My grandparents did have a claim on the villa and farm … It's also true I now have it." I waited for a response, but his face was a mask I couldn't read.

"It's all true," I rushed on, trying to ignore his piercing gaze. "Initially, I thought I might have some legal claim to the villa and the farm and wanted to see them, but when I found Marielle was still alive, I couldn't have been happier." Still no response; his eyes were mesmerizing, breaking my train of thought. "I want you to know I have no intention of doing anything with the claim. No intention of ever doing anything to hurt Marielle … and I definitely didn't steal Rosa's necklace." The words came out in a rush.

The hardness of Antonio's jaw softened. His hands slid from his hips. "I appreciate you telling me this, Catalina. There is no doubt that the missing necklace is a mystery, and the timing? You have to admit, it is not good."

I waited for the wave of relief I was expecting at his words, but they held no reassurance.

"Do you think I had something to do with the break-in?" I asked.

Antonio frowned while I waited for his response. "I don't think you stole the necklace," he said. "But …"

One word with the impact of a sledgehammer.

"But the break-in happening so soon after your arrival in Havana leaves many unanswered questions."

"What are you saying?"

"That I don't believe chance is at play here."

"You think that there's a connection between my arrival and the missing necklace?"

"Only because no one really knew about the necklace until you arrived, and Marielle brought it out of its hiding place."

"Well, I haven't told anyone about it."

"No one?"

"No one! So that leaves you, Haydée, and Marielle," I replied with confidence, even though there was a whisper of a doubt in my mind that I might have mentioned it to Liam. "Any other coincidences you feel like sharing?" I asked.

"There are currently foreigners buying up property claims like your grandmother's and selling them to developers, hoping one day they'll make a lot of money."

I thought of the conversation I'd had with Liam about selling my grandmother's claim. The heat of guilt burned my neck and cheeks. "But I've told you that I'd never do that. You have to believe me."

Antonio searched my eyes for the truth. "And that's not the only scam operating. Foreigners are buying property and getting local people to put their names on the deeds to make it look like they own it when they don't. We hear whispers of some deal that's about to be done, but we're still having difficulty working out their networks."

"And you think that all of that has something to do with the break-in and the missing necklace?"

Antonio shrugged off my question. "It's just interesting that you and your fiancé turn up in Havana with a property claim and then Rosa's necklace goes missing."

"I've explained all that. I only have the claim because my grandmother has just passed away. I don't see how these events could possibly be connected."

Antonio frowned. "Neither do I … yet." He stood up and

walked to the door, before disarming me with one of his smiles, the kind that sent my heart racing. "But don't worry—I will."

With that, he disappeared, leaving me just as determined to solve the mystery of the missing necklace. He wanted to solve a mystery—I wanted to clear my name.

Chapter Eleven

The front door clicked shut behind Antonio. I glanced around the gallery of photographs hanging on the wall—my family, my past—which provided a sense of belonging I'd never felt before.

I wasn't totally convinced that Antonio believed I had nothing to do with the stolen necklace, but at least he seemed to listen. Now, I needed to talk to Marielle, so I headed straight to the garden, hoping to find her in her usual place. I'd almost reached the kitchen door, which opened onto the veranda, when hushed voices crept up the stairs from the garden.

"I'm telling you that nothing good can possibly come of it." Marielle's whispered words were just audible.

"But she has a right to know." Isabelle's voice was almost outside the door. I backed away.

"But after all this time, what can it possibly matter?" A pause.

"I made a promise, and I won't break it." Marielle's voice was insistent.

Any second now, and they would be inside. I'd have to either make my presence known or leave completely. But still I remained.

"Marielle, Alicia is gone now, and there's no reason why you shouldn't tell her. The time for secrets is over."

I inched closer; I couldn't help myself.

"There are some secrets that can never be told—and some promises that can never be broken," Marielle replied.

I opened the kitchen door just as Marielle and Isabelle stepped onto the veranda. As soon as they saw me, they stopped talking. "Good morning, anyone interested in coffee?" I asked.

Isabelle shook her head. "*No, gracias.* I just called in to drop off some cakes for Marielle. They're her favorites." She leaned over and kissed Marielle on both cheeks. "And anyway, I've already kept Marielle long enough from her gardening."

"Yes," Marielle recovered quickly from my unexpected appearance. "Antonio was going to do it, but he is so busy with his work."

"I can help," I said.

"Are you sure? That would be wonderful. Those dead palm fronds have to go, and there are branches that need to be pruned. It's all getting a bit too much for me to manage by myself."

"I'll leave you two gardeners to it, then." Isabelle disappeared with a wave.

I helped Marielle down the steps to the garden. The shade thrown by the palm trees and the African tulip tree shielded us both from the direct sunlight, but there was no relief from the humidity weighing me down and slicking my skin with a faint sheen of perspiration.

Mariposa lilies were flowering under the protection of the tall trees, their white butterfly wings delicately nestling amongst the green leaves. I reached down and picked one, tucking it through the clip that held up my hair.

"Marielle, you sit here in the shade." I dragged one of the cast-iron chairs further into the shade, then picked up a palm frond in each hand. "Where do you want me to put these?" I asked.

"Over there, near the front gate. Antonio can take them away later after he finishes work."

I had no idea what work Antonio did, so I grabbed the opportunity to find out more. "Where does Antonio work?" I asked, putting my quickening pulse down to the physical exertion of cleaning up the yard.

"He works for the government … a very good job."

"The government?" I stopped, the palm fronds I held resting on the ground. She had my full attention now. "What does he do?"

"He coordinates special projects in Habana Vieja, the old city, but he's involved with many things: restoration work, building projects. It's getting harder to remember everything he tells me."

I wiped the perspiration from my face.

"You need to take a break. I'll get you some water," Marielle said.

I threw the last of the palm fronds onto the pile and

glanced up in time to see her struggling down the steps with a tray holding a jug of water and glasses.

"Here, let me help." I rushed over and took the tray from her. When we sat down, I poured two glasses of water. "Marielle … about last night." I hesitated, gathering my words and my courage.

"If you're referring to Haydée's outburst, then you don't need to say another word." The tone in her voice called "time" on our conversation.

"But I want to explain."

Marielle held up her hand.

"I want you to know that I'd never do the things Haydée accused me of." I couldn't slow down; couldn't let Marielle believe Haydée.

Marielle reached out and took my hand. "Catalina, stop there." Her bony fingers gripped mine. "I may be old, but I'm still an excellent judge of character. I know you would never do anything to hurt me." She gave my hand a squeeze. "Now, I don't want to talk about this again."

I stood up and put my arms around her, squeezing her as tightly as I dared. She seemed so fragile. Relief rode the waves of my emotions, cutting through my frustration and fear of losing the family I had just found.

"Thank you," I whispered, giving her another quick hug as tears pooled in my eyes. "I guess I should get rid of the rest of these fronds. Is there anything else you'd like me to do?"

"Haven't you had enough for one day? It's very hot."

"I'm just getting started."

"If you're sure … Those bushes over there could do with a

prune. There are some shears in the shed." Marielle pointed toward the back of the garden.

I pushed my way through the overhanging branches and followed an overgrown path through the trees to the far corner, where a wooden shed was positioned between the stone wall and the boundary of the neighboring fence.

Pushing the door open, I felt for a light switch and flicked it on. I picked my way through the shapes and objects scattered across the floor until I reached the workbench against the far wall. If this was where Antonio kept his tools, it could certainly do with a clean-out.

The shears were easily recognizable, lying among all the other tools scattered on the bench. I grabbed them and hurried back to Marielle, who by this time was on her feet and inspecting the bushes to be pruned.

We worked as a team, she directing me to the branches, which I snipped. Eventually, I gathered the courage to mention her conversation with Isabelle.

"I overheard you and Isabelle talking earlier," I said, glancing up at her.

Marielle's eyes darted away for just a moment, then met mine without flinching. "I wondered how much you heard."

"Is there something you would like to tell me?"

"It was nothing … really."

"Isabelle said there was something I needed to know."

"Isabelle should not interfere." She waved her hand sharply, as if swatting away both Isabelle and her suggestion. "There are many skeletons rattling around in the closets of Cuban families, and ours is no exception. I'm of the firm belief that there's no point in digging up the past."

"Does it have something to do with Rosa?" I persisted.

Marielle sighed and shook her head. "My dear, it really is nothing. Besides, it would involve breaking a promise I gave to my sister many years ago. And I intend to keep my word."

I tried joining the dots of the clues I'd collected but wasn't having any luck. "Does it have anything to do with Rosa's disappearance?" I pressed.

Silence.

No sound except my heart pounding the seconds in my ears.

Marielle bent to pick up some of the stray twigs on the ground and threw them on top of the pile of palm fronds.

"Why do you ask that?"

I hesitated, summoning the courage to reveal the truth.

"You said that the last time you saw Rosa was in January nineteen fifty-nine, but I know that she was still alive in August of that year." There, I'd exposed the lie.

Marielle looked at me wide-eyed, shaking her head. In denial? Or defeat?

"I have a letter."

"A letter?" Marielle's voice was whisper-low.

"Yes, a letter from Rosa to my grandmother. It was among the things she left for me. I can show you?"

Surprise flickered across her face, and I saw something else. Was it fear? Dread? Remorse? Or all three?

She nodded. "I'd like that."

I raced up the stairs to my room and took the letter from the locked cupboard, which Antonio had repaired after the break-in. Then rushing back, I handed it to Marielle and sat in the chair opposite to watch her read it. I studied her face, tracking the movement of her eyes across the page, but it remained expressionless. She folded the paper and handed it back to me. A bird flew from the tangle of trees, landing on the side of the chipped birdbath, splashing water as it ducked its wings and beak into the bowl.

"I was telling the truth when I said that I haven't seen Rosa since nineteen fifty-nine. But it wasn't January when I last saw her." Marielle paused. "It was in May, after she went to live at the farm with Alicia and her husband Eduardo before they both moved to America." Sadness flooded her voice.

"And that was the last time you saw her?"

"The very last time."

"And you never looked for her?" I smothered the disbelief and judgment from my voice.

"It wasn't that …"

In that moment, Antonio rushed into the garden before Marielle could finish. He was wearing the same white shirt he'd worn to the station, but now the sleeves were rolled up against the heat of the day and he'd undone the top button. Marielle's shoulders relaxed with relief at her reprieve.

"Has anyone seen Haydée?" he demanded.

"I haven't seen her at all today," Marielle said.

"I was supposed to pick her up at the university, but she wasn't there. I managed to find a couple of her friends, but they said she hadn't turned up at all this morning." Antonio turned toward me. "Have you seen her?"

"Not since this morning. She's probably gone out and just lost track of time." I was anxious to get back to the conversation about Rosa. Questions were lining up like marchers at the May Day parade.

"It's strange," Marielle said. "Haydée normally lets me know her plans because she knows how much I worry."

"She was pretty angry last night … Maybe she needed some time to calm down."

"I'm sure she'll turn up," Marielle said cheerfully, although the furrow forming above her eyes betrayed her real concerns.

My cell phone cut into our conversation. Liam's photo flashed on the screen as I picked it up. "Hello," I said, walking over to the stone wall for privacy.

"I had a couple of minutes between meetings and thought I'd ring. How's everything?"

"I've been working in the garden helping Marielle clean up the backyard."

"Isn't that something that 'dear old Antonio' should be doing?" Liam asked, sarcasm dripping from his words and sparking indignation in me.

"I don't mind helping. It gives me a chance to spend more time with Marielle."

"I thought you'd be out sightseeing, making the most of your time in Havana."

"Getting to know Marielle is more important to me." I searched for a change of topic to lead us onto safer ground.

"Haydée told Marielle and Antonio about my grandparents' claim. I told you she had something against me and was up to no good. And now, she seems to be missing in action."

"What do you mean?" His voice sharpened.

"Antonio was supposed to pick her up at the university, but she wasn't there."

"No one's seen her?"

"I'm sure it's no big deal. She hasn't even been missing

twenty-four hours. I think she's probably out enjoying herself with some friends."

I expected Liam to agree, but there was silence on the end of the phone.

"Liam. Are you still there?"

"Yeah, I'm here. I spoke to the boss and it looks like I can head back to Havana earlier than I thought. I'll check the flights and let you know when I can get one."

A ball of tension fell to the bottom of my stomach as I thought of Liam returning. I should have been excited and happy that he was able to get more time off work, which was exactly what I wanted. Maybe he was finally starting to listen to me, but I wondered if it was too late.

"Sure," I replied, realizing I wasn't that sure of anything, including my relationship with Liam.

I returned to the garden and Marielle. "That was Liam. He's able to get away from work for a couple of days," I said, sitting down in the chair opposite her.

"That's nice. You'll have someone to take you around."

I thought about Liam returning and forced a smile. Our relationship was "complicated," a term used in Cuba to describe situations that were difficult to manage and even more difficult to explain. I realized now that our relationship had been complicated for a long time, and I was beginning to have serious doubts about our future together.

"I'm going out for a while." Antonio was speaking to both of us, but his eyes never left mine. My heart picked up its pace. I waited, hoping for an invitation to join him.

"I'll be back in a couple of hours. Will you be around?" His eyes were still locked on mine.

"I don't have any plans at the moment."

"Good. We can talk when I return." He gave a wave and left.

I happened to glance over at Marielle, who was looking at me and smiling.

I touched Our Lady of Regla hanging around my neck and thought of my grandmother, of Rosa, and of Marielle—three sisters separated by time and distance…and the choices they'd made.

Then I thought of Liam and Antonio and the choices I was going to have to face.

I prayed Yemayá would guide me.

Chapter Twelve

From my bedroom window, I could see a dark purple bruise of cloud hanging low over the ocean, turning it almost black. The smell of salt clung to the air and settled on my skin. Sticky and clammy. The threat of storms had everyone on edge. It had been two days since Haydée had disappeared, and at some stage, I'd have to admit that I was possibly the last person to speak to her.

Haydée's disappearance was affecting everyone—no one more so than Marielle. Jumping at the smallest noise, she would often walk to the front door and stand on the veranda, one hand shielding her eyes from the sun as she looked up and down the street. Even visits from Isabelle failed to distract her.

Marielle was convinced that something had happened to Haydée—I still thought she was likely to turn up at any minute with some lame excuse. But it was upsetting to see Marielle so distressed, and I vowed I would make more of an effort to get on with Haydée in the future. After a quick shower, I made a coffee and joined Marielle, who was enjoying breakfast in the garden.

Marielle looked at me and smiled. A smile that barely made it over the line.

"What are your plans for today?" she asked, but the tone in her voice told me she had other things on her mind.

"We could do a bit more work in the garden," I suggested. "Another couple of hours should finish it."

Marielle's face lit up at my suggestion.

"Why don't we tackle the section near the stone wall on the ocean side?" I asked. "I'll get the tools from the shed."

I walked down the path I'd cleared earlier and found the door to the shed slightly ajar. Strange. I definitely closed it when I was last here. I pushed the door open and fumbled for the light switch inside the door, but I couldn't get it to work. I felt my way to the shelf where I'd placed the shears, but now there was only an empty space.

My fingers trailed through piles of dirt, scraping against the wooden splinters as I searched the shelf. I touched something wet and yanked back my hand, striking a tin and knocking it over. I scrambled to catch it before it landed on the ground, but as I went to grab it, the shovel and pick that were leaning against the edge of the shelf clattered to the floor.

"Are you okay?" Marielle's voice, just outside the door.

"Yes," I called out. "The light's not working."

"That happens sometimes. There should be a torch hanging just inside the door."

I continued my search, not wanting to waste time looking for the torch. My hands closed around the handles. "Found them!" I turned toward the door, blinking at the bright light shining in my eyes.

"I've found the torch," Marielle said, moving closer. I took a step toward her, tripping over the tools that had fallen and grabbing the bench to stop my fall.

"What's that?" Marielle asked, her torch pointing at the tin I'd knocked off the bench. The circle of light from the torch pooled around my feet. And in the middle of it—a tumble of rubies and diamonds sparkled.

I picked them up, held them at arm's length, watched them slither in the torch's beam like a snake ready to strike. I looked from the necklace to Marielle, whose eyes were stretched wide.

"Rosa's necklace," she whispered.

"Marielle!" Antonio called from outside.

My heart slammed into my throat at the sound of his voice, then lost its footing and hit the bottom of my stomach. "In here," I called.

He came inside and looked at me, at my face, my hands. "What's this?" He snatched the necklace from me.

I wiped my hands on my shorts as if to wipe away any trace of its existence. "You know what it is. It's Rosa's necklace. It must have been in the tin I knocked off the shelf while trying to find the shears," I explained.

Antonio took the torch from Marielle. "Let's get out of here," he said, slipping his hand under her elbow and leading her outside to one of the garden chairs. He placed the necklace on the table.

The three of us sat in silence, staring at it. I glanced at Marielle and Antonio, trying to interpret their thoughts. Did they think I'd stolen the necklace?

"Was the tin in the shed when you were last there?" Antonio asked.

I tried to remember. "It could've been … I'm not sure."

"Who could have put the necklace in the shed?" Marielle asked, knowing there weren't a lot of candidates for consideration. Although all the evidence might be pointing to me, my money was still on Haydée. She didn't like me, and I was sure she would have done anything to discredit me and destroy my relationship with Marielle.

"I don't know, but I think we should put it somewhere more secure now that you have it back," I said.

The phone in my pocket started ringing, and when I checked the screen, I saw it was Liam calling.

"I'd better get this." I moved away so that I could speak privately. "Liam?"

"Hi, Cate, can't talk for long—just letting you know I've managed to get an airline ticket for the day after tomorrow."

"So pleased you rang. I found Rosa's necklace." I couldn't wait to tell him the news.

"Where was it?"

"In the shed at the back of the property."

"Have you told anyone?" he asked.

"Marielle and Antonio."

"Any news of Haydée?" His question was as unexpected as a punch I didn't see coming.

"No. Why?" Why was Liam so worried about Haydée? I'd just told him I'd found Rosa's necklace, and he already knew the false allegations Haydée had made against me.

"Okay, I've got to go now, but I'll be there in a couple of days. Will you be okay till then?"

"Yes. I'm just a bit shaken—"

"Sorry, Cate. The boss is calling. I'll be there soon." He disconnected the call, and I walked back to Marielle and Antonio, trying not to feel annoyed with Liam about his concern over Haydée.

"What do we do now?" I asked, looking from Antonio to Marielle.

"Contact the police," Antonio said. "Let them know that we've found the necklace."

"Who could have put it in the shed?" Marielle asked.

Antonio shrugged. "The police will find out." He took out his phone and walked around the back of the house toward the stone wall to make his call. He put one foot up on the wall, and I caught a couple of Spanish words on the breeze as he spoke.

His back stiffened. Shouting into his phone, he jumped on top of the wall, balanced for a brief second, then sprang onto the rocks below. I ran to the wall to see what had grabbed his attention.

Antonio was below me, kneeling, examining the ground in front of him. A leg lay wedged between two of the rocks.

"What's going on?" Marielle appeared beside me. I turned quickly, standing in front of her to prevent her from seeing anything, then put an arm around her shoulders. "I think we should wait for Antonio in the garden," I said, gently turning and leading her back to the table and chairs.

Within a couple of minutes, Antonio had climbed back over the wall. I walked over to him so I didn't have to speak in front of Marielle. His jaw was clenched tightly, turning his expression stony.

"Who?" Icy cold fingers of premonition crept up my spine. "It's Haydée, isn't it?" I reached out to touch him but pulled my hand away, scared that my gesture of kindness might be misinterpreted. I knew what it was like to lose someone you loved. Guilt about my dislike of Haydée burned around the edges of my compassion, curling and blackening my good intentions.

Antonio nodded, his face still expressionless. "Can you take Marielle inside? Díaz is on his way." His voice demanded that emotions be put on hold.

"Should I tell Marielle?" I asked, dreading the devastation the news would bring.

"I will."

We both returned to Marielle, who looked at me and then Antonio. "What's wrong?"

"It's Haydée," Antonio whispered.

"Haydée? Where?" Marielle asked, pulling herself up from her chair.

"There's been an accident," Antonio said.

"We need to ring someone, get some help," Marielle cried.

Antonio gently put his arm around her shoulders. "Marielle, it's too late." His voice softened.

Marielle's face fell, and she slumped in her chair, her face buried in her hands. "No…it can't be."

I pulled my chair closer to her and rested my hand on her back. Her sobs pulled at her body… pulled at my heart. There was nothing I could say to take away her pain. I glanced over at Antonio, who was watching me.

"I'll ring Isabelle and see if she can come over. Díaz will be here any minute."

Antonio left to phone Isabelle and let her know what had happened while I stayed with Marielle in the garden—the place where Isabelle eventually found us. She rushed over and wrapped Marielle in a hug.

"What a terrible shock," Isabelle said.

"I knew there was something wrong." Marielle's thin voice was filled with vindication. "I knew she wouldn't just run off like that." She shook her head slowly. "No one would believe me." Her voice dropped, and more tears filled her eyes and slid down her cheeks. "No one would believe me." Her body shuddered under her grief. "Why wouldn't anyone listen?"

Isabelle took Marielle inside while I went outside for Antonio.

The crashing of the waves and the lone cries of seagulls were soon replaced by the sounds and movements of crime scene investigators, ambulance drivers, and Díaz. Police tape and barricades now blocked access to the rock wall and the back of the house. Díaz stood beside Antonio, his hand on Antonio's shoulder. A shawl of guilt hung around my shoulders; guilt about not making more of an effort to get to know Haydée; guilt for not taking her disappearance seriously.

My cell phone rang—Liam again. The second time in less than an hour.

"They've found Haydée." No introductions. No pleasantries. Just the hollow sound of my disbelief.

"That's great." His voice filled with an excitement I didn't understand.

"No, it isn't. She's … dead." I forced myself to say the word.

There was a pause at the end of the line. I waited for Liam to say something. He didn't. "You still there?" I asked.

"Of course, I'm bloody here!" His voice attacked without warning.

"No need to yell," I retaliated, aware that both Antonio and Díaz were looking over at me. "Were you ringing for a reason?" The tone in my voice was angry and hurt.

"Yes. Sorry. I forgot to mention that I might have a buyer for your grandmother's claim." His voice steadied, regaining its even keel. "Should I tell them to go ahead?" he asked.

I dragged my thoughts away from the discovery of Haydée's body to focus on what Liam was saying. "I don't want to talk about it now."

"But they want an answer. And we could certainly do with the money."

I turned and walked further away from Antonio and Díaz. "Liam, I've said I don't want to talk about it now. Haydée is dead, Marielle is distressed, and the police already think I had something to do with the theft of Rosa's necklace. Can't you understand?"

"No problem. We can talk about it more when I get to Havana."

"I don't want to talk about it at all. I've decided—"

"Sorry, I've got to go. Talk later." His voice was so tense it sounded like it was ready to snap.

"Liam, are you okay?"

There was a slight hesitation. "See you soon." He disconnected the call, leaving me hanging on the other end of the line.

"Something wrong?" Antonio appeared beside me.

"Nothing." I slipped the phone into the back pocket of my shorts. "Nothing at all." But there was. Liam had ended the call, the distance between us even greater than before.

"Díaz wants to talk to us at the station," Antonio said, breaking into my thoughts.

Apprehension slithered up my spine, chilling every nerve it touched. Was Haydée's death an accident, or was there something more sinister going on?

"Of course. But are you okay to talk now?" I asked him. It seemed like a callous move to expect Antonio to give a statement so soon after finding Haydée. "Surely, it could wait until tomorrow?"

"It's better to get it over with," he replied.

"I'll grab my bag and see if Isabelle can stay until we get back." Both women looked up when I entered the living room. "Antonio and I have to go down to the police station for a little while. Will you be alright here until we get back?"

"Yes, you go. I'll wait here with Marielle until you return," Isabelle reassured me, reaching over and holding Marielle's hand.

* * *

There was only one person waiting on the bench in the police station, and the officer behind the counter recognized us immediately. He picked up the phone on his desk and nodded toward the vacant bench on the other side of the room. We'd just sat down when Díaz opened the door to the interview rooms and beckoned us in. Antonio accompanied me this time.

Díaz waited for us to walk past him, then shut the door firmly, leading me to the same interview room we'd used last time and directing Antonio to the room opposite. "Can you wait in there?" he asked Antonio.

Two hours of questions and I was exhausted. I'd relived the morning's events more than a dozen times, trying to find something, anything that might help with the investigation. Díaz had fired questions, one after another, often repeating the same one. I refused to get flustered and wondered if it was a ploy to see if I changed my responses. I focused on each question, taking my time and breaking the rhythm of his interrogation.

When we'd exhausted all avenues of questions relating to the discovery of Haydée's body, Díaz stopped, and I managed to squeeze in the question that had been bothering me since Antonio had found her. "Was it an accident?"

"We won't know for sure till the medical examiner talks to us, but at this stage, we are treating it as suspicious."

"Someone killed her?"

"We're waiting on the results of the autopsy to be sure, but it's beginning to look that way."

I thought that we'd finished the interview, but Díaz moved quickly onto a new line of questioning.

"When was the last time you saw Haydée?" he asked.

"The morning she went missing."

Díaz's eyes narrowed, and he leaned forward in his seat. "Go on."

"It was only for a minute." He waited for me to continue. "She didn't like me staying at the villa," I explained.

"Why was that?"

I shrugged. "I'm not sure. I thought she might be jealous."

"Jealous? Of what?"

"Jealous of me being here in Havana and in the villa. She knew I had my grandparents' claim for their property. Maybe she thought I could somehow take the house from them."

"And is that something that you intended to do?" he asked.

"Of course not," I blurted out. I thought of my recent conversation with Liam and could feel a guilty heat rise up my neck.

Díaz narrowed his eyes further as he tapped the pen on the desk. "Were you aware of anyone who would want to do her harm?" he asked.

"I told you, I only recently met her. I don't know anything about her except she didn't like me."

Díaz wrote down something on the paper in front of him. "Did you notice anything strange in the lead-up to Haydée's disappearance?"

I remembered the conversation I'd heard under my window. "I did hear her arguing with someone one evening. I was in my bedroom, and they were standing below. I could hear her voice clearly. She sounded angry."

Díaz's eyes widened slightly. "When was this?" he asked.

"A couple of days after I arrived." I counted back in my head. "Maybe Saturday evening … or Sunday?"

"Did you recognize the other person?" he asked, his eyes boring into mine.

"No."

"You're sure?"

"Yes."

"What were they saying?" he continued his questioning.

"The only thing I heard was that Danny was ready to sign. I couldn't hear anything else because their voices were muffled."

"But you could hear enough to be sure that it was Haydée?"

"I'm sure."

"Just a few more questions. Do you know how the stolen necklace came to be in the shed?"

"I have no idea."

"You didn't put it there?" The question was direct, hitting hard.

"Absolutely not."

Díaz turned off the recorder. "Thank you for your cooperation, Ms Johnson. Someone will type up your statement. I'll let you know when it is ready to sign."

He packed up his notes and led me out to the reception area, where Antonio was staring out of the office window. When he heard Díaz's voice, he turned toward us, glancing briefly at Díaz, who was standing at the door, and then at me.

"Everything okay?" he asked.

"Sure. I told them everything I knew," I said.

"Are the police finished with the villa?" Antonio asked Díaz.

"They've finished with the villa, but the area below the wall is still a crime scene. They won't be finished till later today."

Antonio nodded, and we both walked out to the car. He held the car door open for me and then slipped into the driver's seat. We sat, neither of us moving.

"This is going to be hard for Marielle," Antonio said.

"It's going to be hard for both of you," I said, still unsure what, if anything, I could say that would be of comfort.

Antonio threw me a glance accompanied by a frown I didn't quite understand. Since I'd arrived in Havana, there had been a break-in and now a murder. Díaz's questions had unsettled me, and I feared the evidence that was building was beginning to implicate me.

I suspected that the argument between Haydée and the mystery man was the key to her murder and far more important than the conversation I'd had with her on the morning she disappeared. I was glad I'd mentioned it to Díaz.

Marielle must've heard the car arrive because she was waiting for us at the top of the steps. Antonio went straight to her and put his arms around her, supporting and comforting her. For the first time since I'd arrived at the villa, I felt like an outsider.

And a little less safe than I'd felt before.

If Haydée's death wasn't an accident, then who else was in danger? And was there a connection between finding the necklace and Haydée's death, or was it just one of those coincidences I didn't like? There was also something about Díaz that I didn't like, and I was concerned that he thought I was involved in some way.

Chapter Thirteen

Morning traffic in Havana was not for the faint-hearted, especially when the waves on the Malecón became so angry the esplanade had to be closed, and masses of cars jammed the narrow backstreets of Vedado—it was absolute chaos.

Combine that with the reappearance of Rosa's necklace, Haydée's death, my suspicion that the voice I'd heard under my window belonged to Antonio, and the villa full of guests grieving for Haydée, and it was no wonder I had a dull, pounding pain that had started at the base of my neck and was being made worse by the heavy humidity.

When Antonio offered to show me some of the sights of Havana, I jumped at the opportunity. But now, he was forced to slow to a crawl, joining a long conga line of cars inching their way toward the Plaza Vieja. We crept forward, fumes seeping through the gaps between the glass and window frames where the rubber had long since perished. The other drivers' impatience grew louder and longer as they leaned on their horns, demanding right of way.

We slowed to stationary, surrounded by throbbing exhaust pipes roaring to be repaired, when a space opened between two cars. Antonio slid into it, turning onto the Prado, then rejoining the Malecón.

A car horn blared beside us. I looked over. Pedro was in the next lane, waving madly. Our lane of traffic moved forward, and Pedro fell behind us. Antonio glanced at me, raising his eyebrows.

"A friend," I explained.

Antonio's eyebrows shot even higher. Vertigo-high.

Detour signs and police cars blocked the road being pounded by waves that were crashing over the concrete wall and flooding the sidewalk. Antonio drove until he found a park near the Plaza de Armas, and we made our way through the cobbled streets toward the Plaza Vieja.

Antonio walked beside me, his eyes fixed straight ahead.

"I know it doesn't make it any easier, but I want you to know that I'm sorry for your loss," I ventured, my voice easing into the space between us.

A horn blared. Antonio grabbed my elbow and pulled me up onto the sidewalk as a car roared past, narrowly missing us, leaving the echo of the car's exhaust pulsing against the stone walls of the buildings on either side. My stomach lurched at the close call and then continued to free-fall at Antonio's touch.

He turned to face me. "Despite what Haydée thought, or wanted, we weren't in any kind of relationship. But she was … family to me."

I released the breath I'd been holding along with some of the guilt I'd been experiencing. A jolt of happiness stabbed my heart at the possibility of a relationship with Antonio, but I was still engaged to Liam. Guilt returned. Intensified.

"But I swear I'll find those who committed this crime, and when I do … those responsible will pay."

Now was my opportunity to ask Antonio if the person I'd heard arguing with Haydée under my window had been him.

"I told Díaz I'd heard someone having a disagreement with Haydée," I said. I wondered what Antonio's response would be, but I wanted to—needed to—make sure it hadn't been him.

Antonio stopped again and faced me, answering the question I couldn't bring myself to ask. "I don't know who this person was, but I know one thing—it wasn't me."

We arrived at the Plaza Vieja just as the blue wooden doors of the school at one end were flung open and children streamed out. Teachers followed like cowboys riding the boundary fences. A couple of the children skirted behind them, conducting their own game of hide-and-seek around the fenced fountain. Their freedom was short-lived as they were discovered and herded back to the others.

One of the boys looked over at us. "Antonio!" he yelled and started running, the rest of the children following. Antonio was suddenly surrounded by a group of children screaming and calling his name.

Antonio reached down, picked up one of the smallest boys, and lifted him into the air. The boy shouted and laughed with delight, ruffling Antonio's dark hair with both of his small hands. Another boy jumped onto Antonio's back, hands clasping around his neck, and legs wrapping around his waist.

"Giddy-up!" the boy yelled.

My heart swelled as I stood at the edge of the circle and watched as Antonio's interaction with the children revealed a side of him I'd never seen before—a gentler, more playful side. I thought of Liam and how he never seemed to feel really at ease with children. I'd always told myself that he'd change and it would be different when we had our own. But now I wasn't so sure. If he was struggling to understand my feelings, how was he going to relate to a child?

A young girl wandered over to where I was standing. I looked down and smiled.

"Are you Antonio's girlfriend?" she asked me.

I glanced over at Antonio, who was still surrounded by children.

"No." My stomach somersaulted like a teenager in love even as I said the word.

"I think you'd make a good girlfriend."

"I'm sure he's already got one."

"No, he doesn't," she jumped in to reassure me. Antonio looked up, caught my eye, and smiled. I glanced down, and the girl was still staring at me intently, her head tilted to one side as if seeing through my denial.

An older woman, dressed in a skirt and blouse, moved from the shadows of the overhanging veranda and clapped her hands to get the children's attention before striding toward Antonio.

"Juan, get down." The teacher's voice was clear and clipped. Antonio's smile vanished, and he quickly placed one boy safely on the ground before kneeling to let the other boy dismount from his back.

The young girl took my hand. "Come, we have to go," she said, pulling me toward Antonio. We reached him in time to hear him apologize.

"I'm sorry, *Señora* Vásquez," he said to the woman.

The woman struggled to keep the corners of her mouth under control. "You are not at all sorry, Antonio. I've never known you to be sorry, even when you were a boy." She reached out and touched his arm. "It's good to see you at last, *mijo*. The children are excited to see you. Are you visiting us today?"

Antonio shook his head. "Not today. I've got some business to attend to in the plaza, and I also have a friend with me. Catalina?" He reached out and pulled me to his side. "Catalina, let me introduce you to the wonderful, formidable *Señora* Vásquez, a teacher at the school. She was also my teacher many years ago."

"*Mucho gusto.* I'm pleased to meet you." *Señora* Vásquez held out her hand. "The children are enjoying their break now," she said. "But I can assure you that they are much better behaved when they are in class."

"You don't have to explain, *Señora*, I'm also a teacher."

Señora Vásquez's smile was wide and genuine. "Good, then you will understand. You'll have to come and visit our little school while you are in Havana."

"I'd love that." I wondered again what it would be like to teach here, so different from the large school where I currently work.

"I'd better get these children back inside. Boys and girls!"

She clapped her hands again, and the children followed her back to the safety behind the blue doors. I turned toward Antonio, who was kneeling and talking to Juan; the boy was refusing to return to class. Juan nodded his head, threw his arms around Antonio's neck for a quick hug, and then scuttled after the rest of the children and *Señora* Vásquez, who was waiting for him.

"Juan seems very attached to you."

"His mother and I are old friends, and I often visit the school."

"Is the school one of the special projects you're involved in?" I asked, trying to ignore the unexpected prickle of jealousy at the thought of Antonio with another woman.

Antonio looked at me blankly.

"Marielle told me that you organized special projects. I thought this might be one of them."

"The projects I'm involved in have more to do with the restoration of buildings, but sometimes I also work with the local children to help them understand the importance of protecting their heritage."

I turned, taking in the renovations in the plaza. "You are involved in all this?" I swept my hand around, indicating the buildings in various stages of restoration.

"It's a slow and painstaking job. It takes years to research and ensure the restoration work is done carefully," Antonio explained.

Houses and buildings lined the plaza. Some had been restored; others were in the process. One of the three-story buildings near the corner of the plaza was almost hidden from view by scaffolding.

"Are people still living in them?" I asked.

"*Sí*. Some of these are still lived in. After the Revolution, families were allowed to stay if it was their primary residence."

"But what happens to the residents while the construction's going on?"

"Other accommodation is found for them until they can return. Speaking of that, I need to speak to Juan's mother while we're here. Just a business call. Do you mind waiting? I'll only be a couple of minutes."

"Of course not." I tried to ignore the jealousy that flickered within me. Looking around the plaza, I saw a coffee shop. "Take your time. I'll grab a coffee and wait on the terrace over there."

Antonio nodded and cut across the paved plaza, stopping outside the door of the house where I'd seen the woman hanging out the washing. I waited. Would the same woman open the door? And what kind of business could Antonio have with her? The strange feeling that Liam knew the same woman returned and niggled at the back of my mind.

I walked over to the café and found a small table cowering in the shade thrown by one of the blue-and-white umbrellas and slid into one of the chairs.

"*Señora*." A woman who'd managed to squeeze herself into activewear three sizes too small stood waiting with a notebook in one hand and a pencil in the other. "Yolanda" was written on the badge hanging from her Lycra top.

"*Un Cafecito, por favor*," I ordered.

I searched for Antonio across the plaza. He was waiting outside the door on the other side of the square. It slid open a fraction, and I leaned forward. He remained outside, but after a couple of minutes, the door opened wider, and Antonio disappeared inside.

Yolanda returned with a cup of strong, dark coffee, which escaped over its rim like a fountain and pooled in the saucer as she placed it on the table. While I was sitting there, a man emerged from the growing crowd of tourists, hugging the sliver of shade thrown by the buildings. He was dressed in a cream suit that was incongruous, given the extreme temperatures we'd been experiencing each day.

Probably linen, I thought, *probably expensive*. My next thought was that it needed a good iron.

He accessorized his outfit with a pair of wraparound sunglasses that swept back and forth across the tables like a pair of searchlights. He walked past, then paused briefly, his glasses fixed momentarily upon me. He'd almost reached the end of the café, then stopped and glanced back before retracing his steps and stopping in front of my table. "Good morning, Ms Johnson."

I squinted into the sunlight, which bounced off the stones beside me. "Good morning," I replied.

He took off his sunglasses. "We met the other night at the restaurant." He paused. "Although we weren't formally introduced." He held out his hand. "Stuart Landrey. I see you're up early, taking in the atmosphere of the plaza. Liam here?" he asked, scanning the other tables before dropping his gaze to the solitary coffee cup in front of me. "I was hoping to catch up with him."

"He's not here." The edge in my voice made it clear I remembered our meeting. Clear that there was something about him I didn't trust.

"No problem. I'll see him tonight. I hope you're coming along too. You can't come to Cuba and not visit the Hotel Nacional."

"I'm sorry," I said when I realized he'd taken me literally. "You misunderstood. Liam's back in the States."

"The States?" Landrey tilted his head. "But we're supposed to meet this evening."

"He'll be back in Havana the day after tomorrow," I said.

Landrey shook his head, went to say something, but closed his mouth, forcing his lips into a straight line.

"Yes, we'll catch up soon, then," he said finally. There was an uncomfortable pause as he glanced at the empty chair beside me, as if hoping for an invitation. He lingered a few seconds longer, wiped the perspiration beading on his forehead with his handkerchief, then started to walk away. After a couple of steps, he returned and sat down in the chair opposite me. Leaning forward, he dropped his voice to a conspiratorial whisper.

"I hear you have a claim to some property in Havana that you're interested in offloading?" He wiped his forehead again. "I can help you with that, if you're interested."

My eyes widened at the unexpected change of subject.

"Liam mentioned it to me," he explained.

Liam had first mentioned selling Ita's claim after I'd returned from her funeral—and he hadn't stopped talking about it since. Was Landrey the one he meant—the person who could handle it for me? I was starting to think Liam and Landrey weren't just casual acquaintances.

"I'm sorry, Mr Landrey, but I have no intention of doing anything with the claim."

Landrey's lips tightened again. "Well, if you ever change your mind …" He stood up and bowed slightly from the waist, lifted his hand in farewell, and moved on.

I watched Landrey skirt the shaded perimeter of the plaza, then disappear down a road at the far corner of the square. My eye caught a movement on the balcony above.

I looked up.

Antonio was standing, both hands on the railing, staring at me. He glanced back over his shoulder, then turned and disappeared inside. A few minutes later, he and Juan's mother reappeared on the terrace balcony.

"*¿Otra taza de café?*" Yolanda had returned, her pencil now stuck behind her ear and her notebook tucked into the waist of her tights. She picked up the empty cup, and I was debating whether to have a second cup when a woman's voice broke through the crowd.

"Juan. Juan. Come back! Stop!" Yolanda and I looked over at the same time. Juan had escaped through the blue wooden doors and was running across the plaza, chasing a small red ball that rolled past a tour group gathered at the fountain before continuing toward the café. Both the ball and Juan skidded to a stop beside my table. I scooped up the ball and handed it to him.

"Where's Antonio?" he asked.

Señora Vásquez arrived quickly, followed by his mother, who gave him a stern reprimand for running away from his teacher and talking to strangers.

"But she is not a stranger," Juan protested in Spanish. "She's a friend of Antonio's."

Juan's mother threw me a sharp glance that would easily

have sliced through ice and grabbed Juan by the arm, pulling him with her toward the school while continuing her tirade in Spanish. *Señora* Vásquez followed a few steps behind.

"Daniela!" Antonio called. Juan's mother turned briefly. Juan held out his free arm toward Antonio, but his mother ignored Antonio and continued across the plaza.

Antonio slumped into the empty chair beside me, his eyes following Daniela as she pushed Juan inside the school's door and slammed it shut.

"A problem?" I asked.

He shook his head. "Some people …" He shrugged off the rest of the sentence like an unwanted coat. I waited for him to continue.

"Juan's mother?" I asked.

His eyes flashed to mine and narrowed. "It's complicated."

"It seems that everything in Cuba is complicated."

"Different from America," he countered. Our eyes met, his narrowing even further as though challenging me to disagree.

"Things are complicated there too." My voice lowered under the weight of my relationship with Liam.

He seemed undecided about whether to tell me more. "Daniela has had an offer on her house, and it looks like she is determined to take it."

"But that's a good thing, isn't it?"

"Not really. Now, she has a roof over her head. But what happens tomorrow? Or the next day? Who knows? She wants to make some money from selling her place, but what she is doing isn't right. I'm sure she's selling to foreigners—something that's illegal." Antonio's eyes bore into mine with a laser focus, holding them captive. "Who was that man who was talking to you?" He leaned forward, waiting for my response. "The one in the cream suit."

"Stuart Landrey?"

Antonio waited for me to continue.

"He says he knows Liam." My cheeks burned when I mentioned Liam's name. "He didn't realize Liam had gone back to the States." My words stumbled as I tried to cover my embarrassment.

Now that I'd found out Liam had spoken to Landrey about selling my grandparents' claim, I was embarrassed and concerned that he might be tied up in one of the scams that Antonio had been talking about. "He had arranged to meet Liam tonight at the Hotel Nacional, and I don't think he believed me when I said he was in the States."

Antonio's expression turned thoughtful. I followed his gaze to the house on the other side of the plaza. The shutters were thrown back against the wall, the sheer curtains floating through the open windows. And the door below? Firmly closed. The scowl that settled on Antonio's face was like a storm ready to break.

He suddenly turned back to me. "If you've finished, we should be getting back to Marielle."

We walked back to the car in silence, but my mind buzzed with the rising clamor of questions about Landrey—the pressure to sell Ita's claim, his plan to meet Liam tonight, and the connection between them.

Chapter Fourteen

Antonio and I drove back to the villa along the Malecón,
which was now open. As we passed the Hotel Nacional, I
couldn't help thinking about Landrey's supposed meeting with
Liam tonight. When Antonio pulled up in front of the villa, he
kept the engine running.

"I've got a few things I have to do," he said. "I'll see you
later."

I lugged my disappointment up the stairs and found
Marielle in the living room surrounded by Haydée's friends. I
said a quick hello and then decided to spend the rest of the
afternoon continuing to clear up the garden. No doubt there
would be some kind of commemoration for Haydée, and I
wanted to make my contribution.

By six o'clock, the visitors had all departed and Antonio
still hadn't returned. After a quick shower, I found Marielle in
the kitchen getting ready to prepare dinner, so I told her I
would do it. Cooking wasn't my forte, but it did extend to

omelets, and while there might be shortages of some foods, eggs appeared to always be available. And there were always spring onions and parsley from the garden. After cooking the omelets, we went into the dining room to eat.

The chandelier still worked, but many of its bulbs had blown, leaving us to eat our meal in a soft glow. Marielle had laid the antique table with a worn linen-and-lace tablecloth, which skimmed the marble-tiled floor. The green-and-gold edging of the china had almost been washed away from generations of use. Our simple evening meal looked at odds with its elegance.

"Should I save some dinner for Antonio?" I asked.

"No. He'll probably get something while he's out." Marielle paused and picked at the omelet in front of her with her fork.

"Is there something wrong with the omelet?"

"No, no, it's great. I'm just not very hungry."

"Marielle, you have to keep up your strength."

When I'd finished eating, I made coffee and insisted on cleaning up. "Ita always said that if I made the mess, then I had to clean it up."

Marielle glanced at the photograph of her family hanging on the wall.

"Your grandmother taught you well," she said. "But I'd have to say it wouldn't be from experience. Alicia very rarely went into the kitchen, and if she did, it was to reassure herself that everything was perfect. She would never have cleaned up anything." The corners of Marielle's mouth softened, but only for a minute. "Of course, times changed, as did our fortunes. But we adapted."

I wanted to ask her more about her childhood and about my grandmother, but Marielle had stopped eating and placed her knife and fork together on the plate beside her unfinished meal. "I'm sorry, I don't like to waste food, but I can't eat any more. I'm so very tired. If you don't mind, I think I'll go to my room."

"I'm going to have an early night too," I said.

Marielle pushed back her chair. "Sweet dreams, Catalina."

"Good night, *Tia*."

I finished the washing up and poured another cup of coffee, which I took to drink in the cool of the garden. The sound of waves lulled me, the warm wind wrapped around me, and the scent of salt from the ocean brought a strange sense of calm. I was going to miss this when I returned to Fort Lauderdale … and Liam.

Liam … Landrey … his insistence that Liam would be at the Hotel Nacional tonight … my grandparents' claim. I was annoyed that Liam had discussed it with him. More than annoyed. I'd told him I wasn't going to do anything with the claim, and he'd let Landrey believe that I was still interested in selling. The realization that Liam was more concerned with getting a good deal on the villa than respecting my wishes created a hollow feeling in my stomach.

Landrey clearly didn't believe me when I said Liam was back in the States. Surely, Liam would've told me if he was arriving tonight. I was intrigued by the comments that Antonio had made about the property scams, and I was beginning to wonder if Liam knew more about them than he was letting on. A sick feeling took root in my stomach and was fed by the growing suspicion that Liam was involved in something he shouldn't be.

I looked at my watch. Nine o'clock. Still early. Decision made.

I gulped down the rest of the coffee, went upstairs to dress before I could change my mind, and searched through my limited wardrobe. After slipping on my favorite black dress, I combed my hair back into a ponytail, which I twisted and then pinned on top of my head. After a final check in the mirror, I slipped downstairs, carrying my shoes so as to not disturb Marielle.

I wondered if it was too late to call Pedro. After all, he did say I could call anytime, and it would save me a walk to the taxi rank. I dialed his number. He could always say no.

"*Pedro, su conductor extraordinario,*" he answered his phone with a voice that smiled.

"Pedro, I know it's late …"

"*Señora* Cate? It is never too late for you. Where you go?"

"The Hotel Nacional?"

"A very good choice, *Señora*. A very nice hotel. I be there in fifteen minutes." I waited on the veranda, my ears alert to the sounds of approaching vehicles. Lights swung around the corner, and I held my breath in case it was Antonio returning. I didn't want to have to explain where I was going.

Pedro pulled over and got out. "*Señora!*"

"Shhh," I whispered.

He cocked his head to one side and immediately dropped his voice. "*Sí, Señora.* I understand. Top secret." He put his fingers to his lips and then opened the door so I could slide into the back seat. Pedro tried to close the door quietly, but after three failed attempts, he was forced to give it one last bash with his hip. The thump of his hip against the door was followed by a clang of metal on metal as it banged shut. Pedro jumped in and then accelerated as quietly and as slowly as was possible in his taxi.

"That's Club 1830," Pedro said, turning tour guide and pointing out the sights as we drove along the Malecón. "And there you see her." He crunched through the gears to slow down, and the engine coughed and growled. "The Hotel Nacional," Pedro said triumphantly.

The hotel stood proudly on top of the cliffs, overlooking the bay, its two twin towers lit like beacons burning in the black sky.

We drove around the block to the main entrance of the building, and Pedro pulled in behind the taxis and cars waiting their turn to stop at the front entrance. Much tapping of the steering wheel with his fingers punctuated our wait. Eventually, we stopped, allowing the doorman to help me out.

"I'll wait for you on the road outside, *Señora* Cate," Pedro said.

"Don't wait for me, Pedro. I don't know how long I'll be," I explained. After paying him, I climbed the stairs and entered the foyer, blinking at the opulence before me. Chandeliers hung in the foyer and down the hallways that spread on either side. Sumptuous leather lounges nestled in private alcoves defined by cream arches. Ceramic tiles from Spain covered the floor and walls.

The foyer was crowded with people—checking in, taking

photos, buying tickets for the after-dinner show, visiting the outdoor bars. I caught sight of a man weaving through the crowd gathering around the reception desk. Liam? *Couldn't be. He was in the States.* I kept my eyes fixed on the back of his head as I pushed my way through the crowd after him.

"Liam!" I called out, disbelief powering my steps as I followed him.

A woman fell into step beside the man. About the same height as Liam, her dark hair was pulled into a ponytail that swung from side to side as she walked. They were moving quickly, but I was gaining on them.

"Liam!" I called out, ignoring the stares of those around me. Something slammed into the back of my legs. My cry of surprise turned to pain as my knees buckled from under me, and I crashed heavily to the ground. A large suitcase pushed by a man in a tailored gray suit passed me without stopping. Hands grabbed at me from every direction, helping me to my feet.

"Are you alright?" A woman in uniform appeared from the crowd gathering around me and steadied me as I pulled myself up.

"I think so." I straightened my dress, wincing as I tried to stand. My embarrassment hurt more than my leg. I tested my knee, putting all my weight on it. I was relieved I could bend it without too much trouble, and while it was tender to touch, I didn't think I'd done any damage.

"I'll get you some ice," the receptionist said.

I scanned the foyer for Liam. If it had been him, he had disappeared. And so had the man with the suitcase.

The receptionist arrived with the ice, and I assured her

that I was fine. I thought my initial assessment had been right: it was probably bruised, but it would be like new in a couple of days. I remained on the lounge to give the ice time to work and grabbed my phone and dialed Liam's number.

His phone rang a couple of times then went to voicemail. I didn't leave a message and waited another five minutes before redialing. The phone had been switched off.

Had my eyes played tricks on me, or had Liam been exactly where Landrey had insisted he would be? And the woman with the dark hair. Who was she? Despite my sore knee, I limped down the length of the foyer past the gift shop to where I'd last seen "Liam" and found two closed doors. I tried both, but neither would budge. Retracing my steps, I located two staircases, one that led downstairs and one that went up. I hobbled downstairs, holding onto the railing for support, but found only the toilets, a restaurant, and another door leading outside. If they'd come this way, they were long gone.

I decided to check the restaurant. The maître d' smiled as I approached.

"A table for one, *Señora?*" he asked.

"I think my friends might already be inside." The lie flowed effortlessly, shamelessly.

"And the name?" He scrolled down the list of reservations on the sheet of paper in front of him.

"I don't think they booked. I'll just have a quick look and see if they're here."

He moved slightly to one side, just enough to block my passage.

"If you'll wait just one minute, I will provide assistance."

He indicated that I wait to the side and then spoke to a group of people who had gathered behind me. As soon as he left his post to show them to their table, I scooted inside and did a quick scan. No Liam, no black-haired woman, and no Landrey.

Disappointed, I returned to the staircase and pulled myself up the flight of stairs to what appeared to be offices, but there was no sign of anyone there either.

"Can I help you, *Señora?*" I jumped at the voice behind me.

"I'm sorry. I thought my friends were up here." I gave a quick description of Liam and the woman, but he just shook his head. "There is no one here. And as you can see," he pointed at the sign, "you shouldn't be either. Perhaps you could look for your friends elsewhere?" he suggested.

He held out his arm in the direction of the stairs, preventing me from going any further. I retraced my steps to the foyer and followed the sound of the music through the large glass doors. A wide veranda ran along the outside of the building, providing shelter over the deep leather lounges.

Ahead of me was a fountain, its surface covered with pink flowers. Some had found safety around the edges of the fountain, but others were left bruised and battered from the spray pushing them under the water.

Beyond the fountain, a row of lights illuminated the cliff's edge. Tables and chairs had been set up under the lights and were filled with people. Peacocks roosted in the branches of the giant banyan fig trees and screeched as I walked under them.

The small tables lined up along the cliffs overlooking the

Malecón were nearly all occupied. A three-piece band was beginning to unpack their instruments. I checked my watch. It was still early. I snagged a vacant chair and positioned myself so I had a view of the Malecón as well as Landrey and Liam should they turn up. I was convinced there was something going on, and I was desperate to get to the bottom of it.

A band started playing in front of one of the tables, while waiters buzzed past, bringing endless mojitos and daiquiris to accompany the full moon, which had risen high over the water. The throbbing of cars driving on the Malecón provided more percussion for the band.

From my cliff-top balcony, I looked down at the scene below. Pools of lights on steel poles spotlighted families and lovers who'd claimed their positions on the wall, while I sat at a table for one, yearning to belong. The loss and loneliness I'd felt when my parents had died had never totally disappeared and had only been partially filled by Ita's love. I was beginning to see I'd been hoping to fill that vacuum by marrying Liam and having my own family. I tried to picture Liam here with me, but the only face I could see was Antonio's.

The band stopped playing, gathered their instruments, and relocated in front of the table next to me.

"You have a request?" he asked the man sitting there.

The man handed him a folded note and asked for *"Guantanamera."*

I'd heard the song a hundred times before but had never really listened to the words. They spoke of love and truth and honesty—values I wasn't sure Liam and I shared—any longer.

When the band finished playing, they packed up and

moved on, and I took that as a cue for me to move on as well. If Liam or Landrey had been here tonight, I doubted they'd still be here. And if they were, I'd have more luck finding *una aguja en un pajar*: a needle in a haystack. I took one last look at the lights playing on top of the fountain and returned to the foyer. The doorman held open the door and nodded as I walked past and down the steps.

Pedro was true to his word. I'd just started to walk toward the taxis when I heard him call my name.

"*Señora* Cate! Over here! See, I wait for you."

"*Gracias*, Pedro." Even though I'd told him not to wait, I was inwardly glad that he had. I was even more grateful when I saw the long line of people waiting for a taxi.

"The car, she is parked on the road outside. Be careful," he warned, moving to walk on the side closest to the road. "Did you catch up with your friend?" Pedro asked.

"My friend?"

"Yes, I was waiting in the street, and I saw him go inside. Not long after you."

"You saw Liam, my fiancé?" The brief triumph I felt at being right was eclipsed almost immediately by disappointment at the thought that Liam had lied and was hiding something from me.

Pedro shrugged. "You know, the one who lives in the villa. *Alto? Pelo negro.*" Black hair. He wasn't describing Liam.

"Antonio?"

"*Sí.* Antonio."

While Pedro drove home, pointing out all the restaurants that he said I would definitely love, I rested my head against the side door and tried to work out what Antonio could've been doing at the Hotel Nacional.

It didn't seem like the kind of place where he'd go to grab a casual bite to eat. Was he expecting Liam to be there with Landrey?

Or was Antonio following me?

Chapter Fifteen

I woke to sunlight dancing across the polished wooden floors
of my room. It shone through the crystal lamp, sending
sunbeams of rainbows shimmering across the opposite wall.
And then I remembered.

Haydée's death cast a black pall over the day ahead, and I
doubted Liam's return would lift it, as I suspected his arrival
was going to bring a showdown that I neither wanted nor was
prepared for. Antonio's appearance at the Hotel Nacional after
I'd told him that Landrey was expecting to meet Liam there
also irritated me. I groaned and went to pull the covers over
my head when I received a message on my phone from Liam.

Feel like going to the beach?

I had been right—he was in Havana. I dialed his number,
and he answered on the third ring.

"Hey, babe, how are you?" If his tone was any cheerier, it would've been handing out party hats.

"Fine." I skipped straight to the point. "You're in Havana already?"

"Got in last night."

"Why didn't you call?"

"It was too late to call," he offered his excuse in a tone that didn't seem to care whether I accepted it or not.

My mind flashed back to the man and woman I'd seen at the Hotel Nacional. "What time did you get in?" I persisted like a pit bull unwilling to let go.

"What time did I get in?" There was a pause. One of those buy-me-some-time pauses people used when they were desperately searching for the words that would be a lifeline to safety.

"I don't remember the exact time, but it was pretty late."

"Really?" I let him flounder.

"I thought we could go to the beach today. What do you think?" He sidestepped my probing, obviously trying to avoid tripping on his lies.

"Sure." I didn't really care where we went as long as we were able to talk and I could get the answers to the list of questions I had.

"How about I pick you up in thirty minutes?"

"I'll be ready." And I'd be ready for more than a relaxing day at the beach…

After Liam hung up, I lay in bed for a couple of minutes longer, thinking about what I wanted to ask him, then I dragged myself out of bed, got ready, and waited for him on the veranda outside.

The humidity hung on everything; even the hibiscus flowers lowered their heads under its weight. So far, there wasn't a cloud in the sky, just an expanse of blue. When Liam arrived, I picked up my bag and swimming gear, pulled the door shut, and slid into his late-model hire car. Liam leaned over and brushed his lips against mine, then swung the car around and headed into the traffic.

The windows were closed, trapping the thumping bass line from the player pumping out rap music into the car. It was strange being in a car and listening to music without the familiar backing of static, and even stranger not having to fight to keep my hair from blowing in the wind. I leaned over to turn down the music.

"How come you didn't ring? Let me know you were back in Havana?" I asked.

We turned into the tunnel heading out of the city.

Liam shrugged. "I already told you. It was a sudden decision. The boss said he didn't need me, and I was lucky enough to catch a late flight. Thought I'd surprise you." He looked over at me. "Did I?"

Surprise? "I'm more than surprised. Were you at the Hotel Nacional last night?"

Liam's smile didn't waver, and only the flicker of his eyes warned me my suspicions might be right.

"Nope. Went straight from the airport to the Copa." He turned and glanced at me. "Were you?" he countered.

"Yes, and I thought I saw you there."

"Wasn't me. Check with the hotel desk if you don't believe me. They'll tell you—I checked in and went straight up to my room. Didn't even have a drink at the bar."

Liam spent the rest of the trip talking about work—his clients, his boss, the bonus he was sure he'd get.

"We're here," he said, pulling up under the shade of one of the large trees in the parking lot behind the beach. We walked over to the wooden fence that separated the parking lot from the sand dunes, and Liam perched himself on the top railing. He took out a cigarette and lit it, flicking the dead match onto the bitumen beside him.

"I didn't know you'd taken up smoking again." Judgment crept into my voice. Liam opened his mouth, then closed it, a straight line of firmly pressed lips. I added "smoking" to the list of things I didn't know about Liam—a growing list of things I didn't like.

"Let's go for a walk along the beach," he suggested, leading the way down the sandy track winding through the overhanging branches of the casuarina trees and toward the sound of crashing waves. We pushed through the last row of green bushes to the waves rolling onto the beach.

I slipped off my sandals, and my feet sank into the loose diamond dust of sand. We struggled through the dunes to the harder sand at the water's edge.

Shielding my eyes, I scanned both ends of the beach. A scattering of people lying in the sun, but no one was swimming. Liam was already walking toward the stack of sun lounges and beach bungalows resting in a cluster of palm trees at the far end of the beach.

"C'mon, I can hear voices," Liam said. When we'd almost reached the deck chairs, he changed directions and ploughed through the sand and bush to a winding track, which, after about a hundred feet split into two—left to accommodation, right to the bar. Liam didn't hesitate; he headed straight toward the bar.

A makeshift café had been set out under the tree. Red-checked tablecloths covering trestle tables had been pinned down by aluminum bowls containing sachets of sugar.

"What do you want to drink?" Liam asked.

I looked at my watch—not yet ten o'clock. "A *cortadito*," I replied.

"Nothing stronger?"

"It's a bit early for me."

He frowned at my comment and went to the bar while I found a vacant table. "*Un cortadito* and a rum and coke," Liam ordered.

The barman reached under the bar and dragged out a bottle of rum, which he poured into a plastic cup. "Armando!" he yelled. "*Un cortadito para el Señor!*"

The coffee came in a plastic cup as well. I took a sip and grimaced at the bitter taste.

"I met your friend Landrey when I was in the plaza the other day." I launched into the conversation I needed to have with Liam in person.

"You know ... he's not really my friend. I told you. He's just someone I met. Said I'd do a bit of work for him to help him iron out some of the technical problems he was having." Liam did another swift sidestep, steering the conversation in a different direction.

"He seems to know you a little bit better than you might think," I said.

"Really?" Liam rattled the ice in his cup and then took another sip.

"He said he was supposed to meet you last night at the Hotel Nacional."

Liam's eyes narrowed, and his jaw clenched.

"And he also seems to know a bit more about me than I'd like," I added.

"Like what?"

"He said you'd told him I'd agreed to sell Ita's claim to him."

Liam looked at me, his mouth open in a liar's gape, scrambling to construct a story on the run. "I don't know why he'd say something like that."

"Neither do I. Because I've said nothing of the kind."

"Well, hang on there just one minute." Liam held up his hands to stop me. "We haven't really had a chance to discuss it in depth, but now that you've brought it up …"

"I don't want to sell the claim." There. I'd said it.

"Not even if it could set us up for the future?" he shot back.

I shook my head. "It's not for sale."

"But it's the right time to sell. And it makes perfect sense." Liam's voice lowered, each word measured, careful not to ruin his chances. "We've got someone who's interested in buying it, and let's face it, we don't know what's likely to happen in the future. The claim might end up being useless. That's why we should take the offer now." He reached over and took my hand, entwining his fingers in mine. "Think of what we could do with the money."

A mental image of the apartment in Fort Lauderdale we'd both been looking at flashed through my head. The one on which Liam had been keen to put a deposit, even though it was far beyond our means.

"We could end up with nothing if we don't take advantage of this offer." Liam's voice broke into my thoughts, playing his last card in a game of dirty tricks. He knew my greatest fear was to be alone, to be left with nothing. But I wasn't folding. I straightened my back.

"It's what your grandmother would have wanted you to do." I thought he'd played his last card, but I was wrong. He touched a raw nerve. Even I didn't really know what Ita would have wanted me to do. I hadn't known about the claim, and I didn't understand why she hadn't told me about it when she was alive.

"How do you know what Ita would've wanted me to do?" Defiance filled my voice.

"She told me."

"What?"

"I told her the same thing I told you—that I could get a good price on her claim—and she was happy for me to go ahead."

"I don't believe it. Why would my grandmother tell you about the claim when she didn't even tell me?"

"She wanted to make sure that you—we—were properly set up. Get married and have our own place."

I picked up the bluff in his voice. I knew that Ita wanted me to be happy, but she would never have pushed me into getting married. Quite the opposite—she was always telling me to take things slowly. And I didn't believe that she would discuss these things with Liam without telling me.

"When did all this take place?" I asked, aiming to punch holes in Liam's story and sink it.

"I called in and saw her when I was down in Miami for business a couple of months back."

I remembered that Liam did go to Miami because I wanted to go with him, but I had to work. "And you saw Ita? Why didn't you tell me?"

Liam shrugged. "You know how it is. You get busy …"

No, I didn't know, and it was sounding like Liam deliberately didn't want me to know anything about his visit. "Anyway, it's pointless discussing this any further because the house isn't mine and Marielle is still alive."

"There's no point in being sentimental. It'll be years, decades even, before the claim is settled and developed."

"What do you mean?"

"Well, these sorts of claims are being sold to people who want to one day build something substantial."

"Substantial? Do you mean they'll knock down the villa and build something like a resort?"

Liam hesitated. "Yeah, more or less."

The last thing I wanted to see was a resort built over the cliffs that I'd come to love. And the villa? I'd never allow that to be destroyed. I shook my head. "The claim's not yours to do anything with," I reminded him. "It was my grandparents' and now it's mine."

"Cate, we don't have to make a final decision now. We can talk about it later," Liam said, waving his arm to take in the view before us. "Why don't we just enjoy the day together? That's what you're always wanting, isn't it?"

"As long as you understand that the claim is not for sale. I want you to make it clear to Landrey."

"So, you're just going to give up your inheritance to virtual strangers." My response reignited the frustration in Liam's voice.

"Marielle's not a stranger. She's my relative. And now that I've found her, I don't want to lose her. She's become very important to me."

"More important than me?" Liam asked.

I paused. A second too long.

"Right. I get the message." He grabbed his towel from where he had thrown it on the chair. "Don't worry, I'll let Stuart know that you're not interested in selling the claim. Now, let's go for a swim. The water looks beautiful."

"When?" I wasn't convinced that Liam would do what he said he would.

"Now." He looked at his watch. "Or do you have somewhere else you need to be?"

"I meant when are you going to tell Stuart?"

Liam took his time answering. "How about tonight?"

"Tonight?"

"Yeah. I was going to catch up with him tonight. I thought we could all go to one of those nightclubs everyone talks about."

The last thing I wanted to do was go to a nightclub. I didn't enjoy them at the best of times, and I definitely didn't feel like going to one tonight.

"C'mon, you'll enjoy it. And you can watch me tell Landrey in person."

It was an opportunity. An opportunity to make sure that

Landrey got the message and to also dig deeper into what they were both involved in.

Liam stood up. "Okay. I'll go."

He rewarded me with a winning smile—probably thinking he'd succeeded in manipulating me and was one step closer to selling the claim.

I slipped my bag over my shoulder.

"Let's check out the water," Liam said.

The sand was so hot that we ran to the water's edge and stood in the shallows. The cool water swirled around me, carving out the sand around my feet.

"You're sure it's safe to swim here?" I asked, noting that no one was swimming, even though it was in the middle of the day.

"Trust me," Liam said. "It's as safe here as anywhere."

Trust? My conversation with Liam had raised a lot of red flags, and I needed time to think about what he'd told me. "You go in. I think I'll go for a walk along the beach. Meet you back here."

"Sure. But you'll regret it." Liam dashed into the water and dived through the waves to the calmer water beyond. I couldn't shake the feeling that he was caught in an undercurrent of deception, drifting toward danger, and if I wasn't careful, it would drag me under too. Our relationship was being destroyed by Liam's love of money and his deceptions.

I spent the next half hour walking on the beach, enjoying the hypnotic effect of the rolling waves. As I headed back, I saw Liam get out of the water. He had dried off and had wrapped a towel around his waist by the time I reached him.

"Feel like another drink?" he asked.

"No, not really."

"We'd better get going, then."

As we walked back to the car, Liam told me about the other apartments he'd been looking at in Fort Lauderdale, which he was sure I'd love. His attempt to get me to change my mind about the claim wasn't working. If anything, it was providing more evidence that we didn't have a future together.

The parking lot was almost full by the time we returned. Liam unlocked the car, and as I went to get in, a blue Chevrolet flashed past us, heading in the direction of Havana. Caught off guard, I didn't see the driver clearly, and although there were other cars like Antonio's, I was pretty sure it was him.

When we arrived at the villa, Antonio's car was parked on the road out front.

"I'll pick you up at eight o'clock?" Liam asked.

Jolted from my thoughts, I looked at him blankly.

"The nightclub tonight?"

"Right, sorry."

I got out of the car and let myself into the villa. The door swung open to reveal Antonio walking down the hall toward me. He stopped as soon as he saw me. "Catalina." He smiled.

My heart skipped a beat, but I refused to be disarmed by his charm. "We have to talk."

My resolve hardened.

And so did my voice.

Chapter Sixteen

I closed the front door and leaned against it, hearing the click of the latch echo in the empty hallway. The doors on either side of the hallway were closed—Antonio and I stood opposite each other, the tension between us strung so tight it pulsed with electricity, ready to spark.

"You want to talk now?" The lines between Antonio's eyes deepened as he frowned.

"Yes, now!"

"What's wrong? You sound angry."

"I have every right to be. You're following me. Why?"

"Catalina …" He shook his head. "I'm not …"

"Don't deny it. I saw you. Just now you were at the beach, and last night you were at the Hotel Nacional."

Antonio held up his hands as if to say, *You win.* But the frown between his eyes remained. "Okay, I admit I was in both places."

"Following me."

"Because I'm concerned about your safety."

"You think I'm in danger? From what?"

"There's already been one death."

I winced at the image of Haydée's body on the rocks below the villa that flickered through my mind. "You don't think Haydée's death was an accident?"

"I found out this morning that Haydée was murdered."

"How?" I tried to keep the panic in my voice under control.

"The damage to her skull was caused by a blunt object, not a fall." He preempted my next question. "They don't know yet who did it."

He looked at me with an expression I couldn't interpret. "You don't think I had anything to do with her death, do you?" My voice vibrated with indignation.

"Maybe not, but I'm not so sure about your boyfriend."

"He's not my boyfriend."

"Your fiancé, then."

"He's not …" I stopped myself from continuing. I hadn't told Liam that I was having doubts about our relationship and didn't want to say anything to Antonio until I had. "How could Liam be involved in Haydée's death? He didn't even know her. What aren't you telling me?"

Antonio hesitated, looking like he was weighing up whether he should continue. "What do you know about the dangerous people with whom your fiancé is involved?"

"I don't know anything."

"Surely you must know that Landrey's involved in illegal activities."

"Only that he's trying to buy claims similar to the one I have on Marielle's villa. I didn't think that was illegal."

"You did know about that?" Antonio's eyes narrowed, and his expression hardened.

"I only found out recently. He wanted to buy the claim I had, but I told him it wasn't for sale."

"You didn't know he's also involved in smuggling merchandise as well?"

"Of course I didn't." The indignation in my voice flared into outrage.

The expression on Antonio's face softened. "I want to believe you, but there are things that don't add up."

"Like what?"

"For starters—what are Liam's explanations for his frequent trips to Havana?"

"What do you mean, frequent trips? He's only been here twice, and both times were to visit me."

Antonio shook his head again. "He's a regular visitor. Ask him. I wouldn't be surprised if he was under surveillance already."

"I don't believe you!" Even as I said it, doubt flickered—could it be true?—but I refused to believe Liam was capable of such dishonesty. "Don't you think I'd know if Liam was a regular visitor to Havana?"

Antonio was silent, but his silence thrummed with accusations, unasked questions, and suspicion.

"Are you inferring that Liam is involved in these illegal activities as well?"

"Haydée's death is still under investigation, but I can tell you one thing, the net is tightening."

"You haven't answered my question."

"And I don't intend to until I know more. Catalina." He stepped closer to me. "It would be wise to not associate with this Landrey." He touched my cheek, his fingers tracing a line down the side of my face, his eyes meeting mine and holding them captive. "I don't want anything to happen to you."

He turned and left me standing alone, my heart hammering in my chest, my thoughts in turmoil, and a shiver of fear flying up my spine.

Antonio had made a lot of allegations, some of which I was struggling to believe. I'd gone to the beach earlier with Liam to ask him the questions that had been gnawing at me, but I still didn't have the answers I needed. Tonight, I'd get proof—one way or the other—of what Landrey was mixed up in… and whether Liam was also involved. And I'd make sure Landrey understood that the claim was not for sale.

Antonio's words that I might be in danger whispered a warning to me. But despite Haydée's death, I knew what I had to do.

The lights of Havana flew past us as Liam accelerated through the narrow streets of Vedado on our way to the nightclub. I finally relaxed, having managed to get out of the house without running into Antonio again. He wouldn't have been happy about my decision to come here tonight.

"There it is." Liam pointed out the club as we drove slowly down one of the narrow streets. "Hopefully, we can find a parking spot close by."

I craned my neck, trying to see where he was pointing, but couldn't see anything that even resembled a nightclub.

Liam drove another two blocks before pulling over and squeezing into a space between a battered Lada and a royal-blue convertible. I regretted my choice of heels almost immediately as I stumbled along the uneven sidewalk. Liam grabbed my arm to steady me, pulling me close to him and enveloping me in a cloud of whiskey fumes in the process. I pulled away, annoyed that he'd obviously continued drinking after he'd dropped me at the villa. He grabbed my hand and pulled me closer again, putting an arm around my waist.

"I don't want you falling and twisting an ankle," he said.

We followed the music snaking its way through the cobbled street, down a narrow lane, and up a wooden staircase. There, we joined the queue of people winding through clusters of potted palm trees dotted along the balcony. As we waited, the line grew longer, stretching behind us and down the stairs. We eventually arrived at the entrance—a set of closed wooden doors and a doorman standing sentinel like a modern-day Cerberus—although he didn't need three heads to keep track of things; his eyes seemed able to scan in all directions at once.

"Good evening, *Señor*," the doorman said, his gaze sharp and quick as it swept over us.

"Good evening." Liam slipped him some folded notes. "A table for four." A demand, not a request.

"*Sí, Señor*, a table for four," the man said, pocketing the notes and pulling open one of the large wooden doors to allow us entry.

A wall of sound enveloped us, and we could barely hear the waiter, who motioned to follow him as he carved a passage through tightly packed tables like an icebreaker. We finally reached a vacant table, which he effortlessly lifted in the air so we could sit down. As soon as we were seated, he replaced the table, smoothing out the white cloth with his hands. There was hardly enough room to breathe, let alone move, but at least we had a perfect view of the band and the dance floor.

White trumpets of flowers fluttered from vines stretched along trellises suspended from the ceiling. A flower floated and landed softly on the table in front of me as an explosion of applause signaled the end of the band's song.

Liam suddenly jumped up, slamming our table against the chairs behind us and waving madly to someone on the other side of the room. I looked over and recognized Stuart Landrey, and assumed the woman with him was his partner. Landrey returned the wave, and they both squeezed their way through the crowd toward us.

Landrey was dressed in an open-necked shirt that stretched over his stomach and barely covered the top of his navy slacks. His partner, by comparison, was dressed in a red Lycra dress that barely covered the tops of her thighs, and with shoes that added another four inches to her already towering frame.

I watched Liam as his eyes traveled over her body, exploring it like a tourist in a strange land, before rushing to assist her into the chair beside him.

"Cate, this is Stuart Landrey and his partner, Inés."

"Mr Landrey and I have met before," I reminded him. "He thought I might be interested in him finding a buyer for my grandparents' claim, but I've let him know that it's not for sale."

The corners of Landrey's lips slowly curved upwards. As

his smile widened, his eyes narrowed until they were no more than slits.

"Well, if you ever change your mind …" he said.

"Drinks for everyone?" Liam asked, frowning as he turned toward me.

"I'll have a glass of red wine. And some water," I added.

"I'll help you," Stuart stood up.

Liam and Stuart disappeared to get the drinks, and Inés and I were left to fill the awkward vacuum their absence created.

"You are Cuban, no?" Inés broke the silence first.

"From Miami," I said. When her eyebrows shot up with surprise, I added, "My grandmother was Cuban-Spanish."

Inés nodded slowly. I could almost see her processing the information. "It is good that you were finally able to come with Liam to Havana this time. We would love to show you the sights."

I frowned, but before I could press Inés about Liam being a regular visitor to Havana, he returned, balancing two glasses on a tray above the heads of the other patrons, while Stuart trailed behind with a drink in each hand. Liam deposited the drinks on the table and then finished his off in a couple of gulps while still standing.

"C'mon, Cate," Liam said. "How about a dance?"

"You know I've got two left feet," I reminded him.

Liam put the rest of the glasses on the table and picked up the tray. "Anyone for another drink, then?"

"I'm still on this one." I pointed to my glass, which was still full. "Why don't you wait for a while?"

"Drink up, Cate, you're lagging behind," he scoffed.

Landrey drained his glass and placed it on the empty tray. "I'll have another," he said.

My sense of foreboding and frustration increased as Liam took off, weaving through the tables toward the bar.

I watched Inés track Liam's progress, then saw her lean toward Landrey and whisper something. He turned and looked as well.

I followed their gaze. As I did, a man strode across the floor to the bar without looking left or right and stood beside Liam. I craned forward. Antonio. He stood a head taller than Liam, his crisp white shirt stretched across his broad shoulders, his dark hair curled slightly over his collar, his presence filling the room. He turned slightly when Liam appeared to say something to him, then Liam returned to the table with another tray of drinks.

Antonio's presence sent a rush of heat flowing through my body, but it was quickly followed by anger fueled by the suspicion that he was following me. Again. Antonio scanned the room in the mirror behind the bar. I shrank lower in my seat, hoping he wouldn't see me with Landrey and jump to the wrong conclusion.

The ceiling fans pushed the hot air through the room. Antonio picked up the drink the barman placed on the bar in front of him, turned around, and scanned the room. His gaze halted when it hit our table. My heart fluttered, then raced to match the beat of the fast salsa the band had started playing.

When the music restarted again, Antonio headed toward us. As he came closer, my heart broke free of the music's rhythm and launched into its own drum solo that drowned out the rest of the instruments, the conversation, and the laughter.

Antonio kept his eyes fixed ahead, continuing past our table to the one behind us, where I could hear him talking to the people seated there. My disappointment that he hadn't acknowledged my presence pulled my heart back into line.

I jumped when I felt a hand rest lightly on my shoulder. "Catalina," Antonio's voice, low and barely audible, whispered in my ear. "Would you do me the honor of having this dance with me?" He stood beside my chair, waited for a response.

I looked at Liam, who was glaring at Antonio. For a minute, I was lost for words, then I managed to shake my head. "*Gracias*, Antonio, but I'm afraid I'm hopeless at dancing."

Liam scraped back his chair, grabbed his cell phone, and answered a call as he pushed his way through the tables and stormed outside.

"I love dancing." Inés gave a little wriggle in her seat, but Antonio ignored her offer.

"I can teach you. It is very easy." He held out his hand toward me. I tried to read the expression on his face, but it was devoid of all emotion. I searched the room for Liam, but there was no sign of him.

I stood up and took Antonio's hand. He led me onto the dance floor, which was crowded with bodies swaying en masse, confirming that I was, as I suspected, way out of my depth. I hesitated, stopping in the middle of the crowded tables.

"Don't you trust me?" he asked.

"Of course." I took a deep breath, swallowed my nerves, and continued to follow him into the middle of the dance floor.

The band switched tempo to a slow bolero, and Antonio

slipped a hand around my waist, gripping me firmly and pulling me close. He took my hand in his, placing it over his heart and holding it there with his own. I could feel his heart beating. Steady. Strong.

Antonio's warm breath caressed my neck, igniting a tingle of excitement that spread through my body. He pulled me even closer. I searched for Liam in the crowd and saw him standing at our table, hands on his hips, watching me. "Relax," Antonio whispered. "You are too tense. Look like you are enjoying yourself."

We danced a few steps, and then he pushed me away slightly and looked into my eyes. "Catalina?" My name rode on a sigh of frustration that escaped his lips.

I looked up at him.

"When a man and a woman dance, the man is in control. It might be different in real life, but it is still this way when dancing. Relax and trust me. Follow my lead."

Gradually, I became less conscious of my feet and abandoned myself to the rhythm of the music and the movement of his body.

"So, you did not think my advice was worth taking?" he said, nodding slightly in the direction of Landrey and Liam.

I floundered for an answer. "Yes … but …"

"But you ignored it?"

"Look, it's not as simple as that. I agree with you. There are too many strange things going on, and all of them have happened since I've arrived in Havana. The break-in at the villa, the stolen necklace, Haydée's death. And you also think that Landrey and Liam are somehow mixed up in it all. I'm sure even Díaz thinks I'm involved as well. I need to find out what's going on and coming here tonight was the only way I thought I could get any answers."

The music stopped.

"Anyway, I'd like to know what you are doing here. Following me again? Don't you trust me?" I countered.

Antonio raised his eyebrows. "Catalina … you are making it very hard for me to do that." He pulled me closer and whispered, "When you are going against my advice and socializing with Landrey. You have to admit it does make me wonder."

"Wonder what? Whether I'm involved with them?" I suddenly realized that was exactly what it looked like to Antonio, and I was deeply offended. I glanced over at the table. "Thank you for the dance. I'd better get back." I turned to leave.

"Of course. Your fiancé is waiting."

Liam glared at us as we approached. Inés greeted Antonio with a very generous smile, but it appeared that her generosity didn't extend to me.

Antonio pulled out the chair for me and flashed a smile at the rest of the table. "*Señoras y Señores.*" He acknowledged them with a slight bow, then turned to me. "Thank you, *Señora.*" He raised my hand to his lips and kissed my palm. A red fire started in the pit of my stomach and spread upwards, burning my cheeks. My heart was thumping, and the eyes of the table were on me.

"I thought you said you couldn't dance," Liam accused.

"I can't."

"Certainly didn't look that way." He grabbed a couple of empty glasses, grumbling something to Landrey as he stood up. Landrey grabbed him by the arm and tried to pull him back into his seat, but Liam shook off his hand and continued to the bar, taking up a position beside Antonio.

"What's going on?" I asked Landrey, sensing that my earlier premonition that the night could end in disaster might come to pass.

"Unfinished business," Landrey said with a shrug.

Antonio and Liam were talking, but I could see from here that it wasn't a friendly chat. I felt guilty that I might have caused the altercation by dancing with Antonio.

Liam started waving his arms and jabbing a finger into Antonio's chest. Antonio looked to be retaining his calm, even though he was now pushed back against the bar. A number of security men were circling in the vicinity, ready to swoop. I grabbed my bag and headed to the bar.

"You can't pretend any longer," Antonio said as I joined them.

"What's going on here?" I asked, looking from one to the other. Neither of them said a word. Liam pushed himself away from the bar. The security guards inched closer.

"C'mon. Let's go," Liam mumbled. He grabbed my elbow and pulled me toward the door. I shook off his grip and glanced back to see Antonio's furious gaze following us. Liam staggered down the first couple of steps, then steadied himself by grabbing the railing. He collapsed on the bottom step, and I sat down beside him.

"What happened up there?" I demanded angrily, embarrassed by his actions.

"Nothing," Liam said, staring straight ahead.

"Liam, look at me." He faced me. "What were you and Antonio arguing about?"

"Nothing."

"It didn't look like 'nothing' to me."

"Cate. Leave it!" he exploded, using the railing to pull himself upright before lurching down the lane.

"Where are you going?" I called after him, frustration spilling into exasperation.

"Home. Coming?" he yelled over his shoulder.

I stood and caught up with him. "You're in no state to drive. You can barely walk. Let's get a taxi and collect the car tomorrow."

"I'm fine to drive."

"Give me the keys, I'll drive." I grabbed at the keys, which were dangling from his hand.

"No, you won't." He snatched his hand back, holding the keys high out of my reach.

"You've had too much to drink. I'm not getting in the car with you."

"Don't, then." He turned away and stumbled toward the car without looking back to see if I was following. Before I could catch up to him, he'd jumped into the driver's seat and roared off down the alley, accompanied by the screech of tires.

I waited for him to return.

He didn't.

Anger turned into rage. How could he just leave me in the middle of Havana, having to find my own way home? I took a couple of deep breaths, and then a couple more.

"Looks like you might need a lift." Antonio stood near me, hands in his pockets, waiting for an answer.

"Thank you." My voice held none of the gratitude it should have—only the sharp edge of annoyance. After all, if he hadn't turned up…if he hadn't asked me to dance…if I hadn't agreed…

We walked to the car with silence on extended play. It settled in for the drive to the villa, and neither of us made a move to break it. When we arrived at the villa, it continued walking beside us to the door.

"Thank you again, Antonio."

"Catalina…"

"Tomorrow. Tomorrow we'll talk."

Tomorrow: Haydée's funeral, facing Antonio and Liam… and the truth.

Chapter Seventeen

Sunlight dragged me out of the heavy slumber that had finally claimed me in the early hours of the morning. It shone through the leaves of the trees outside, dappling the floorboards around my bed. It was already hot and sticky, the kind of hot and sticky that usually preceded a storm.

I showered and dressed, pulling my wet hair into a ponytail, the cool water dripping down my back. I crept downstairs, not wanting to disturb the others on my way out. I needed some time alone to process last night. A door closing hurried me along. While I'd have to face Antonio eventually, I wanted to delay it as long as possible. I was grateful that he hadn't abandoned me as Liam had, but I was still annoyed that he appeared not to trust me.

Marielle came out of the living room holding a vase. "Catalina, you are up early. I'm just getting some flowers ready for the wake."

"Do you need help with anything?"

"No. Everyone has been kind and has offered to bring food, and I'll make some *galletas* this morning."

"I can bring a few things on my way home."

"You don't have to," she said, but the tone in her voice told me that my contribution would be gratefully received.

"There's a café in the Plaza Vieja that has beautiful pastries," I said.

"Don't forget we're leaving for the service at the Colón Cemetery at one o'clock."

I gave Marielle a kiss and a quick hug, and left to go to the taxi rank at the Copacabana.

A black blanket of clouds was beginning to roll in from the ocean, hauling the humidity along with it. Perspiration dripped between my shoulder blades, and my dress clung to my legs as I strode toward the taxi rank. It hadn't been long since I'd showered, and I already felt like I needed another.

My phone started ringing, and Liam's face appeared on the screen. I let it ring. Pedro drove past just as I was almost at the Copa, his horn blasting a fanfare into the street as he whizzed by. Within a couple of minutes, he'd driven around the block and returned to a slow crawl beside me.

"*Señora*, you need a lift." It was a statement of fact, not a question, launched from the open window of his taxi. He stopped and jumped out of the car to open the back door.

"Pedro, you're a lifesaver."

"No, *Señora*." He flashed his white teeth and pushed his limp dark fringe off his forehead. "A simple taxi driver. But a very good one, no?"

He waited until I was settled in the back seat before slamming the door and giving the now routine double shove with his hip.

"Where you go?" he asked, leaning through the window.

"The Plaza Vieja, Pedro … I need a coffee."

"My cousin has a place near here. He make great coffee. And very cheap. Do you need breakfast? He make a great omelet also."

"Not today."

"My cousin, he is a very good cook," Pedro persisted.

"I'm sure he is, Pedro, maybe another time."

"My cousin's place has *mucho* atmosphere. Very *historico*. Famous people lived there. Gangsters, you know gangsters? Meyer Lansky and Al Capone?"

"Pedro." I used the same voice I sometimes used in class to get my point across.

"Okay, *Señora*, you wear me down. Habana Vieja it is. Maybe you would like to go to my cousin's place another time. He always has room for a friend of Pedro's."

I smiled at the thought that Pedro considered me a friend. Perhaps my only friend in Havana.

Pedro let me out on the Malecón, and I wound my way through the narrow streets that were becoming as familiar as my own neighborhood. I went straight to my now favorite café, and because it was so early, I had my choice of seats. The umbrellas were still folded, leaving the front tables in full sunlight, so I opted for a table at the top of the steps, shaded by the balcony above.

Yolanda greeted me with a wide, generous smile.

"*Señora*, welcome back. Café?" Yolanda looked genuinely

pleased to see me. All was not lost. Maybe Pedro was not my only friend.

"*Sí, Yolanda, gracias.*"

Her smile grew wider when I used her name. She disappeared into the growing crowd of people inside the café buying the pastries for which it was renowned. The smell of coffee drifted onto the terrace, tempting those who were greeting the new day and those who were reluctant to say goodnight to the old. I breathed in the rich aroma, which found a hollow space in my stomach that I was sure only a croissant could fill. I waved Yolanda over and added one to my order, then settled down to wait, knowing that in Cuba, good coffee could never be rushed—and neither could the staff.

I looked over at Daniela's house. The shutters were closed, and today there was no washing drying in the breeze. No sign of Juan or his mother.

A van squeezed through the cobbled road and tried to round the corner, making four attempts before finally pulling up in front of Daniela's house and blocking my view of the front door. A couple of minutes later, the shutters were flung open, and five men poured out onto the veranda, checking the roof above and then the plaza below. Huddling together and gesturing sharply, their voices wrestled with each other and echoed through the plaza.

Three of the men disappeared inside and then reappeared beside the truck below. Within minutes, a rope was hung from a fixture on the roof, and large pieces of furniture were attached to it and hoisted over the side of the veranda.

Yolanda wandered past and stopped beside my table, as fascinated by the spectacle as I was.

"What's happening over there, Yolanda?" I asked.

"The owners are moving," she said.

I remembered how angry Antonio was when he found out that Daniela might be leaving. "Where are they going?" I asked.

She shrugged and rubbed her thumb and third finger together. "Who knows?"

"Who bought it?"

Yolanda put her index finger up against her lips, giving me a sign that whatever the answer, I wouldn't be getting it from her.

As I sat and watched the men load the furniture, I thought of Antonio's anger at Daniela selling her house, the pressure to sell my grandmother's claim on the villa, and the conflict between Antonio and Liam. Last night, I'd had high hopes of finding out what Landrey and Liam were involved in. High hopes that had crashed and led nowhere. I grabbed my phone and dialed Liam's number.

The phone had almost rung out when he finally answered.

"Thought you might have disowned me," he said. His voice was gravelly and rough, sounding like it needed a grease and oil change.

Yolanda placed the coffee in front of me, and I took a sip before answering.

"How do you know I haven't?" I asked.

"You rang me, didn't you?" His voice held an I-knew-you-would tone. "Where are you?" he asked.

"Having coffee in the Plaza Vieja."

"Coffee's just what I need," he replied.

"I'm not surprised, considering the state you were in last night."

There was a pause.

"I could probably be there in an hour. Are you happy to hang around until I get there?" Liam asked.

"I can fill in time till you get here." I had a million things I wanted to ask, but not over the phone. I needed to see Liam's face when I asked them.

"Okay. See you in an hour." He ended the call.

I finished my coffee and started walking. I loved watching Havana waking up and preparing for the day, and I was more than happy to wander through its streets until I had to meet Liam. I ended up in the Plaza de la Catedral.

Although it was still early, people were scattered throughout the plaza and around its perimeter. Tables and chairs were set out in front of the mansion-turned-restaurant. Two women were sprawled between the pillars, their billowing dresses cascading over the stone steps, lace shawls covering their shoulders as they puffed on cigars. No doubt they were preparing themselves for the onslaught of tourists desperate for a photo with a national icon.

I walked past one of the fortune tellers dressed in white, who was sitting with her talismans laid out in front of her. "Come, lady, and I will tell your future. Come, come. It will be lucky for you."

I didn't believe in fortune tellers, but for some reason, I allowed myself to be persuaded to join her. My skin scraped against the rough sandstone as I squeezed onto the top step beside her, careful not to step on her flowing dress.

"Carmelita," the woman said, patting her chest and introducing herself. She held out her hand. Her long, curved nails were blood red and a perfect match to the red flowers cascading from her white turban. A square of blue silk was spread out before her, shells scattered around its edges. A set of cards was positioned in the center.

Carmelita's jewels flashed in the sun as she shuffled the cards. Without skipping a beat, she stopped, put the cigar in her mouth, and then laid out the spread. I studied her face closely and wondered why I was sitting in the middle of a square hoping a woman with a cigar would be able to help me find the answers I needed. Carmelita's frown was replaced by a smile and the nodding of her head, as if the cloud between her and my future had suddenly disappeared.

"You have a man?" She leaned over the cards, studying them closely, before lifting her gaze to my eyes as if she'd find the answer there.

I hesitated. I had two.

"You'll be very happy together," she said.

With Liam or Antonio?

Carmelita closed her eyes and started rocking back and forth. A low keening sound escaped before her rough voice rasped out a warning. "Lady." She gripped my hands tightly and slipped into Spanish. I only understood her final words. "*Usted debe tener cuidado, Señora.*"

"I'm sorry," I said. "*No hablo español.* I don't speak Spanish."

Carmelita's eyes flashed open. She looked confused and disoriented.

"*Más despacio, por favor,*" I said.

The woman nodded her head and then her eyes flicked upwards, as if searching for the English words.

"You must be careful, lady."

A prickle of fear started at the base of my spine.

"Danger is near."

The chill crawled slowly up my back.

"It is someone you trust."

I shivered.

Her eyes opened wider. "But there is someone who loves you and cares for you. It is him—not the other man—you must trust."

I could've asked for more details—about the danger I was in, or the man I could trust— but I didn't.

Couldn't.

In case I heard the wrong answer.

I gave her a ten CUC note, which she tucked into the bodice of her dress. It was only then that I noticed the chain she was wearing. Hanging around her neck was a medallion— Our Lady of Regla. I instinctively touched the one that I was wearing.

Carmelita reached over and held the medallion tightly in her hand and nodded. "*Sí*. Yemayá, she will protect you." She released the charm, scooped up the cards before her, and placed the deck on the blue silk square in front of her to wait for her next customer. It was time to go.

I looked at my watch. Liam would probably be there by now, so I picked up my pace, hurrying down Calle San Ignacio past La Bodeguita del Medio—a small bar with a huge reputation as one of Hemingway's favorites. It was on my list to visit, but Liam was waiting—and so were my questions. Questions that were racing through my head, colliding with the ones my conversation with Carmelita had raised.

Liam was already there when I arrived and gave me a sheepish smile. He stood up, his lips brushing my cheek as I sat down. The tables around us were now full, and conversations buzzed around us in all languages. Havana had woken up and was thirsty and hungry.

Yolanda saw me immediately and bustled over. "*¿Quiere otro café?*" she asked.

"*Sí.*" I nodded. She looked at Liam, who ordered a black coffee. He was sporting red eyes, black bags, and a five o'clock shadow, even though it was only ten o'clock in the morning. His shirt looked a lot like the one he was wearing last night.

"About last night …" He raked his hand through his hair, pushing it off his forehead where beads of sweat were forming. His eyes met mine, and then flicked to Daniela's house, then back to me. "I drank a bit too much," he said.

I didn't argue.

"You deserve an explanation."

I waited.

"I've been under a lot of pressure," he explained.

"What kind of pressure?" I asked.

He grabbed my hand and leaned toward me. "Let's get out of here. Go back to the States."

I felt my jaw drop with surprise. No apology for embarrassing me last night, no explanation about what was going on. Just a *let's skip town* like it's not a big deal. "But you just got here—and you're going back after the weekend, and I'm leaving in a week."

His hand rubbed the stubble on his chin. "I meant leave earlier. I've checked and we can get seats on this afternoon's flight to the States."

I held out my hands in protest. "This afternoon! I can't just up and leave this afternoon."

"Why not?" Liam asked.

"Well, for a start, Haydée's funeral is this afternoon, and I can't walk out and leave Marielle at a time like this. Anyway, why the sudden rush?"

Liam took a slurp of coffee. "It's a long story," he said.

"I've got plenty of time. Does it have something to do with what you and Antonio were fighting about last night?"

"That? That was nothing." Liam sat still, shoulders hunched, his eyes staring into the distance.

"Liam, what is going on?" My voice was impatient, sick of playing twenty questions.

His eyes flashed at me. "It's nothing to concern yourself about."

"Liam, we're supposed to be starting a future together. It does concern me. We shouldn't be keeping secrets from each other."

Liam straightened in his chair and squared his shoulders but still avoided looking at me. "It's nothing really. Just dabbling in a bit of commercial trading."

"Trading in what? Real estate?"

"Yeah, sort of."

I immediately thought of the allegations that Antonio had made, and my stomach churned.

"You're involved in something illegal," I challenged.

"No, not illegal."

"What do you mean?"

"There are always loopholes in the law, you know that."

"I'm not sure I do, Liam. Is that what you're involved in? Loopholes? Is Landrey involved in these 'loopholes' as well?"

"Kind of. You could say he's the banker. My job is to make connections."

"So, you knew Landrey before you came to Cuba. He wasn't just someone you met on the plane coming here. Why don't you tell me exactly what these 'loopholes' are?"

"I keep telling you—there's huge interest in Cuba right now, from all around the world. It's more than just selling claims to people on the off chance that Cuba will open up. That's only part of it. People everywhere are desperate to own a piece of paradise. And they take risks to get it."

"Antonio says that it's impossible for foreigners to own property in Cuba."

"It is … technically. But there are ways around it. For a start, there are plenty of Cubans prepared to put their name on the official deeds—for a good price. And often, as well as getting paid, they end up with a somewhere to stay. Everyone's a winner!"

"It sounds risky to me."

"I knew you'd say that. That's why I haven't discussed it with you."

I stared at Liam and felt the ground shift. At that moment, I realized that my suspicions had been right—our relationship and our future had been built on lies. My stomach lurched, and dread clawed its way up my throat, threatening to choke me. I swallowed and took a deep breath.

"So, getting me to sell Ita's claim to the villa was part of this scheme?"

Liam hung his head and avoided meeting my gaze. "I needed some money."

"For what?" I asked.

"I owe Landrey money. Money he lent me to buy a couple of properties."

"Where? In Miami? Fort Lauderdale?" I pictured the photos he'd shown me of apartments he liked.

"Here actually."

"In Havana?"

"Shhh," Liam said.

I glanced over my shoulder and noticed that people were staring at us.

"You're telling me that you've already committed to selling the claim without my permission? That's why you didn't want to tell Landrey that it wasn't for sale. By the way, how did you find out about my grandmother's claim? I know she wouldn't have told you about it without mentioning it to me."

Liam looked down at his coffee, avoiding my eyes challenging him for the truth.

"Landrey told me about it."

"How did he know?"

"He said there was some kind of register he could access."

Yolanda appeared at our table with the coffees. "Would you like anything else?" she asked.

"No." Liam waved her away. "Don't worry, Cate, I know I can get the money from somewhere else."

I was beginning to understand Antonio's distrust of foreigners. If I'd been in any doubt before or been slightly tempted to change my mind about marrying Liam, this conversation had cemented my resolve. My future with Liam, the future we'd planned together, wasn't possible any longer. Liam's lack of integrity left me speechless, but his inability to admit he'd done anything wrong stunned me even further.

Liam leaned forward, took my hand, and squeezed it.

"Things are going to work out just fine. We'll be back home in a couple of days, with all our friends, and life will get back to normal. We can buy our own place, get married."

I pulled my hand away. "I don't think so, Liam—this is too big to put behind us."

"Nothing is that big. I love you, Cate." He leaned toward me, but I moved away. Liam might love me, but he'd made it clear he loved money more.

"I'm not even sure that I want to go back to the States," I said quietly.

"What's that?"

"I'm not sure I'm going back to the States," I repeated.

"What do you mean?" Liam asked.

"I've just found my great-aunt. She's the only family I have. I want to get to know her while I can."

"You're going to stay in Havana?"

"I don't know if it's possible, but I do know that I need to take one step at a time."

Liam looked at me as if I'd gone mad. There was no easy way to say it, but I needed to be honest with him—and with myself. "I just think we've become different people, we want different things from life, and … we have different values. I think we should go our separate ways."

I stood up and pushed back my chair. "Goodbye, Liam."

Liam didn't look at me as I went to leave—just continued to stare straight ahead, a frown creasing his brow and a sneer lifting one corner of his mouth. I didn't know if it was because I was leaving him or because I'd ruined his plans. I didn't care. I left and didn't look back.

I walked away, and with every step I left the past behind me—and the fear I'd always had of being alone. It disappeared and was replaced by excitement as a new beginning took its place.

I had no idea what the future was going to hold, but I was certain now that it wasn't going to include Liam.

Chapter Eighteen

A convoy of cars, some older than others, greeted me as I arrived back at the villa. Drivers were giving their cars a last-minute polish, including the windows, chrome, and even the plastic-covered upholstery. I walked past the cars, their bright colors creating a festive air that gave my spirit a burst of lightness. As soon as I opened the front door, I saw Marielle.

"Catalina, *mi vida*."

"Where do you want these sandwiches?" A woman I didn't recognize stopped beside us.

"In the fridge until we get back," Marielle said, before turning to me. "Catalina, you're here!" She gave me a quick hug. "We're leaving soon. Go and get ready, *mi cielo*, but before you do, meet Frida, Haydée's mother."

Haydée's mother was slight, her long black hair swept up in a tight chignon at the nape of her neck. Her black dress was as severe as the expression on her face as she looked me up and down. "The girl from Miami."

"Frida's mother was a dear friend of mine." Marielle ignored Frida's comment. "When we were girls, we were part of the literacy campaign, and we lived with farming families in Matanzas. That is why we have permission to have the service at the chapel in the cemetery. But we will talk of this another time. Now, you must go and get ready."

I was just putting the last touches to my makeup when I heard Antonio's voice below. I raced downstairs to find he'd already gathered everyone outside and was allocating them to the cars lined up beside the curb.

"You can ride with Marielle and Frida—my car is over there," he said when I reached him.

Marielle and Frida were already in the back seat. I slipped into the front with Antonio. I caught a faint tang of his cologne as he leaned over me to open the glovebox. His hand brushed my knee, sending a jolt of electricity through me.

"Sorry," he said, grabbing his sunglasses and slamming the glovebox shut.

I threw him a glance, but his eyes were already fixed on the rearview mirror and the road behind as he waited for a break in the traffic. He led the funeral cortège to the cemetery, pulling up behind a bus that was parked on the side of the Avenida Cristóbal Colón. Mourners streamed out of the bus and through the pale-colored arches circling the chapel.

Antonio assisted Haydée's mother, while I helped Marielle into the chapel and to the front pew. The gold-and-blue-painted chapel provided a sanctuary, a cool respite from the sun. Small stained-glass windows and doors were large enough to be impressive but small enough to lessen the power of the sun. Incense wafted through the chapel, heavy and pungent, reminding us of the purpose of our visit.

Frida sat in the front row with other relatives and friends, and Marielle sat between Antonio and me, staring straight ahead at the giant fresco covering the wall behind the altar … and Haydée's coffin. I felt uncomfortable being here, almost like an imposter, but reminded myself that I was here to support Marielle.

Before I knew it, tears welled up in my eyes. I tried blinking them away, but when they persisted, I scrambled to find a tissue to wipe my damp cheeks. I hoped no one noticed because I would have had difficulty explaining that I wasn't crying for Haydée, that I was crying for Ita. And if I were being honest, a few of those tears were for myself.

The service began. While I couldn't understand everything the priest was saying, there was a familiarity about the service that I recognized. The ceremony was shorter than I expected, and when I made my way outside, I was relieved to escape the smell of incense and breathe in the fresh air.

A Cuban flag fluttered in the breeze, and through one of the arches, I could see an angel standing tall, arm stretched toward the heavens. Other mourners moved outside and were clustered in small groups talking with the solemnity that signified such an occasion. I remembered my last visit to the cemetery and quickly glanced over my shoulder to check that the man in the white hat wasn't still following me.

I looked back at the chapel. Marielle had followed me outside and was talking to a group of people.

"I didn't know that you knew Haydée?" a voice interrupted my thoughts.

I turned and recognized Daniela, Juan's mother, immediately. "Marielle and my grandmother were sisters. I'm staying with her while I am visiting Havana."

Daniela tilted her head, as if trying to accommodate the information I'd just given her. The two lines between her eyes deepened, giving me the impression that she was having some difficulty.

"You are from America? I am going to America," she said confidently.

"For a holiday?"

"No, no, no." She shook her head emphatically. "I go to live … one day."

I wondered if that was why she'd sold her house.

"Have you moved?"

Daniela glanced around us. "It was necessary. I move in with my relatives. It is good because I get much help with Juan."

"He's a lovely boy."

Another deepening of the lines between her eyes. "He doesn't like school. But it is important. He must learn many things before we go to America, including English."

"I could give him a couple of English lessons while I'm here, if you would like?"

"You would do that?"

"Of course."

"*Gracias*," she said, then flashed a wide smile.

"Danni!" a voice called from a car parked near the church.

"Sorry, I must go," she said before disappearing.

Danni. The pieces were beginning to fit together, beginning to make sense. The voices below my window were talking about Daniela, not Danny. The document to be signed was probably something to do with the house she wanted to sell. Of course, Daniela would know Haydée because both she and Haydée were Antonio's friends.

I felt a growing apprehension stealing over me at the thought that there was a connection between the property scams and Haydée's death. I pushed the information to the back of my mind to think about later.

Marielle was still occupied talking to the other mourners, so I grabbed the opportunity to revisit Amelia's grave. There was something about her husband's enduring love, constant and loyal, that gave me comfort and hope, especially after spending the morning with Liam.

I retraced the steps of my earlier visit through the gravestones until I reached the marble statue of Amelia and her baby.

Two women sat on the grave opposite, their legs dangling over its edge, flowers clasped in their hands. A third woman was standing in front of Amelia's grave. She picked up the iron ring attached to the marble slab in one hand and held a bunch of wilting gladioli in the other. I could hear the hollow knock of brass on stone, once, twice, three times. With whispered words, the gift of flowers, and the light touch of her hand caressing the rough stone, the woman reluctantly left her wish behind and began the wait for it to be fulfilled.

One of the women noticed me standing in the scrap of shade thrown by a tree and waved me over to the grave. I shook my head, but she maneuvered herself off the edge of the grave on which she was sitting and walked toward me. She took me by the hand and led me to Amelia's grave, folding my fingers around the brass ring and knocking it three times. A shiver ran the length of my spine, raising the hairs on the back of my neck. The woman gently pushed me forward, closer to Amelia and her baby.

"*Pide un deseo*, a wish." She placed her hand over her heart. "You wish, now."

I placed my hand on the statue of Amelia as I had seen others do and closed my eyes. What did I want? I still wasn't sure. I knew what I didn't want. I didn't want to be with Liam any longer.

Even as I thought this, a stone of hardened resolve replaced any feelings I once had for Liam. I wanted, and deserved, someone I could trust, someone who trusted me. Someone I could depend on and who valued the same things I did. I closed my eyes and whispered the words that came from my heart. An image of Ita, smiling and nodding, appeared in my mind.

"I hope you were careful." Isabelle's voice startled me. I looked behind and felt heat warm my cheeks.

"About what?" I asked.

"Your wish." Isabelle pointed to Amelia's grave. "You have to be sure it is what you really want."

"I can assure you that there won't be any complaints from me if it comes true. Is everyone ready to go?" I asked, thinking that she'd been sent to get me.

"They'll be a while yet. You know, people catching up, remembering."

"Last time I was here, I visited the Marquez-Fuentes crypt,

but I had help from the guide. I don't think I could find it as easily as I found Amelia's."

"I can show you, if you like."

"Do you think we have time?" I asked. I looked back toward the church, but Marielle was still engaged in talking.

"*Un montón de tiempo.* We have much time." Isabelle took off, moving deeper within the cemetery, and we wound our way slowly through the marble angels and wreaths. This time, I was able to look at the graves we passed more closely.

Scattered among the well-maintained family crypts decorated with fresh and artificial flowers were the resting places of those who'd been abandoned after the Revolution. Openings boarded up, holes and steps leading down into darkness. We reached the Marquez-Fuentes crypt, and Isabelle seemed so at home here that I wondered if she was a regular visitor.

We stood together in the shade of the lone tree, its branches shielding us from the unrelenting sun.

"I wish my grandmother had spoken more about her … my family … and about her life here. I feel I've missed out on so much, not knowing Marielle."

"Your grandmother had reasons for her silence."

"Knowing Ita, she probably did, but I can't imagine what they were," I said.

"Maybe she was scared that she would lose you," Isabelle said. "Scared that if you came to Havana, you might get to love it in a way that she no longer could … scared you might even get to know and love Marielle."

"Why would she be concerned about that?" I asked.

If Isabelle had an answer to my question, she wasn't sharing. Had Ita been scared that I would find out the family secret

I'd overheard Marielle and Isabelle talking about? A secret that I was pretty sure involved Rosa. If Marielle wasn't going to tell me, maybe Isabelle would.

"Why isn't Rosa buried here with the rest of the family?" I asked.

Isabelle shook her head. "You'll have to ask Marielle."

"Isabelle, I need to know." My voice was filled with a raw urgency that surprised me. "Please tell me."

Isabelle studied my face, paused as if considering my request and the cost she'd pay for telling me. "The family could never forgive the shame Rosa brought on them." Isabelle hesitated, and I thought for a minute that she wasn't going to say any more. "Rosa had a baby, but no husband. In those days, a woman either got married or had to give up her child. I know it's hard to believe that now, but that's just the way it was."

"But where did she go? What happened to her and the baby?" My voice grew louder with excitement and the hope that all was not lost, and I could find Rosa.

"I looked after Rosa at the farm during her pregnancy. It was a sad and lonely time for her."

"Where is she?"

"Both Rosa and her daughter, Luisa, are buried at the farm in Matanzas," Isabelle continued.

"Rosa's daughter was called Luisa?"

My memory flashed back to the grave on top of the hill at Matanzas, to the white angel weeping in the shade of the giant trees. "I've visited the farm there, and I saw Luisa's grave, but it was the only one."

"Rosa's name wasn't put on the headstone. The family

wanted to give the impression that she had left Cuba and had gone to live in America."

"But …"

"So, this is where you both got to." Marielle's voice interrupted Isabelle's story.

"Catalina wanted me to help her find the Marquez-Fuentes crypt," Isabelle explained.

Marielle let go of Antonio's arm and used a walking stick to negotiate the uneven cobblestones in front of the crypt. Antonio handed her a bunch of mixed flowers, heads already fatigued with heat, which she placed on the grave. She stood silently for a few seconds before stiffening her back and turning to rejoin us.

The four of us walked back to the chapel together; a solemn group lost in our own thoughts. Mine were about three sisters and a woman who knew their secrets. I wondered just how many secrets Marielle was keeping, and if Rosa and Luisa's deaths were what I'd overheard them discussing. And how many more secrets was Marielle keeping from me?

We returned to the villa after the funeral, and I assisted Marielle by refilling cups of coffee and handing around the cakes and *galletas* that had been provided by the other guests. The sadness of someone dying so young, and in such tragic circumstances, hung in the air. As soon as I could, I fled to the garden outside.

I'd pushed thoughts about my conversation with Liam out of my mind, but now that the guests were leaving and I'd almost finished my hosting duties, they returned. I began to feel the weight that accompanied the need to make another difficult decision. Should I tell Antonio what Liam had told me about the real estate scam, or should I keep quiet? If I shared the information with Antonio, I knew there could be far-reaching implications for Liam.

"Thank you for being here for Marielle." I turned at the sound of Antonio's voice, low and tender. "It's been a pretty awful day."

I wasn't going to disagree … and Antonio didn't even know the half of it. I wondered if Liam had caught the plane to the States as he had intended.

Antonio stepped toward me so that only a couple of inches separated us. He ran his fingers through my hair, tucking the loose strands behind my ear and caressing the side of my neck with his fingers.

I looked up at him, held captive by his dark eyes, their intensity lighting a fire in my stomach. Every thought of Liam and my indecision about what to do disappeared.

"Catalina …" He bent his head, and his lips touched mine, gently, at first. I could feel myself trembling as his lips awoke a recklessness and depth of desire I hadn't felt in a long time. I reached up, entwining my arms around Antonio's neck and pressing my lips against his. Our bodies melted into each other as his arms enveloped me.

We parted slowly, his hand cupping the side of my face and tilting it upwards.

"Why are you frowning?" He swept his thumb along my bottom lip. "There's something wrong."

I shook my head and pulled away from him, even though

my body ached to be closer. I didn't trust myself, my emotions, or my actions. I'd been attracted to Antonio ever since I'd met him, and now there was no reason why we shouldn't act on that attraction.

But I'd just escaped one relationship and wasn't going to fall into another—especially since I knew I'd be returning to the States in a week. Long-distance relationships didn't work. We were from different worlds—and I knew Antonio would never consider living in mine.

"I understand. You're engaged. I'm sorry." He stepped away from me.

"Liam and I are no longer together," I said. As if on cue, my phone started ringing.

"Aren't you going to get that?"

I shook my head, scared that answering the call would interrupt our conversation. "I'll ring them back later."

Isabelle came out onto the veranda and walked down the stairs toward us. "I'm leaving now, but I wanted to say goodbye."

"Isabelle, thank you for telling me about Rosa and her daughter. I understand why Marielle doesn't want to talk about them, and I'll wait until she's ready." I gave her a quick hug. When she left, I turned to tell Antonio what I'd learned about Rosa's disappearance, but he'd already vanished.

I took my phone out of my pocket. Just as I thought, I'd missed a call from Liam. He'd also sent a text message:

Ring me. Need to speak to you. URGENT.

I rang back immediately, but there was no answer.

Chapter Nineteen

It was seven in the morning, but I'd already been awake for an hour waiting for the sun to rise. I dialed Liam's number again. I'd tried calling him several times last night to no avail. The phone rang out, so I left a message for him to call me back.

I threw on some clothes and headed straight to the Copacabana in case Liam was still in Havana. It was early and cool enough to walk, but I'd still worked up a sweat by the time I passed through the glass doors.

The foyer of the Copacabana was almost empty. I knew that would change as soon as the buses arrived to pick up the tourists for their day trips and airport drop-offs. I walked up to the reception desk.

"*Señora?*" the receptionist looked up from the paperwork in front of her and smiled, a half-smile, telling me I was interrupting important business.

"I'm looking for *Señor* Liam Rochester? Can you tell me which room he is in?"

The receptionist checked the computer in front of her, her fingers dancing over the keys.

"Sorry. No Liam Rochester is registered here."

"He must've checked out yesterday. Can you tell me what time he left?"

A few more taps and the beginning of a frown started between her eyes.

"Can you spell his last name for me?"

"Rochester. R-O-C-H-E-S-T-E-R."

"*Señora* …" Her tone slid down a register—an aha moment turning confusion into condescension. "I think maybe you have the wrong hotel. No one by that name has stayed here all week."

"But that's impossible."

She looked at me, a glare that demanded how dare I doubt her computer, or even herself for that matter.

"Good morning, *Señora*." Her tone left no room for discussion. She dismissed me and redirected her attention to the papers beside the computer. Our conversation was over.

I stood there. Speechless. Motionless. The burning acid in my stomach rising in my throat. The receptionist glanced up after a few minutes. This time, there was no smile, fake or otherwise, just the tilting of her head to one side, asking what I was still doing there. I moved away from the desk and sank into one of the lounges.

If Liam wasn't staying here, where was he staying? Could he have used another name? I looked over at the reception desk, but the receptionist was now drowning in waves of people with matching suitcases.

I dialed Liam's number again. Still no answer.

I checked my options, which I had to admit appeared limited. I grabbed one of the taxis waiting at the rank because I'd wasted enough time. After paying the driver, I jumped out of the cab, ran up the steps, and let myself into the villa. Marielle was up and enjoying breakfast in the garden as usual.

"Catalina." Marielle put down her coffee. "Come, join me."

I looked around. "Is Antonio here?" I asked.

"*Mi corazón*, you just missed him. He said he had to go out for a few minutes, but you know Antonio. Always something to be done."

I groaned and flopped down into the chair across from her.

"He'll have his cell phone on him. Why don't you ring him?"

"No, it's best if I speak to him in person," I said.

"You look like you could do with a cup of coffee. Let me get you one."

My stomach grumbled, reminding me that I hadn't had anything to eat yet. "No, Marielle, I'll get it."

After making myself a cup of coffee, I cut the end from the loaf of bread and rejoined Marielle in the garden.

"Is something wrong?" she asked.

"No … maybe … not sure."

"Is it about your fiancé?"

"Yes and no. Liam and I have decided to go our separate ways."

"I'm very sorry to hear that," she said, reaching over and squeezing my hand. "But you know, time … passes, and each day it will hurt less. You'll find someone else."

"We've grown apart, and it's become really noticeable

since I've been in Havana. We definitely aren't right for each other. But that's not the real problem. I'm concerned that he's in some kind of trouble."

"Perhaps you should speak to the *policía*. By the way, Capitán Díaz called and said that your statement was ready to be signed at the station."

I felt a lot better for having a caffeine hit and something solid in my stomach. I looked at my watch. I would wait and see if Antonio returned, and if he didn't, I would go and see Díaz.

By mid-afternoon, Antonio hadn't returned, and Liam still wasn't answering his phone. A sense of dread was growing in my stomach, and Díaz was looking like my only option to find Liam. I had to sign the statement at the police station anyway. I let Marielle know where I was going and dialed Pedro's number.

When he pulled up a couple of minutes later, I jumped into the back seat. He turned around, waiting for instructions.

"Can you take me to the police station, Pedro?" I asked.

He scrunched his eyes together in a frown. "You are in trouble, *Señora* Cate?"

"No, nothing like that, Pedro. Everything is fine."

He turned around and crunched the gear into first, but I could see in the rear-vision mirror that the frown on his face hadn't moved. Pedro drove past the aquarium and down a couple of backstreets before pulling up outside the station with a squeal of tires. He jumped out and opened the door for me. "I wait for you."

"Don't bother waiting, Pedro. I'll call you when I'm ready to leave, and if you're free, you can pick me up." I walked inside, leaving him leaning against his car.

The station was almost empty. I recognized the officer guarding the front door from my last visit, and a man was hunched on one of the benches in the furthest corner. I hesitated briefly inside the door.

"*Señora?*" The officer at the door began, but I continued past him and headed straight to the officer behind the counter. He looked up as I reached him.

"Is Captain Díaz in?" I asked.

"What did you want to see him about?"

"I have to sign the statement I gave a few days ago," I said.

"I can get someone to help you."

"The message was from Díaz, and he took my original statement. Can you tell him Catalina Johnson is here to speak to him, please?"

He hesitated briefly, then lifted the receiver of the phone and dialed a number. We waited. Either Díaz was busy or wasn't in his office. Just when the officer began to put the phone down, he pressed it back to his ear and I heard him tell the person on the other end that I was waiting, then he hung up.

"He will be here in maybe thirty minutes?" the officer said. "Please, take a seat."

"Thirty minutes?" I repeated.

The officer simply shrugged and went back to the papers

in front of him. Thirty minutes dragged. I walked outside, but the heat forced me back into the air-conditioning. When I returned, the man who was sitting in the corner had disappeared, and the officer behind the desk was so engrossed in his work he didn't acknowledge my presence. I checked my watch. I'd been waiting forty minutes when Díaz opened the door to the offices and beckoned me to follow him down the now-familiar hallway.

We ended up in a room at the very end, which was furnished as an office. A massive wooden desk took center stage, almost filling the whole room. In one corner, there was a filing cabinet, and a bookshelf was squeezed between the desk and the wall behind.

Díaz sat in a comfortable leather office chair on one side of the desk and pointed to the synthetic molded chair on the other. "Good. You got my message and have come to sign your statement," Díaz said, pulling some sheets of paper out of the folder he'd brought with him. "Please read it carefully to make sure it is accurate."

I read through it. Everything was there—except any reference to the argument I'd overheard between Haydée and the unidentified man. I looked up and caught Díaz looking at me, an expression on his face I couldn't interpret. "You haven't included the argument between Haydée and the unidentified man."

He shrugged. "Do you have a name for this unidentified man?"

"No. I don't."

"Did this man make any threats?"

"Not that I heard."

Díaz shrugged again. "As you can see, it didn't provide any additional information. Of course, I can include it, but you will have to come back again to read and sign the statement."

"No, it's fine. I can see I wasn't able to provide anything specific that would help." I took the pen he gave me and signed and dated my statement.

Díaz took the pen and statement and stood up. I remained seated.

"Anything else?" he asked.

I took a big breath. "Well, there is something …"

Díaz sat down again and drummed his fingers on the table.

"My friend, Liam Rochester, has been visiting me in Cuba."

He nodded. "Yes, *Señor* Rochester, your fiancé, no?"

"When I went around to his hotel, I was told he wasn't staying there … that he had never stayed there."

"Could he have used a different name perhaps?" he asked.

I'd asked myself the same question. "There has to be some mistake. I thought … Could you perhaps contact the hotel? They weren't very forthcoming with any information, but it might be different if you ask."

"Of course, I know the manager there very well."

"Thank you. I'd appreciate that."

Díaz stood and walked to the door.

"Aren't you going to take down the details of the hotel?"

"Of course. Where was your friend staying?"

"The Copacabana."

He scribbled the name on the notepad in front of him. "Is there anything else?" he asked.

I hesitated, the knowledge of what Liam had told me

about his dealings with Landrey weighing heavily on my mind. And I couldn't escape the thought that it had something to do with his disappearance. "I think that Liam might be involved with some property dealings that might be …" words raced through mind … *illegal … immoral … unethical*, but I settled for "questionable".

"Really?"

I outlined everything Liam had told me, and as I did, Díaz sat down and leaned back in his chair, clasping his hands behind his head.

"I see," he said. "And you think he is in some danger?"

"He could be …" I hesitated to reveal my personal situation and the fact that we were no longer together.

Díaz nodded his head slowly as if in thought. "Well, Ms Johnson, your friend hasn't been missing for twenty-four hours yet, so why don't we wait a little bit longer before we start jumping to conclusions?"

"If we'd acted earlier, we might have been able to save Haydée," I said.

Díaz's eyes narrowed to calculating when I mentioned Haydée's name. "You think that Haydée's murder and the disappearance of your fiancé are connected?"

"Of course not!" I retorted. "I was pointing out the importance of acting quickly when a person goes missing. Something's wrong. Liam sent me a message yesterday to call him urgently. And now he's disappeared." I showed him the text.

"Have you told Antonio about this?" he asked.

I shook my head. "He wasn't at home, and I was coming here to sign the statement."

"I see. Now, why don't I give you a lift home, and we'll see if *Señor* Rochester turns up tonight. If not, we'll put some of our resources into finding him. But I'm sure that won't be needed."

"Thank you … and if you wouldn't mind calling the Copacabana in the meantime, I'd be very grateful."

"*Ciertamente.* Wait here for a minute," he said, picking up my statement and pushing his chair back against the wall before disappearing into the hallway. He returned a couple of minutes later and stood at the door, jingling a set of keys. "The car's out the back."

Díaz led the way to the back door and strode to the late-model car parked at the far end of the parking lot. At least I wouldn't be arriving at the villa in a marked police car.

My hand rested on the handle of the front door.

"If you don't mind, could you sit in the back? Police protocol," he explained.

"Of course."

He shut the door behind me and jumped into the front seat. As he turned up the radio, I heard the door locks click.

"I hope you don't mind, but I called Antonio just to let him know what's going on."

I did mind. I was sure Antonio would wonder why I'd gone straight to Díaz and not spoken to him first. "Why did you do that? If I'd known that, I would've waited and spoken to him myself."

"My apologies, *Señora.* I thought I was doing the right thing."

We sped through the streets until we reached Fifth Avenue

and stopped at the intersection. Díaz waited for the lights to change, then he turned left.

"Aren't we going to the villa?" I asked.

"Sorry. I started to tell you and got sidetracked. When I told Antonio what has happened, he asked if we could meet him at one of the stations near where he's working today. Is that okay with you?"

"Sure. I guess." I tried to keep the hesitation out of my voice, but even I could hear it.

We passed suburbs I'd never seen before and through streets where the houses were in such need of restoration that Antonio would never be out of work.

As we drove further, the traffic thinned, and the multi-lane roads gave way to a single, winding one. Trees and smaller houses replaced blocks of apartments as we continued out of Havana. We'd been driving for about twenty minutes.

"Where are we meeting Antonio?" I asked.

"In Regla, a small suburb on the edge of the harbor."

My hand instinctively flew to the medallion of Our Lady of Regla I was wearing.

"I thought you had to go by ferry."

"You can," he said, turning to me, "but we have to take the long way around because of the car."

Díaz slammed hard on the brakes. I gripped the front seat of the car, hitting my head against the window as the car skidded and fishtailed on the dirt beside the bitumen. We came to a stop in a cluster of bushes at the side of the road.

"You okay?" Díaz asked.

"I think so," I said, rubbing my shoulder, which had smashed into the door. "What happened?"

"Wait there." He jumped out, rushed around the back of the car, and wrenched open my door.

"I think I…" I began. And then I saw it.

The gun.

Pointing straight at me.

Chapter Twenty

Trapped, I was pressed against the door. Díaz grinned, the gun still pointing straight at me. My insides somersaulted and landed heavily in the pit of my stomach.

"Give me your phone," Díaz demanded. "Don't make me do anything I'll regret."

I took the phone out of the pocket of my cargo pants and threw it at Díaz. He ducked, buying me valuable seconds to scoot over to the other side of the car. I pulled the handle and slammed it with my good shoulder, willing it to open. It didn't budge. I grunted through clenched teeth.

I tried again.

"No use trying to get away." I looked at Díaz, who was leaning down, one hand on the top of the car, the other still holding the gun—still pointed at me. His face was contorted into an ugly scowl.

Fear pumped its way from my heart through my veins. *Run! Run!* it pounded.

"Get over here! Now! You don't want to end up like Haydée."

"Haydée?" I asked, my stomach clenching. The seriousness of the situation hit me with force. Díaz was involved in Haydée's murder. Had he been the unidentified man I'd heard arguing with Haydée, and was that why he hadn't included it in my statement?

"I said, get over here and shut up."

I inched across the back seat and struggled out of the car, wincing at the pain that jolted through both shoulders. My head was throbbing. I gingerly touched my forehead and the lump forming over one eye. The blood pumping through my body contained a cocktail of fear and panic, but I tried desperately to remain calm. Díaz pulled a set of handcuffs from his pocket.

I checked the road in both directions. Díaz had chosen this place well. No houses. No cars. He'd also managed to angle the car behind a hedge of bushes, making it difficult to see it from the road.

"Did you kill Haydée?" I was playing for time. Surely, a car would drive past soon. I visualized making a dash to safety and prayed Díaz would think twice about using a gun in front of any witnesses.

"I'm not going to tell you again!" Díaz warned. "Turn around and put your hands behind your back."

Dismay sent a shiver of apprehension down my spine as I realized my situation was going to get a whole lot worse.

Díaz's phone started ringing. Maybe someone was already looking for me. The flare of optimism didn't last long. No one knew that I was with Díaz—except maybe the officer at the front desk and Marielle. I had no idea who Díaz had spoken to or what he'd said in those few minutes when he'd left me alone in the office.

Díaz waved the gun menacingly in front of my face, and I thought of Haydée and her twisted body on the rocks below the villa. I turned around and placed my hands behind me.

The handcuffs ratcheted shut, pinching my skin.

"This way!" Díaz demanded, turning me around to face him.

He tore a section of tape from a roll and placed it over my mouth. "Now, get inside and lie down on the floor."

I wriggled along the floor between the front and back seats. Díaz tore another piece of tape and wrapped it around my ankles.

I watched in horror as he picked up my phone, checked it, and then turned it off. All too late, I realized that Liam was the only person who knew my number. Why hadn't I bothered to give it to either Marielle or Antonio?

Díaz's phone began ringing as he slammed the back door of the car closed. I struggled to sit up, to find a position to ease my throbbing shoulder.

Díaz ignored the phone and started the engine, and I felt the car swing onto the bitumen. I screamed as my shoulder was pushed against the back seat, but my cry of pain was muffled by the tape.

I guessed we'd been traveling for about ten minutes when Díaz's phone rang again. Someone was trying to locate him, and it appeared they weren't giving up. My hopes grew that they were also trying to find me. This time he answered.

"Díaz!" he barked into the phone. Silence, as he waited for

the person on the other end to finish speaking. "I'm out on a job, but I should be back in the office in an hour or so."

Another lengthy silence.

"Don't worry. I'll deal with it when I get back."

Díaz swung the car into a side road. For a while, I tried to keep track of the direction and distance we'd traveled, but I soon became disoriented, with only a continuous loop of trees and bushes flashing past the car window.

Pieces of information and events started to fall into place. Díaz hadn't written down any of Liam's details because he had no intention of contacting the Copacabana. He'd taken me out through the back door so no one could see us together. No doubt the unmarked police car was also part of the plan. Why hadn't I seen this coming?

The dark thought that Antonio might also be involved with Díaz smoldered in my mind. I stamped out the thought before it could catch fire and do any damage. I trusted Antonio and refused to believe he would do anything illegal—anything to hurt me.

The trees disappeared and were being replaced by large apartment blocks. It was getting darker, and the traffic sounds were getting louder. With my hands and feet tied together, there was no way I was going to escape.

The panic I'd felt at first seeing Díaz's gun was increasing with each mile. I guessed we'd traveled another fifteen minutes before we slowed, bumped our way over rough ground and came to a stop. The sun had totally disappeared, but I could see the outlines of what looked like warehouses. We stopped, and Díaz jumped out of the car.

I heard three loud thumps on metal.

"Stevie, open up!"

The clanging of a chain and the sounds of a roller door groaning split the silence. I felt the car rock as someone flopped into the front seat and drove it into the shed. More clanging reverberated around the walls of the shed as the door was lowered.

"We've got a problem," Díaz stated. He opened the back door, grabbed me, and pulled me to my feet. My cry of pain was stifled by the tape over my mouth. The man I assumed to be Stevie slid the bolts into the side of the roller door and turned to face us.

"What's she doing here?" he asked.

I stared at Stevie—the mystery man from the cemetery and the police station. I'd been right, there were no such things as coincidences.

"She knows too much," Díaz said. "You're going to have to keep her here till we're ready."

Ready for what?

"What am I supposed to do with her?" Stevie asked.

"Let the boss decide," Díaz said.

"He's not going to like it."

"He doesn't have a choice." Díaz waved the gun at me and pointed to the back corner of the empty building. "Over there," he said.

Feet still bound together, I hopped in the direction that Díaz pointed. I looked around me, and my heart plummeted. I had no chance of getting to one of the exits without being shot.

Stevie grabbed my arms and shoved me into the corner of the building. Bracing my back against the wall, I slid down onto the cement floor. The pain in my shoulder stabbed like a knife as I struggled to keep my balance, to keep myself upright.

Even though it was dark, the shed was like an oven—even the wall against which I was resting radiated heat. My mouth was dry, and I was having trouble swallowing. Díaz's phone began to ring. He walked away to take the call, but I could still hear him.

"I don't know. I dropped her home after she came to the station," Díaz said. My head jerked up at his words. Someone was looking for me. I strained to hear the conversation and hoped it was Antonio on the other end of the line.

I screamed through the tape gagging me, but Díaz put his hand over his phone, effectively deafening my muffled cries.

"I'll be back by the end of my shift. Just following up on a few loose ends in Cojímar." He ended the call, and my stomach sank. If we were in Regla, we were nowhere near Cojímar.

"I'd better start heading back before they send out a search party," Díaz said. "I'll take the cuffs. Don't want to raise any suspicions." He gave the keys to Stevie, who took off my cuffs. "Don't leave here until you hear from me. Take this." Díaz handed him the gun. "Use it if you have to."

I rubbed my wrists where the cuffs had dug into my skin and waited for them to find another way of securing my hands, but obviously Díaz thought the leg restraints would be enough.

He stood over me. "You should've minded your own business," he said as if I was to blame for my situation.

I had a retort ready to go, but my words were strangled by the tape covering my mouth.

"Open the roller door," Díaz instructed Stevie while he kept an eye on me.

Stevie tucked the gun in the back of his jeans and rolled up the door, closing it as soon as Díaz had driven out.

Only Stevie and me.

He walked to a stack of chairs along one of the walls and dragged one over, setting it down in front of me. Then he pulled an empty wooden crate closer to use as a footstool and made himself comfortable.

I mumbled into the tape again. This time, he walked to me and ripped the tape off my mouth. I yelled as it tore out strands of hair that had been caught with it.

"No point in yelling because no one will hear you in here."

I swallowed. "Water?" I whispered the word through dry lips.

Stevie stood for a while, looking at the tap on the far side of the building, then at both doors, safely secured. I guess he realized, as I did, that I wasn't going anywhere fast.

With the gun in one hand, he grabbed a plastic cup and filled it with tap water. He shoved it against my lips, and most of the tepid water dribbled down my face and onto my top. He threw the cup onto the ground, then resumed his seat, feet on the upended box and gun resting on his stomach. He wriggled, looking like he was making himself comfortable.

All the windows had been blocked out with black paint,

and there was only a naked bulb for light. If anyone was looking for me, they weren't going to look for me here—in an abandoned building.

A couple of hours later, I heard the rattle of the key in the lock of the side door. Someone was coming.

The door opened, and Landrey walked through, pulling it shut behind him. Another piece of the jigsaw fell into place. Stevie jumped to his feet, almost stood to attention, and saluted, the gun resting loosely by his side. Landrey looked at me, the corners of his mouth turning upwards in a sneer. "You should have left Havana while you had the chance."

I thought of Liam's desperate plea to go back to the States.

Landrey folded his arms and stood towering over me with his feet apart and a patronizing look on his face that made me want to slap him.

"As it turns out, I don't need to collect your claim from you —I'll get it from your fiancé."

A glint of hope flashed, sparking the thought that Liam was okay and might be looking for me as well, but I was soon plunged back into darkness as I realized he probably didn't even know I was missing. There was no point in pinning my hopes of being rescued on him—or on Antonio. The reality was that only one person could help, and that person was me.

I rested my head on my knees, trying to work out how I was going to escape. I knew Landrey and Díaz had no intention of letting me go. They were waiting for something—I just wasn't sure what it was or how long I had. I'd have to grab any opportunity that came my way.

"I'm going to check how long they're going to be,"

Landrey said. He went outside, pulled the door closed, and locked it.

"Who are they?" I asked.

"Shut up," Stevie said. His phone rang, and I watched him fumble with the gun as he changed hands to answer it. Confusion and concern seemed to fight for a place on his face. "Right." He looked over at me, ended the call, and pointed the gun. "Get up!"

I struggled to stand up, inching my way along the wall by pressing my back against it and trying to get some traction with my feet. I only managed a couple of inches before falling hard on the floor. I shook my head at Stevie. "I can't."

He waved the gun at me. "Up," he insisted.

I tried again and ended back on the cement. Stevie crossed the floor to the desk in the corner, reached into the top drawer, and took out a knife. He came toward me and sliced through the tape tying my legs.

"I'm not going to carry you to the boat," he said. "Now get up." He kicked my shins, and I winced at the pain. "Just remember the gun is loaded, so don't try anything." He grabbed me with his free hand and hauled me to my feet.

I stumbled, pins and needles cramping my legs, which refused to hold my weight. I fell against the wall, then regained my balance. He pushed me in front of him toward the door. My heart was pounding, my throat tightening.

Time was running out.

Stevie opened the door and checked the area before shoving me outside. The saltwater smell of the ocean hit me first, and I took a deep breath. It was pitch-black. No moon yet, just a light sprinkling of stars across the sky. My eyes took time to adjust to the dark, but eventually, I could distinguish the outline of derelict buildings on either side of the shed.

Stevie seemed to be having difficulty locking the door. He took his eyes off me for a second. But a second was all I needed.

I saw what might be my only chance. And I took it.

Chapter Twenty-One

I dived into the darkness, a black curtain enveloping and hiding me. There was only one way to go. I fled down the side of the warehouse, away from Stevie.

"Hey!" Stevie yelled from behind me. Stones scattered under my feet, threatening to throw me off balance as I ran. I could hear Stevie's footsteps on the gravel behind me and the thundering of blood in my ears. Waiting for the gunshot, I skirted around the front of the building and slammed into a wire fence.

I raced along its length, one hand outstretched to guide me until I felt a break in the fence. Broken wire scratched me, and I felt my palm sticky with blood. The wire had been pulled away from the steel poles, exposing a small gap. I reached down and yanked the wire back further.

The ends tore my skin, and I gritted my teeth to stifle my cry of pain. I steeled myself, ignoring the pain in my shoulder and pulling the wire with all my strength. It finally gave way, and I lunged through the hole. I felt my shirt rip as I tumbled to the ground on the other side.

I took a couple of deep breaths to slow my heart and get my bearings. The humming of engines from the nearby boats in the port and the smell of salt in the air told me the water was close. Nothing in front of me, except tall grass and stumps indicating where a house had once stood.

No hiding places, just an empty block with houses on both sides. I could see a road ahead of me that looked like it led to the ferry. If I could make it to the terminal, I was sure I could find someone who would help me. The street wasn't an option —I'd be an easy target. It would be safer to cut through the backyards of the houses for as long as I could.

"We've got to find her. The boat will be here any minute." Díaz's voice boomed through the night. My heart raced even faster, knowing he'd returned—and was joining the hunt.

"How was I to know there was a hole in the fence?"

Díaz's voice was getting closer and louder. "Leaving without her isn't an option."

"Let's split up, then," Stevie suggested.

I slipped into the yard next door to the vacant block. The low-set *casa* was in darkness except for a dull light shining in one of the rooms. I could keep going and run the risk of being caught, or I could try to get some help.

Getting help seemed to be a better option, so I raced up the steps. I looked over my shoulder for any sign of Stevie and Díaz. The door opened easily. I stepped inside and closed it quietly behind me, before creeping down the hall toward the light.

I stopped in the doorway. "*¿Hay alguien aquí?* Is anyone

here?" I called out *"Ayúdenme, por favor!* Help me." The light I'd seen from outside turned out to be the flickering of the television. The volume had been turned off, and the glow from the streetlight outside slid through a gap in the curtains. Two vinyl armchairs faced the television, sandwiching an iron coffee table between them. A lonely cup stood in the middle of the table. I reached over and picked up the half-full cup, which was still warm to the touch. The owner must be nearby.

The hairs on the back of my neck stood to attention as fear crept through the semi-darkness and took hold. I slipped into the hall and returned the way I'd come.

"¿Qué hace aquí? What are you doing here?" a voice, low and threatening, followed from behind. I glanced behind me and could see a man, his shirt unbuttoned and hanging loosely on his large frame. In his hands, he held a piece of wood, which he waved through the air.

"¡Salte! Get out," he said. He started to move toward me, his weapon poised to strike. I practically flew through the door, my heart in my throat and survival my only thought.

I was going to have to make a run for the ferry and try to get back to Havana. I ran down the back steps and into the yard next door, my heart pumping adrenaline and fear. No time to think. I crossed the backyard and then hit another fence.

This one was too high to scale, and it was too dangerous to retrace my steps. I had to keep going. I hedged my way down the side of the house until I reached the front yard. I peeked around the corner of the building, checking for Stevie and Díaz.

I looked up and down the road. Stevie was standing not

more than a hundred and fifty feet away, talking on his phone. A car rumbled past, coughing its way down the street. His head jerked up, and he looked in my direction as the car passed me. I pulled back into the shadows, my heart in my throat, beating so loudly it almost deafened me.

A church stood on the corner of the street opposite me, lit by the streetlights and the cars roaring past. I looked back to see if Stevie was still on the phone. He'd disappeared. I didn't know in which direction to head. And then I heard it. The sound of the ferry docking, bringing the commuters home from Havana. Waves of voices rippled toward me, followed by a group of twenty or thirty people. I was one block and a stream of people away from safety.

As soon as the first of the commuters reached my side of the road, I dived into the middle of the crowd and pushed my way through them. I searched their faces as they passed, trying to find someone who looked like they could be approached for help, but most were either talking to each other or looking straight ahead.

I was still in the middle of the crowd and had almost reached the queue waiting to get on the ferry when I saw him. Stevie. My escape route was blocked, and chances of getting to Havana dashed.

Stevie had anticipated my move. He leaned against the railing of the pier, arms crossed, scanning those ready to board the return ferry to Havana. Ready to pounce. There was no sign of his gun, but I suspected that it wouldn't be far away. I looked around me, desperate to find an alternative way to get on the ferry.

All the arriving passengers disembarked and the ferry

would be boarding any minute now. I stopped and then darted across into the shadows of one of the buildings close by. I needed time to think.

I closed my eyes and tried to calm my breathing. The ferry was no longer a viable option. Stevie and Díaz were both waiting for me. But for how long? They said they had a boat to catch. Diaz's words—that leaving without me wasn't an option—rang in my ears, but I refused to be beaten. I needed to find somewhere to hide until morning and then make my way to Havana or somehow contact Antonio.

I raced out from the side of the building and joined the last of the stragglers heading away from the ferry. When we reached the front of the church, I split from the group and took off, skirting around its side and up a couple of steps to the wooden door. My hand gripped the cold iron handle. Closing my eyes, I touched the charm Ita had left for me, whispered a silent plea to Our Lady of Regla for help, then pushed. The door swung open. I squeezed through and pulled it shut behind me.

Listening. Watching. Adjusting to the semi-darkness. No movement. No priest. Only silence. Our Lady of Regla, Yemayá, framed in gold, floated in a sea of blue robes gathered in waves around her. She held the baby close, protecting him as she does all women. I prayed she would do the same for me.

An altar stood in front of Our Lady of Regla, and an aisle ran the length of the church, separating two rows of pews. Stained-glass windows stretched around the walls on either side. I rushed to the altar and grabbed one of the large candlesticks, weighing it in my hands, judging how much damage it was likely to inflict. It would be no match for a gun, but it was all I had. At least it was something.

I knew that as soon as Stevie and Díaz realized I wasn't getting on the ferry, they would be back to continue their search.

Voices. Coming closer. Footsteps.

"Hey, this door's open." Stevie and Díaz.

My heart leaped into my throat, threatening to suffocate me. I couldn't leave the same way I'd come in. I raced down the central aisle, desperate to find a hiding place before they came inside. Then I found them. Stairs. Tucked away in the corner. I slipped into the shadows and scrambled up them.

I'd no sooner reached the top when the closed fist of reality sucker-punched me. I'd expected there to be another set of steps from where I could escape, but there was only one way up—one way down. My safe haven was no better than being exposed on the streets outside. In fact, it was worse. I was trapped.

"Do you think she came in here?" The sound of a door slamming.

I dived to the floor. Bright lights flooded the church. I crawled between the chairs to the back corner.

The banging of doors and the scraping of furniture being shoved signaled Stevie and Díaz's movement through the church. It would be impossible to get down the stairs now without being seen.

I tried to slow my breathing, to think, to find an escape route. My chest tightened, and my stomach turned to stone—I was cornered. It was only a matter of time.

"She's not here. I think we should forget about her and get to the boat before it leaves without us."

"Are. You. Crazy?" Díaz's voice roared from beneath me. "You can be the one to tell Landrey."

There was complete silence. I imagined Stevie thinking about what Landrey would do to him. And then I heard it … the creaking of a floorboard to my left. Then another. I held my breath, scared that even from this distance, Díaz would hear my heart hammering nail-gun fast. I pushed myself to my feet and pressed against the back wall, determined to at least put up a fight. If Díaz decided to come all the way up, I'd be ready.

"Díaz!" Stevie's voice called out.

There was no reply from Díaz, just another creak. One step. Closer.

"Díaz!" Stevie yelled.

"Well, well, well." Díaz stood in front of me. "Who do we have here?" His slow and measured voice sent chills down my back.

I couldn't see Stevie, but I had a good view from above of the front of the church.

"Díaz," Stevie called out. A change in his tone made both of us look down at the same time.

Stevie wasn't alone. Antonio was standing beside him, looking up at both of us.

"What's going on, Díaz?" Antonio's voice exploded in the empty church, and the sight of him below released a tidal wave of emotions that left me powerless to say or do anything. A flicker of hope was glinting at the end of a very long tunnel of terror. I gripped the railing to steady myself.

"Keep out of this, Antonio, it's none of your business." Díaz swung his gun in an arc and pointed it in his direction.

"No!" Adrenaline tempered by a calm detachment surged through my body, powering me. I heard my voice echo through the church as I lunged, my full weight barreling into Díaz. He tried to regain his balance and grabbed at the railing, but it was too late. He started to fall down the stairs, his gun slipping from his grasp, clattering to the floor below.

I looked down and saw Antonio surrounded by a dozen men in uniforms, guns ready. A couple of them reached Díaz before he had time to recover, and another came through the side door, pushing Stevie in front of him. Antonio rushed up the stairs, climbing over the police and Díaz in the process.

"You okay?" He grabbed me by the shoulders.

I nodded, ignoring the pain that shot through my arm.

"Thank heavens!" Antonio folded me into his arms and crushed me against him. He gently pushed me away, his eyes checking me over. "You're not. You're bleeding," he said.

"It's just a scratch."

Díaz and Stevie were both handcuffed and being escorted from the building. A couple of the officers remained below, waiting for instructions from their commander.

"Did they catch Landrey?" I asked.

"Landrey's here too?"

"He was. They've got a boat."

"Slowly, slowly," Antonio said, taking both my hands in his. "Come and sit down for a minute. You're shaking." He helped me to one of the chairs.

"You have to get them before they get away," I said.

"Do you know the name of the boat?"

Rifling through the files of conversations in my memory but coming up empty, I shook my head.

Antonio leaned over the railing and called down to the officers still gathered below. "You need to find Landrey. He could be on a boat moored somewhere near here!"

The officer in charge spoke rapidly to his men, and they all rushed outside to search for the boat and the remainder of the gang, leaving us alone. Antonio turned to me.

"How did you know where to find me?" I asked. I had so many questions.

"I'd like to take the credit for running a successful intelligence operation, but to be honest, it was Pedro," Antonio said. "He was parked on the road outside the police station waiting for you when he saw you leave with Díaz."

I thought of Pedro, always waiting patiently for me, even when I'd tell him not to, proudly polishing his car, proudly claiming me as his friend.

"He thought it was a bit strange, so thank heavens, he decided to check on you later in the day. Luckily, I was at the villa when he called and told me you'd left with Díaz."

"How did you know Díaz had taken me to Regla? I heard him telling someone he was going to Cojímar and I thought for sure that's where they'd be searching."

"Well, for that, you have to thank Liam."

"Thank heavens he's safe, but how did he know I was in Regla?"

"He'd been trying to get in touch with you because things had become serious with Landrey, and he thought you might be in danger. When he couldn't get you, he came looking for you at the villa. As soon as I told him that you were with Díaz,

I could tell that there was something wrong. He told me every-thing he knew, including the address of the place Landrey used at Regla to store the merchandise they'd smuggled to and from the States."

I couldn't help feeling relieved that Liam wasn't all bad. "Where is he now?"

"Said he was leaving Havana and returning to the States to avoid prosecution. As soon as I realized you were in danger, I notified the police, then raced here. It was a relief to see the police when I arrived. They scoured the warehouse, and when you weren't inside, we spread out and began a search of the area. It was then we saw the lights in the church."

Antonio read the confusion written on my face.

"It wasn't a Saturday or Sunday, so there shouldn't have been anyone inside. We decided it was worth investigating."

"I'm glad you did!"

"I think our first stop should be the hospital. You need to be checked out."

I moved my shoulder and winced at the pain. At least I could still move it. "I'm fine—just a little tender here and there, but I can still move it. To be honest, I just want to go home."

"I'll clear it with the captain." Holding my hand tightly as if he was afraid to let me go, he helped me climb down to the ground floor. After clearing the last few steps, Antonio wrapped his arms around me, holding me so closely I could barely breathe.

"I'm glad you're safe," he whispered.

"Ain't this a touching scene?"

I recognized the voice straight away and pushed myself

away from Antonio, who turned around at the same time. Landrey was standing in front of us, his gun ready.

Antonio pushed me behind him as he spoke. "It's over, Landrey."

"It sure is."

"You need to leave while you've still got a chance. You know what's going to happen if you get caught."

"That's exactly why I need to get both of you on that boat before it sails."

"You know that's not going to happen," Antonio said.

"I'm going to give it a damn good try. Now, we're going to walk out of here nice and calm, as if nothing's wrong. Like you said, I've got nothing to lose. Now you"—he waved the gun at Antonio—"you go first. And, Ms Johnson, you're going to walk real close here next to me."

Pain ratcheted the length of my arm when Landrey grabbed it and pulled me tightly against his side. The gun dug into my back, and I saw Antonio tense in front of me.

We walked out of the side door, following Antonio. I'd just reached the first step when lights blinded me, and I halted.

"*¡Policía!*" a voice yelled from behind the searing lights. We were no longer alone. Landrey pulled the gun away slightly, enough that it no longer dug into me.

It was now or never.

I dived off the side of the steps, pushing Antonio to one side as I did. I bit back a scream when we hit the ground amidst a volley of shots.

Landrey's body hit the ground with a thud beside us. Voices yelled and hands clawed at me, dragging me to my feet. One of the officers rolled Landrey over with his foot and trained his gun on him, while another bent over to check his pulse.

"He's dead," the officer confirmed. "We'll need to speak to you both."

"Now?" My voice was thin and weak.

Adrenaline had fueled my body for nearly ten hours, and the tank was now empty. I could feel the ground swaying under my feet, and I struggled to keep my eyes focused.

"Tomorrow will do."

Chapter Twenty-Two

Darkness had become my companion, my friend, shielding me from danger, and now soothing me as Antonio drove from the clinic where the doctor had checked me over toward the lights of Havana. I closed my eyes and let its silence settle around me, comfortable and warm. Even so, the night had outstayed its welcome and I wouldn't be sad to say farewell.

By the time we reached the tunnel, the first rays of the sun were creeping over the horizon and spreading their fingers of light over the water. A new day had arrived. A new beginning.

"Home?" he asked.

I nodded. "Please."

We drove along the Malecón toward Miramar just as the sun was rising.

"Can we stop for a minute?" I asked.

"I thought you were in a rush to get home?"

"Just for a minute. To enjoy the sunrise. Last night, I wasn't sure I'd see another one."

Antonio found a park on the Malecón near the Hotel Nacional. We got out and found a place on the wall where the waves couldn't reach us.

"I've worked out some of the puzzle, but I still don't understand it all. What was Haydée's involvement in all this?" I asked.

Antonio looked out to sea. "Haydée … had a dream. And that dream was always going to be out of her reach."

I waited for him to continue, wondering if her dream had included Antonio.

"She wanted to go to the States."

Just like his ex-wife.

"She thought she'd found a way to make it a reality, but she didn't realize the danger she was in."

I thought back on the events of the last couple of weeks. I was sure that Haydée had something to do with the stolen necklace. "Did Haydée steal Rosa's necklace? Was that how she intended to get some money to go to the States?"

Antonio nodded. "She probably had more than one motive—to sell it on the black market and cast you in a bad light at the same time."

"I knew she must have had something to do with it."

"And then she discovered a way to make even more money."

"How was she going to do that?"

"While you were in the clinic, I spoke to the police captain. He said Díaz had already confessed that both he and Haydée were involved in Landrey's property scheme. She was the one who located Cubans willing to sell their properties—and she also facilitated the deal with Landrey and your fiancé. But after she found out about the smuggling operation, she thought she could get extra money by blackmailing Landrey and Díaz.

"It would have meant more than the end of Díaz's career if she revealed his involvement, so Haydée had to be silenced. Landrey made sure of that, and I guess we'll find out more details as the investigation continues."

"I can't believe I trusted Díaz."

"You know, I think Díaz got in over his head. What started out as a bit of extra money for turning a blind eye ended up getting out of control, and before he knew it, he was forced to do what Landrey wanted or meet the same end as Haydée."

"What about Stevie, the man following me?"

"When you decided to come to Havana, Liam realized that things could get a bit 'complicated' and he let Landrey know. Stevie was told to keep an eye on you. He's also cooperating with the police."

"So, I was right. He was following me."

Antonio nodded, and I thought about what he'd just told me. The last piece of the jigsaw fell into place, and I could see everything clearly. It was all beginning to make sense now.

We leaned against the wall, beside each other. Antonio's arm touched mine, and a tingle of excitement chased away the exhaustion of the last twenty-four hours. I leaned against him, and he put his arm around my waist as we looked out to the ocean. Beyond the horizon lay Miami.

"So close and yet so far," Antonio said, looking toward the coast of Florida.

"And not just in miles," I mused.

"What do you mean?"

"I'm thinking that … thinking how … I'll be sorry to leave Havana."

"You could stay longer, no?"

The thought had already crossed my mind.

"But of course, that would be difficult. You have many responsibilities," he said.

"Not so many." My only commitment was work. And I was pretty sure I could get leave. I was a free woman now, and I liked the feeling. I could do what I liked.

Antonio pressed me closer against him.

"The sunrise looks even more perfect after the events of last night, don't you think?" I asked.

"Everything looks perfect after last night." His voice, low and husky, sent shivers down my spine. He turned me toward him, his lips brushing mine, lightly at first. I lifted my head, eager for more. Even as he pulled me closer, I warned myself that this was not a good move, but I couldn't help myself. My body had taken over.

A group of young people walked past, yelling and cheering.

"I think I need to get you home," Antonio said.

In the car, I rested my head against the back of the seat and closed my eyes. As we drove along the Malecón, the events of last night flashed through my mind, a series of images randomly spliced together. The memory of Díaz pointing the gun at me in the church elbowed the images of the new day's sunrise from my mind.

Things could have turned out very differently. Someone had been looking out for me. I touched the charm hanging around my neck.

We pulled up outside the villa. "We're home now." Weariness had crept into Antonio's voice. He helped me out of the car, slipping his arm around my waist to help me up the steps to the front door and into the kitchen.

"What's that?" I asked. "Someone's left a note on the table."

Antonio picked it up and read it. "It's from Isabelle. She says that Marielle has been taken to hospital and she's gone with her. I'll ring and find out what's going on."

"No, let's just go there," I said.

We jumped into the car and rushed to the hospital.

I caught myself gripping the charm around my neck and saying a silent prayer for Marielle. Panic was rising in my throat and threatening to unleash all the emotions I'd been suppressing for the last few hours. What if something happened to Marielle? I refused to give the idea any airtime. Not after I'd just found her. I looked over at Antonio and caught the flash of fear in his eyes. Haydée was dead, and now Marielle was ill.

"I'm sure she'll be okay," I said, reaching over and grasping his hand.

When we arrived, Antonio asked for directions to the ward. We found Isabelle sitting in one of the steel chairs lined up against the wall. She stood up as soon as we arrived, and I rushed over to her and hugged her.

"What's happened?" I asked. "Is Marielle okay? How serious is it?"

"I don't know. The doctors think that she's had a heart attack," Isabelle replied.

Every time someone pushed through the swing doors near

us, I would jump and move toward them, hoping they would have information. Each time, they would stride past, avoiding eye contact.

"Will you be okay here for a while?" Antonio asked, nodding toward Isabelle. "I'll see if I can find out what's happening."

I nodded and sat down with Isabelle, who put her face in her hands.

I wrapped my arm around her shoulders. "Marielle will be fine. You'll see," I said.

"I'm not so sure." She looked at me and shook her head.

"Nothing can happen to Marielle, not now when I've just found her." I spoke with conviction, defying anyone to contradict me, but a small doubt grew with every slamming of the swing door against the wall and every staff member who rushed past.

We waited in silence for Antonio to return with some news.

"Catalina." Isabelle shifted in her chair, turning to face me and taking my hands in hers. "There's something I've been wanting to tell you for a while now, but Marielle thought that I should say nothing. But now …" She glanced around the waiting area. "I think that it is time to say something. Marielle may have made a promise to her sister, Alicia, but there are some promises that shouldn't be taken to the grave. You have a right to know." Her trembling hands squeezed mine.

For a minute I was confused, but then dread began a slow crawl through my veins. What was she going to say? It sounded serious. I leaned forward, waiting for her to continue.

"Alicia—your '*Ita*'—raised you and loved you. But she is not your grandmother. Your real grandmother is Marielle."

Despite her efforts to soften the blow, her words were unexpected, hitting me in the stomach like a runaway train. I felt rudderless, at the mercy of the past.

"I don't understand. How can this be possible?"

"After the Revolution, after Alicia and Eduardo left Cuba, Marielle was alone, her two sisters gone. She joined the literacy campaign and then ... she fell in love."

"With whom?" I asked.

"One of the other teachers. He was killed in an accident, never knowing Marielle was pregnant with your mother. No one knew. No one except me and Alicia."

"No one?" I asked.

Isabelle thought for a minute. "Only one other person knew. Father Paul. He and Marielle grew up together."

"Father Paul? In Miami?"

Isabelle nodded. "After the Revolution, the church didn't have a place in the new order, so he left Cuba with many other priests."

I was shocked. I remembered Ita's funeral, Father Paul clasping my hands, inviting me to come and see him. Had what I'd thought been a polite request to visit really been an invitation to find out about the past?

"Why did Marielle keep her pregnancy a secret?" I asked.

"Marielle saw what Rosa's pregnancy had done to her parents, and she was determined not to let them go through it a second time. Besides, she was very independent and was determined to see this through herself."

"But surely, questions were asked about how Alicia ended up with a child when she obviously wasn't pregnant."

"Alicia cut off all contact with her relatives and friends in

Cuba after they left. And many children were taken from Cuba and resettled in the States after the Revolution, so it probably didn't seem so strange to anyone."

"Marielle is my grandmother." I tested the sound of it, but my voice was thin and barely audible. I looked at Isabelle. "How did she manage to keep such a secret for so long?"

"Marielle worked for as long as she could, and then when that was no longer possible, she came and stayed with my family. Her parents still thought that she was working in the country. After Rosalita, your mother, was born, Marielle went to the States to see Alicia, and when she returned, she returned alone. Rosalita stayed with Alicia and Eduardo."

My mother was Marielle's daughter? The shock had eased slightly, but I still felt numb. My mind was jumping between thoughts, but I wasn't feeling anything. "How could she have given up her own child?" I thought of my mother never knowing who her real mother was.

"It was complicated," Isabelle said.

There was that word again.

"According to Marielle, Rosalita was only supposed to be in the States for a short time," Isabelle said, "until Marielle had the means to bring her back and support her here in Havana."

"But that didn't happen."

"I suspect that Alicia never really intended to let Rosalita return. And as time went on, Marielle knew she would never be able to give Rosalita the kind of life that Alicia and Eduardo could provide. She coped with the loss of her daughter by throwing herself into her work and devoting herself to others, helping those less fortunate. I can assure you, though, she always held you and your mother both close in her heart. She was so happy and excited when you came here. It was like a gift from heaven."

"But why hasn't she said anything?" I asked.

"She promised Alicia that she would never disclose it. And she's been true to her word. She didn't want to say anything in case it upset you. Finding out after all these years … Maybe she would've told you once you got to know each other better."

Inside, my stomach was churning. My loyalties were torn between the grandmother I had known all my life and my real grandmother. I felt betrayed by both. Resentment at not being told the truth collided with the relief I felt at finally knowing the facts about my family. And yet now, there were still more questions to be answered.

I'd survived the last twenty-four hours only to find out my grandmother had been lying to me all her life and that my real grandmother was lying in a critical condition in hospital.

Antonio returned, followed by one of the doctors. "This is Dr Ortega," he introduced. "He's going to try to find out about Marielle's progress."

"*Un minuto*," Dr Ortega said, holding up his index finger before disappearing into the wards.

Not long after, Dr Ortega returned and led us through the swing doors. He pushed through the curtains separating Marielle from the other patients and then disappeared.

Marielle looked so thin and frail. The sheet was tucked under her chin, and tubes and wires connected her to machines that beeped and flashed.

"Marielle," I whispered, standing beside her bed. I gently touched her brow, pushing strands of hair back from her forehead. My heart clenched at the sight of her. Leaning over, I kissed her lightly on her forehead. *"Mi abuela,"* I whispered.

I'd found room in my heart for both Marielle and the sister who'd raised me and would always be my grandmother. I searched among the tubes and wires, and when I found her hand, I clung to it, her bony fingers resting in mine. I felt her fingers tighten slightly. Her eyelids fluttered behind closed lids.

"Antonio is here too, Abuela."

Marielle's eyelids fluttered again and opened slightly. She stared straight ahead, so Antonio moved around the bed to allow her to see him.

Her lips struggled to say something. I leaned closer to try to hear what she was saying, but her words disappeared among the beeping and whirring of the machinery before I could catch them. Her eyes closed again, her chest rising up and down.

Voices sounded on the other side of the curtain, and a nurse appeared. *"Por favor,* you will need to leave now. The doctors are coming," she said.

I leaned over so Marielle could hear me. "We'll be back soon. I love you." I kissed her forehead, my lips brushing her cold skin.

"You can come back tomorrow," the nurse said, ushering us out.

Antonio shepherded us out of the hospital and back to the car, and after dropping Isabelle at her home, we returned to the villa. I was so consumed by Isabelle's revelation and Marielle's illness that I couldn't speak. Antonio finally broke the silence.

"Are you feeling hungry?"

I shook my head. I was beyond hungry and almost beyond tired. "I'm in desperate need of a shower before I do anything."

"Catalina?"

"Yes?"

"We didn't really finish our conversation on the Malecón." He bent down, and his lips brushed mine lightly. "But we can finish it later."

I pulled myself up the stairs to my room, one foot slowly in front of the other, remembering the conversation we hadn't finished.

Was coming back to Havana a possibility? I let the hot water soothe my aching shoulders, then struggled into a pair of shorts and T-shirt and lay gingerly on the bed. *Just a couple of minutes and then I'll get up.*

Chapter Twenty-Three

My eyes flickered open. I tensed, springing upright, pain racking my body. The curtains billowed, floating on the ocean breeze. I was safe. From Landrey. From Díaz. And then, the weight of remembering Marielle lying in the hospital crushed me, making it hard to breathe. The gentle touch of the breeze turned into a sigh of sadness. The happiness I'd felt at finding Marielle looked like it might be torn away from me again just as it was within my grasp.

A light tap at the door. I found it difficult to move.

Another knock, louder. I struggled out of bed, padded across the cool floorboards, and opened the door. Antonio was there, balancing a tray, which held a cup of coffee and a sandwich. "I thought you might be hungry," he said, holding out the tray toward me.

"Thank you, Antonio. Any news about Marielle?"

He shook his head. "Nothing yet. I guess they'll let us know if there's been any change and when we can see her."

"Let's go down to the garden?" I suggested.

"I'll take this down and come back and help you manage the stairs."

"You go. I'll be fine." I dressed as quickly as my sore muscles would allow and then negotiated the stairs, leaning heavily on the railing and gritting my teeth with each step. When I reached the garden, I lowered myself into one of the chairs.

I couldn't remember how long it had been since I'd eaten. I took a bite of the ham-and-cheese sandwich, savoring the soft, smooth slices of cheese sticking to the roof of my mouth. I followed it with a mouthful of strong coffee. Butterflies played hide-and-seek through the branches of the shrubs, and birds sang their presence accompanied by the breeze whispering through the palm fronds. Things were almost as they should be. Almost.

When we'd finished, I struggled out of the chair and walked around the back of the villa to the rock wall and the soothing sound of the ocean's rolling rhythm. Antonio followed and stood beside me, leaning against the wall.

"Isabelle spoke to me at the hospital."

Antonio turned slightly so that we were facing each other.

"She told me that Marielle is my real grandmother."

His eyes widened and his eyebrows shot up. He appeared just as surprised as I was. "How could that be?"

I told him what Isabelle had told me.

"How do you feel about that?"

"I'm not sure … confused, angry, overwhelmed."

"That's natural. You've gone through a lot in the last couple of days. And now this."

"I'm going to try to extend my visa. I can't leave Marielle like this. Even if I didn't know she was my grandmother, I still wouldn't leave her. I need to be here with her."

"I'm sure Marielle would appreciate you staying."

We leaned against the seawall, the ocean spray showering us with droplets.

"And you, would you appreciate me staying?" I asked.

Antonio's eyes filled with sadness, his expression almost apologetic for what he wasn't saying.

I pushed myself off the wall, preparing to return to the garden, but Antonio held his ground in front of me, barring my way.

"Do you want me to stay?" I asked.

"Of course I do. Why do you have to ask?"

"Well, one minute I get the impression that you like me, the next, I'm not so sure."

"It is complicated," Antonio replied.

I let the silence hang heavy between us.

"You know I've been married," he said.

"Being married isn't on my agenda if you are trying to warn me off. Or are you telling me you're still in love with your ex-wife?"

"No. She no longer has a place in my heart. I never felt I would ever be able to trust anyone enough to remarry."

"Antonio, trust is something that grows with time. And you can't predict what will happen in the future."

"I think I can." He shook his head and pressed his lips together to underline his comment. "Life in Cuba is not easy. It is very, very hard, and many Cubans want to live somewhere else, where there are no shortages of food, where there are plenty of opportunities, plenty of everything. You say you love Havana now, but I know that when things get difficult, you will return to your home. You will leave for a better life, just like my wife."

"I'm not your wife, and I'm not Haydée."

His eyes penetrated mine as if searching for the truth in what I was saying.

"Then, I would love for you to stay," he said.

Antonio's phone rang, and he pulled it from his pocket. "Yes … I see … oh … okay … thank you." He hung up. "That was Dr Ortega."

"We can go back? I'll get my—"

Antonio pulled me toward him and folded his arms around me. "*Mi corazón.* I'm so sorry."

The words stabbed my heart like a knife. I shook my head and pulled back, putting my hands out to stop the words I knew were coming. "No. No."

Antonio held my shaking hands. "Dr Ortega rang to let us know … that … Marielle … has passed away."

"No." I pushed myself away from him. "I don't believe it. She can't die. Not yet."

Antonio gathered me in his arms and held me while I sobbed. Ita. Marielle. My losses were a burden almost too heavy to bear.

Antonio and I stood before the Marquez-Fuentes crypt, the unyielding sun pounding us as we stared at the bronze plaque shining with newness.

Marielle
Sister of Alicia and Rosa
Mother to Rosalita
Grandmother of Catalina

Twelve words, not nearly enough to capture the lives of three sisters separated by time and distance … and a secret. Although united in spirit, they would forever be apart; Rosa in Matanzas, Alicia in Miami, and Marielle here in Havana.

At least I had the knowledge that Marielle knew that the silence they'd shared had been shattered and the secret revealed. I was able to tell her I loved her and acknowledge her as my grandmother. There was some sadness at the thought that they would never be together, but mine wasn't the only family where history and choices had intervened to change lives forever.

I placed one of the two mariposa flowers from Marielle's garden on the masonry slab in front of me.

"*Mi abuela*," I whispered and touched the marble.

I wiped the single tear from my cheek, and Antonio reached for my hand and took it in his. We walked toward the car, and when I was near Amelia's grave, I turned to him. "I need to do something. I won't be a minute."

As I neared the statue of Amelia and her baby, I passed a tour group leaving after having made their wishes. When I passed the group leader, a flicker of recognition flashed between us. Marco. Without stopping, he nodded in my direction, giving me the briefest of acknowledgments.

A small cluster of women standing near Amelia's grave parted as I walked over and placed the second mariposa on Amelia's grave, whispering, "*Gracias.*"

I returned to Antonio, who was looking at me with a smile I could only describe as indulgent.

"Did you make your wish?" he asked.

"Of course I did." I reached up and kissed him.

"What was it?"

"I can't tell you that. At least not yet."

"I don't want you to leave. Stay here in Havana," he said suddenly.

"I'll be back in a couple of weeks. As soon as I speak to the lawyer about Ita's will and apply for leave from work. And I'd also like to speak to Father Paul."

"It sounds like you won't be back till Christmas."

"I'll be back—and it'll be long before Christmas, I promise you."

"I'll be waiting. But should you have second thoughts, I want you to know—"

I slipped my arms around his neck and silenced him with my lips.

One year since Marielle's passing, and it was fitting that those who loved her should gather to honor her in the place she loved most, her beloved garden. The heady perfume of the mariposas clung to the ocean breeze, pushing its way through the palms.

The screen door from the kitchen slammed behind me. I turned in time to receive a hug and a plate of *galletas* from Isabelle. I balanced the plate while she kissed me warmly on both cheeks.

"Her favorites," Isabelle reminded me proudly. My heart clenched with the loss I still felt. We stood looking over the guests gathered in the garden. "So many people …"

"Quite a few of Marielle's old friends are here from Miami," I said.

"It's a shame that they didn't bother visiting earlier when she was still alive."

"She would've liked that, but you know how things are …

complicated. At least they have come now. Father Paul is even here."

"Father Paul?" Her hand flew to her chest. "From Miami?"

I nodded. "When I went to the States last year, I told him I planned to return to Havana, and when I invited him to come, he was delighted. I'm sure he'd love to see you."

I left Isabelle with Father Paul and placed the plate of *galletas* on the large oak table, which had survived generations and the efforts of Antonio and five of his friends to maneuver it into the garden.

Two small arms grabbed at my legs from under the table. I reached down and lifted the tablecloth. Juan jumped out, grabbed a biscuit, and took a bite.

"Found you!" Antonio yelled. Juan screamed and ran off into the thickest part of the garden. Antonio and I shared a smile and a shrug, then he continued the chase. "I'm coming to get you."

I watched him race after Juan. Yes, Antonio would make a wonderful father.

Daniela, Juan's mother, appeared beside me, her voice dragging me back into the present. "Catalina, thank you for helping Juan with his English. It is much improved."

"Juan is a very bright little boy and learns quickly."

She beamed at my comments. "It's a shame that you do not work at the school. You could help more students."

"I love what I'm doing at the moment. Antonio's idea of me volunteering and teaching English to the young children of the neighborhood was brilliant. I feel I'm doing some-thing worthwhile and also giving something back to my adoptive country. Who knows, maybe one day I will end up teaching in a school." I thought of the school in the Plaza Vieja.

Juan's screams interrupted us.

"I'd better go and see what is going on," Daniela said. "Make sure Antonio is safe."

"*Señora* Cate!" Pedro rushed down the veranda steps and through the guests, one hand waving his white hat over his head, the other gripping a bunch of flowers.

"*Señora.*" He took off his white hat and bowed low, then handed me the flowers. "For you, *Señora* Cate ... the most beautiful flower." His smile stretched from one side of his face to the other.

"Thank you, Pedro. My friend."

I would be forever grateful for the role he had played in my rescue. There were still times when my nightmares would wake me in the middle of the night, but Antonio would soothe me and remind me that Díaz and Stevie were safely behind bars and would be remaining there for a very long time.

"*Señor* Antonio. He is here?" Pedro asked, searching the crowd.

"I think he might be playing hide-and-seek."

"Hide-and-seek?"

I was just about to tell him the Spanish equivalent when Daniela, struggling with a wriggling Juan, passed us and caught the end of our conversation.

"No more hide-and-seek for today. Antonio is showing your guests from Miami the villa."

"I'm not surprised. Antonio is so proud of his efforts to restore the villa that he insists on showing everyone who walks through the door." I set off to find them but was stopped by Father Paul.

"Catalina, thank you for inviting me. It is such a joyous occasion." He took my hands in his and leaned closer. "And I'm so happy that you now know the truth of the past."

"I know what Isabelle has told me and what you've told me."

"I'm so sorry I wasn't able to tell you more while Alicia was still alive, but we were all sworn to secrecy."

"I understand."

"We must make time before I go home to continue our talk about our lives growing up in Havana."

"I'd like that, Father."

"I'll leave you now to your guests. Keep safe, Catalina."

Father Paul left to search the crowd for faces from his past while I went searching for Antonio. I found him with a group gathered in Rosa's room. Unlike other areas of the villa, this room remained untouched. I couldn't bring myself to make any changes, not yet. When I arrived at the door, the mood inside was somber, far too somber for the celebration I'd planned.

"I just wish I knew what happened to Rosa," Dolores, one of Marielle's friends, said.

I knew the time was right to tell them about Rosa and Luisa, about Marielle being my grandmother. I wasn't sure how many of them already knew the secrets my family had kept, but by discussing them openly, I was acknowledging that any skeletons lurking in the closet had finally been laid to rest. I had nothing but pride and love for my family.

I moved in front of the small group next to Antonio, and

began the story of Alicia, Marielle, and Rosa. My voice caught on the facts, and at times Graciela nodded as if confirming what I was saying, but most of the faces of those present displayed varying degrees of surprise. I paused for a minute to let them digest what I had said. "While you are all here, we should go for a drive to Matanzas so you can see the farm."

"You still own the farm?"

"No. But I've contacted the people living there, and they don't mind me visiting Luisa and Rosa's grave. I'll eventually move them to the family crypt in Havana."

"Will you do the same for your family in Miami?"

"No. They made their decision to leave and not return, and I wouldn't want to disobey their wishes."

A moment of awkwardness followed, and then Graciela stepped forward and put her arms around both Antonio and me. "My children. It is so good to see you so happy. And I'm sure Alicia and Marielle would also be happy with the way things have turned out."

I had my doubts about Ita, but I knew that above all she would've wanted me to be happy. "Come, let's go. Everyone else is waiting in the garden."

As our guests filed down the staircase after Antonio, I closed the door gently behind me. There was no need to lock it any longer; Rosa's memory had been set free.

I stood at the top of the veranda steps. Isabelle was sitting at one of the tables, engrossed in conversation with Father Paul, and the other guests visiting from Miami were mingling and searching for old friends. Voices buzzed around me, almost drowning out the crashing waves.

The lure of the waves and the ocean was too strong, and I

slipped past the chatter to the stone wall at the back of the villa and the familiar, soothing sounds. I looked toward the horizon and the future. I'd begun the process of proving my Cuban descent and hopefully, one day, the villa would be ours. Then it would be safe.

Antonio appeared behind me, slipping his arms around my waist and resting his chin on top of my head.

"Are you happy?"

I turned toward him and slipped my arms around his neck.

"I've never been happier."

"Not sad for Marielle?"

I thought for a minute. Images flashed through my mind—Marielle sitting in the garden… smelling the scent bottles in Rosa's room… lying in the hospital. There was sadness, yes, but there was also love—and gratitude. I shook my head. "We are celebrating the life of a wonderful woman who was also my grandmother, and I'm surrounded by friends… and the man I love. The man—"

Antonio's lips crushed mine before I could finish.

"Our guests will be missing us," he murmured after a while.

"They can wait just a little longer."

"I love you, *mi amor*," he whispered, his voice catching with emotion.

I didn't need him to say the words—his eyes, his touch, said everything. I'd found happiness where I'd least expected it. "*Yo también te amo.*"

Antonio kissed me again and pulled me to his side. "Do you think now is the right time to say something?"

"Now? Are you sure?"

"Why not? Our friends are here," he said.

I rested my hand on the new life growing inside me.

"You're right. A new life… and a new beginning."

Hand in hand, we followed the laughter and voices back to the garden. Antonio led me to the top of the veranda steps.

"*¡Mis amigos, por favor!*" His voice—strong and powerful—hushed the crowd as everyone turned toward us. I looked at Antonio, and he nodded.

"*Mis amigos,*" I began. "We are so glad you have been able to join us this afternoon to celebrate the life of Marielle Marquez-Fuentes… and to share our good news."

THE END

Acknowledgments

Set in 2016, *The House in Havana* is my thank you to Cuba and to the people who have welcomed me during my visits over the last twenty years. There have been many changes during that time, and more recent visitors may notice that certain details differ from those portrayed in my novel. For example, Cuba no longer operates under a dual currency system, several landmarks have since been renovated or altered, and travel regulations around people traveling from the United States have tightened.

While the villa and all the people in this story are fictional, the story was inspired by research and real conversations with people about foreign ownership of property, the Helms–Burton Act, disputed property claims, smuggling, and irregular land transactions in Cuba.

I'd like to thank my editor, Alex Nalhaus, who continues to work with me on my novels, sharing her expertise and suggestions. Thank you also to Annie Seaton for proofreading my work and ensuring it was up to standard.

My appreciation also goes to the sensitivity reader who helped me ensure cultural accuracy and appropriateness throughout the novel.

To my favourite haunts—the libraries and cafés—and the

staff who provide the space (and the coffee and tea) that fuel my creativity—thank you.

And finally, my heartfelt thanks to my loyal friends and supporters, who show just as much excitement for each new milestone as I do. Your encouragement means more than you know.

Book Club Questions

1. Which moment in the story made you most emotionally connected to Cate—and why?
2. The novel blends mystery, family drama, romance, and cultural history. Which thread resonated most strongly with you?
3. What details made Cuba feel alive and authentic to you?
4. If you've never visited Cuba, what assumptions did the book challenge or reinforce?
5. The entire story is built on family secrets. Do you think keeping Rosalita's parentage hidden was justified?
6. Which plot twist surprised you the most?
7. Many characters do morally gray things—Haydée, Liam, Díaz, even Father Paul keeping secrets. Who do you think made the *worst* choice? Who made the *most understandable* wrong choice?

8. How does the novel explore the idea of belonging
    — culturally, romantically, and personally?
9. If the author wrote a spin-off or sequel, whose
    story would you want next?
10. What do you think Antonio and Catalina's "good
    news" was? Do you think the story should have
    revealed more about it, or was it better left implied?

About the Author

Annette lives in Brisbane, Australia. A passionate traveller, she draws inspiration from her experiences to create her Destination Mysteries and Romances. When she's not travelling or writing, Annette loves spending time at the beach with a good book, enjoying the company of friends, and experimenting with recipes inspired by her travels.

She has published two series—the Three Wishes series and the Bayswater Series and has now launched the first book in her new Havana series.

As part of the Bayswater Crime series, Annette has also published two novels—*The Whispering Palms* and *The Curlew's Scream*—set in tropical North Queensland, as well as a novella, *The Raging Fire*, set in Melbourne.

The Three Wishes is a series of destination romance novellas—*A Christmas Wish* is set on a South Pacific cruise; *A New Year's Wish*, set in Paris; and *A Valentine's Wish*, set in Venice during Carnevale.

Stay tuned for information about her new novel in the Bayswater series, also due for release in 2026. Sign up for

Annette's monthly newsletter to receive a free digital copy of *The Raging Fire* by copying this link into your browser:

https://dl.bookfunnel.com/ov4vrxh1gc